sammy keyes
AND THE wild things

Also by Wendelin Van Draanen

Sammy Keyes and the Hotel Thief
Sammy Keyes and the Skeleton Man
Sammy Keyes and the Sisters of Mercy
Sammy Keyes and the Runaway Elf
Sammy Keyes and the Curse of Moustache Mary
Sammy Keyes and the Hollywood Mummy
Sammy Keyes and the Search for Snake Eyes
Sammy Keyes and the Art of Deception
Sammy Keyes and the Psycho Kitty Queen
Sammy Keyes and the Dead Giveaway

◆ ◆ ◆

Shredderman: Secret Identity
Shredderman: Attack of the Tagger
Shredderman: Meet the Gecko
Shredderman: Enemy Spy

◆ ◆ ◆

How I Survived Being a Girl

Flipped

Swear to Howdy

Runaway

sammy keyes
AND THE wild things
THE

by WENDELIN VAN DRAANEN

ALFRED A. KNOPF
New York

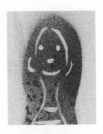

THIS IS A BORZOI BOOK PUBLISHED BY ALFRED A. KNOPF

All rights reserved. Published in the United States by Alfred A. Knopf, an imprint of Random House Children's Books, a division of Random House, Inc., New York.

KNOPF, BORZOI BOOKS, and the colophon are registered trademarks of Random House, Inc.

www.randomhouse.com/kids

Educators and librarians, for a variety of teaching tools,
visit us at www.randomhouse.com/teachers

Library of Congress Cataloging-in-Publication Data
Van Draanen, Wendelin.
Sammy Keyes and the wild things / Wendelin Van Draanen. — 1st ed.
p. cm.
SUMMARY: While on her first hiking and camping trip, thirteen-year-old Sammy tries to solve a mystery involving endangered condors while avoiding scorpions, ticks, and embarrassment.
ISBN 978-0-375-83525-4 (trade) — ISBN 978-0-375-93525-1 (lib. bdg.)
[1. Camping—Fiction. 2. Hiking—Fiction. 3. Condors—Fiction.
4. Endangered species—Fiction. 5. Southwest, New—Fiction.
6. Mystery and detective stories.] I. Title.
PZ7.V2857Sar 2007
[Fic]—dc22
2006029261

Printed in the United States of America
May 2007
10 9 8 7 6 5 4 3 2 1
First Edition

For Wendy Thies, an insightful news anchor, condor aficionada, and good friend

Acknowledgments

As always, I would like to acknowledge my editor, Nancy Siscoe, and my husband, Mark Parsons, for their invaluable input. Additionally, I want to thank Kevin Cooper, forest biologist and BAER Team Leader for the Los Padres National Forest, for sharing his condor expertise; my parents for all the camping and backpacking adventures; my siblings, with whom I've hiked many miles through scrub, ticks, and poison oak in search of condors; and my devoted leaders and fellow Scouts from Santa Anita Council Troops 86 and 10.

sammy keyes
AND THE wild things

PROLOGUE

Summer's supposed to be a time of freedom. Freedom from school, from homework, from junior high head games . . . freedom to hang out with your friends without adults constantly hovering around, telling you what to do.

But it seemed like school had barely let out when all my friends suddenly flew the coop. Marissa's family went to Las Vegas. *Again.* Holly took off on some road trip in a motor home, and Dot went to Holland to visit her grandparents. *Holland.*

Me, I was left trapped in this freak-fest of a town, in an old-folks' apartment where I live with my grandmother, next door to a whale of a woman who has supersonic hearing and the charming habit of falling off her toilet.

I was desperate to get away.

The trouble is, when you're desperate, you do dumb things.

When you're desperate, you might as well face it— you're doomed.

ONE

If Marissa *or* Holly *or* Dot had been around, I wouldn't have been thinking about Casey Acosta at all. But since they weren't around, and since Casey *does* qualify as a friend (even though he's my archenemy Heather's brother), okay, I admit it—he had crossed my mind.

More than once.

Partly that was because I'd seen him at the mall a couple of times during the first few days of summer break. Marissa was with me the first time, and she practically choked my arm off with her grip when she spotted him coming out of Sports Central. "Sammy, look! It's *Casey.*"

I wanted to say, So? but it just didn't come out.

Then *he* spotted *us,* and the three of us wound up cruising through the mall, laughing the whole afternoon away.

It was fun.

Like being with friends should be.

The *second* time I was by myself. I'd escaped the Senior Highrise, cruised the whole town on my skateboard looking for something, *anything* to do, and finally I'd wound up at the mall.

Did I go to the arcade?

No.

Did I go to the music store?

No.

To any of the clothing stores?

No.

Like a moronic moth to the flame, I fluttered over to the only place I'd ever bumped into Casey at the mall—Sports Central.

Now, I've got every right to go into a sporting goods store. I *like* sports. But I didn't go inside. I stood *outside,* pretending to window-shop, with my heart racing and my hands sweating, a shouting match going on inside my head.

"What are you *doing*?"

"I don't know!"

"Why don't you just go inside!"

"Because I don't need anything!"

"So what! Just go inside!"

"Why?"

"Because standing out here is the lamest thing you've ever done in your whole entire life!"

It was, too. I felt like one of those dingbat girls who walks back and forth past some guy's house, hoping he'll notice her. How stupid did I want to be? And what were the chances of Casey being here again? Why didn't I just call him up if I wanted to hang out with him?

So there I was, in the middle of a total mental spaz-out, when all of a sudden someone sneaks up behind me and pokes me in the ribs.

Before I can even think about what I'm doing, my elbow jabs back, punching deep into someone's stomach, and then *wham,* my fist flies up and back, smacking them in the face. And when I spin around, who do I see doubled up on the floor with blood coming out of his nose?

Nope, not Casey.

It's his goofball friend, Billy Pratt.

Casey *is* there, though. And even though his eyes are popped wide open, his words are really calm. "Dude, I told you not to startle her."

I drop to my knees and say to Billy, "Oh, man! I'm so sorry!"

He chokes out, "I'm good," but he's still totally winded, and blood's getting everywhere.

So I run to the pretzel stand, snag a bunch of napkins, and run back. "Here. Put some pressure on your nose. It'll stop the bleeding." Then I add, "I'm *really* sorry! It was . . . you know . . . a reflex."

He pinches the napkin against his nose and sits up, moaning, "No problem." He gives me a goofy grin. "I've had a stomach massage and a realignment. . . ." He shoves a corner of the napkin up his nose, and with the rest of the napkin dangling, he staggers to his feet and says, "I am totally ready to rock."

The thing about Billy Pratt is, you can't *not* laugh when you're with him. He is always, *always* "on," even when he's just been smacked to the floor by a girl. So being around him made the spastic thoughts I'd been having magically disappear. I followed him and Casey into the sporting goods store, where Casey picked out camping supplies while Billy harassed a clerk, acting like he was some hoity-toity British polo player instead of a kid with a bloody napkin dangling from his nose. "I say there, chap! These shorts say 'one hundred percent cotton,' but I must have combed *Egyptian* cotton or I break out in rashes. Absolutely wretched rashes! You wouldn't want to see, not at all! So I must know. I absolutely *must* know . . . are these combed Egyptian cotton?"

I whispered to Casey, "Do they even grow cotton in Egypt?"

"You got me," Casey whispered back. "Probably just Billy being Billy."

He'd turned and looked me in the eyes when he'd said that, only he didn't look away when he was done talking. He just kept right on looking me in the eyes.

Which of course made my heart skip around funny while glands everywhere burst forth with sweat. "Uh . . . so you're . . . uh . . . going camping, huh?" I said, showing off my brilliant intuitive talents.

He laughed, "Yup," and went back to picking out freeze-dried food. "Backpacking, remember?"

He had mentioned it at the end of the school year. Like twenty times.

"You've really never been?" he asked.

I shook my head.

He shrugged. "My dad and I got into it a few years ago. It's like camping, only cooler."

I hesitated, then said, "I've never been camping, either."

He stopped flipping through foil packages. "*You*? Never been camping?"

I shook my head again.

He stared.

I shrugged.

He went back to his freeze-dried selections. "Sorry. You just seem like . . ." His voice trailed off, and then he chuckled and said, "Now, *Marissa*. That I would believe. But you? You'd love camping."

"I don't know." I picked out a foil pouch of vegetable lasagna. It weighed hardly anything. "You actually eat this stuff?"

"That right there's pretty vile. But some of these are almost good." He grinned. "And after about day four, even the vile ones start tasting all right."

"You going with your dad?"

"Nah. He was planning to come, but then he got some big audition in L.A." He hitched a thumb in Billy's direction. "So now it's just me and Mr. Entertainment."

"You and *Billy*? And you expect to survive?"

He laughed out loud. "Yeah, my dad wasn't too hot on the idea, either. But I know what I'm doing, and he trusts me. And Billy's a good camper, believe it or not." He hesitated, then eyed me and said, "I don't suppose your mom would let you come along?"

It was my turn to laugh out loud. "I don't suppose . . . !"

And see? That's the stupid thing about trying to be friends with the opposite sex. How can you be friends when you can't *do* anything together? Even going to the movies becomes a big deal. Voices drop. Eyes bug. Gossip flies. "She went to the movies with him?

Alone?" All that gasping and gossiping over what? A movie? Sharing some popcorn? Sitting next to each other and laughing? Maybe accidentally touching elbows?

Hmm.

Anyway, it made me mad that I couldn't go camping. Not because I wanted to go and couldn't, but because I couldn't go even if I wanted to. I was a girl and he was a boy and the idea of going camping together was just insane. No, it'd have to be just him and Napkin Nose in the woods eating from shriveled foil pouches, warding off bears with nothing but sticks and their wits.

Okay, so it was probably a good thing that I couldn't go, but still, it didn't stop me from being royally ticked off about it.

So a couple of days later I went *back* to the mall because I was bored to death, and I went *back* to Sports Central. It was on beyond insane, because yes, I was hoping to run into Casey again, and no, I had no idea when he was actually leaving on his backpacking trip or how long he'd be gone.

Little details I'd neglected to gather.

I can be so bright.

Anyway, this time I didn't stare at the lime green biker shorts display and have an argument with myself. This time I just moseyed inside. And who did I find over in the camping department holding on to an empty shopping basket?

Not Casey.

It was a girl from school named Cassie Kuo. Or Cricket, as she likes to be called.

And maybe she wasn't Casey, but at least she was someone I knew.

Sort of.

I mean, I'd had her in homeroom all year, and she had been my Secret Santa at Christmastime. She'd made me a little macaroni angel to hang on my tree, so I probably *should* have known her better than I did, but she's quiet and shy and I never saw her at the lunch tables or after school; she didn't hang out around town or at the ballpark. . . .

Not that this was anything I'd ever given any thought to, but now all of a sudden there she was, sifting through the same foil pouches that Casey had gone through, and it hit me that it was truly weird to see her anywhere outside of homeroom, especially here.

"Cricket?" I asked, because I still couldn't quite believe it was her.

She jumped a little, then her head snapped to face me. "Sammy?" she gasped, like I was a long-lost friend. "It's so great to see you! What are you doing here?"

I shrugged. "Trying to get over perpetual boredom."

"You're bored? How can you be bored? It's summer!" Then her eyes got really big and she said, "Oh! It's because Heather's in England, isn't it? She's gone and you just don't know what to do with the peace and quiet, is that it? But where are Marissa and Dot and Holly and . . . all your friends?" She looked around, like, where was I hiding my posse of friends.

I couldn't help laughing, because (a) she was being really hyper and (b) the stuff she'd said about Heather was so . . .

bizarre. Like I would be bored because the world's most evil, conniving, mentally deranged teenager was half a world away?

I don't think so!

Cricket leaned in and said, "I bet Heather comes back with a phony English accent! I bet she tells everyone that she had breakfast with the queen and a private tour of Buckingham Palace. I bet she starts complaining that there's no high tea offered in the school cafeteria! I bet she starts using words like *brilliant* and *loo*! I bet—"

I busted up so hard that everyone in the store turned to look at me. I mean, Heather's *my* archenemy, not hers, but everything she was saying was so spot-on that it was like *she'd* been the one harassed by Heather all year.

When my laughing wound down, I asked, "What did she do to *you*?"

"What did she do to *me*?" She seemed to take a step back, even though she stayed right where she was. "She tortured *you*."

"But . . ."

"She was evil! Awful! How can anyone be so terrible?" She shook her head. "All year I just wanted to smack her." She grabbed my arm. "But you stood up to her and won! And now her brother likes you and she's insane over *that*." She rubbed her hands together. "It's all so . . . satisfying!"

All of a sudden I was not laughing. I was staring at Cricket and feeling very, very weird. She was treating me like the star of some teen-drama reality show that she hadn't missed one episode of. She knew a *lot* about my life—about my archenemy and her brother and my friends and all the action that had gone down at school—but I knew nothing about her.

She was just Cricket Kuo, Quiet Girl.

Macaroni Angel Girl.

"So what are you buying?" I asked, suddenly wanting to change the subject.

"Backpacking food!" she said, like she'd been saving up all year for this very moment. "We're hiking out to Vista Ridge to see condors!"

"Condors? I thought they were extinct or . . ."

Her eyes got wide. "They were *almost* extinct, but they're making a comeback! We hike out to a tracking station where we can monitor them." She tossed a couple of freeze-dried pouches into her basket. "Everyone who's seen a condor soaring over the canyon says it's the most amazing sight, and this time I'm not leaving until I spot one!"

"So how far do you have to hike?"

"Aaaactually . . ." She pulled a little face. "We drive most of the way. There's a road clear up to the tracking station, but it's steep and full of potholes, and there's a gully you need a four-wheel drive to ford. So we just get as close as we can and hike the rest." She shrugged. "It's only about five miles."

"Your whole family's into this?"

She stopped cold, then seemed to thaw from her fingertips, up her arms, to her shoulders. "I'm going with my Scout troop," she said quietly, then gave me a shy smile. "Remember? I told you about it once?"

I racked my brains, and yeah, I kind of remembered her inviting me to go on an outing with them. It was when she'd given me the macaroni angel. Or thereabouts.

"We don't wear uniforms or anything. We're just a group that likes to camp." She was looking down, and her voice had dropped to a whisper. "We don't look like the girls you see on cookie boxes."

I didn't know what to say. She was acting apologetic and so *embarrassed*.

"You would like it, Sammy," she whispered. "You really would."

I shrugged. "Probably so."

Mis-take! All of sudden her face is twitching and popping and lit up like fireworks, and she says, "Why don't you come! You'd have a blast! Vista Ridge has the most amazing views! You could share my tent! You could share my food!" She turns over a pouch of freeze-dried Santa Fe Chicken with Rice. "See? Serving size: two! I don't mind! I'll buy more!"

"Whoa, Cricket, hang on! I've never been backpacking. I don't know how. I don't have any gear!"

And what does she do with this camp-killing news flash?

She looks at my feet.

"What's your shoe size?"

"A seven . . . ?"

She hops up and down. "You can borrow boots from me! And a pack from my brother! And Robin has extra sleeping bags! You'll love Robin—she's our leader and she's good friends with Coach Rothhammer!"

Now, the fact that her leader was good friends with my softball coach was a plus. I respect Ms. Rothhammer. As Grams says, she's got backbone. But still, it wasn't reason enough to go backpacking.

So while Cricket's whipping around the store, tossing one thing after another into her basket, I'm trailing behind her going, "But I, um . . . I don't know if I can. . . . Cricket . . . ? Hey, Cricket! Hold on a minute. . . . Cricket?"

But there's no stopping this girl. When she's done filling up her basket, she grabs me by the arm and yanks me toward the checkout line. "Come on! There's a ton to do before tomorrow!"

"You're leaving *tomorrow*?"

"*We're* leaving tomorrow."

I didn't really want to, but I *was* desperate to do something, *anything*, besides hang around the mall.

So yeah, I was doomed.

I was *so* doomed.

TWO

I learned more about quiet little Cricket Kuo that one Wednesday afternoon than I had the whole school year. The biggest shock was that she's *not* quiet. She talks faster than anyone I've ever known, and *boy,* once she starts, she doesn't stop. The whole way over to her Scout leader's house, she yammered about condors and camping and the joys of feeling like you're living with nature, not just visiting it. And then, *ding-dong,* before I'd had the mental space to really process what I was getting into, we were inside the house and I was being introduced to a woman with long salt-and-pepper hair wearing an oversized T-shirt and baggy jeans.

"Sammy, this is my leader, Robin Terrane. Robin, this is Sammy Keyes! *The* Sammy I've told you about? And guess what! She's coming with us!" She hesitated. "If that's all right?" But before Robin could say a thing, Cricket barreled ahead. "She doesn't have any supplies, so we need to borrow a sleeping bag and a pad, and maybe some utensils and stuff. I have everything else at home! What do you say? Is it all right?"

Cricket was chirping so fast and Robin was giving me such a sharp once-over that I felt more like an item up for auction than a kid gathering camping gear. Then Cricket added, "She'll do great, I promise! Sammy's tough! Ask Coach Rothhammer. Sammy plays catcher for her!"

Robin's eyebrows went up. "Catcher, huh?" She finally smiled and said, "Well, why not?" and led us to her garage. "Take what you need. I'll get the forms."

Cricket rummaged through the garage like it was her own, and in less than five minutes we had a down sleeping bag, a thin pad of dense foam, a plate, a cup, and utensils, plus medical release papers and a permission slip from Robin.

"Six-thirty a.m., right here. Don't be late!" Robin said as we left with her stuff through the roll-up garage door. The door was halfway closed when suddenly it stopped and went back up. "Don't be early, either!"

Cricket called, "I know, I know! Sorry!"

I eyed her as we zipped up the sidewalk. "You've been early for a six-thirty start time?"

She laughed. "I get excited."

This was definitely an understatement. And on the long walk back to her house, she seemed to get even more wound up, chattering a million miles an hour about Robin and her daughter, Bella, who's best friends with some girl named Gabby who both go to Bruster, which is our rival junior high.

And *then* she went on and on about Robin's nephew, Quinn—how smart and strong and passionate about condors he is—until finally she wound down with, "He knows everything about the wilderness, Sammy. Everything!" She let out a dreamy sigh. "He's amazing."

Her cheeks were all rosy, and she was practically skipping down the sidewalk. "And cute, too?" I asked with a smirk.

She blushed. "You have no idea."

There was a white pickup truck parked in the driveway of Cricket's house, and when she saw it, she said, "Oh, good. Gary's still home."

Gary turned out to be her brother. Sixteen or seventeen, round face, lots of acne, and hair shooting out all over the place. He looked like a pimply porcupine that had had its quills dipped in black ink.

"Hey!" Cricket said, leaning into his dungeon of a bedroom. "Can we borrow your backpack?"

The minute it registered that there were intruders in the dungeon, Gary shrank the page on his computer quick. "Huh?"

"You haven't been out of this room all day, have you?" Cricket asked, stepping inside it.

He ignored the question and asked one of his own. "Who's your friend?"

He was talking about me, but he sure wasn't looking at me.

"Her name's Sammy. Can she borrow your backpack?"

Now he looked at me. For all of a nanosecond.

"Sure." He got up and started rooting around his closet, and that's when I noticed that his dungeon walls were decorated with—not swords or shields or random medieval weapons—no, they were covered in *butterflies.* Cases and cases of real butterflies.

Well, real *dead* ones, anyway.

There were small ones, big ones, colorful ones, plain ones . . . and at first I thought it was kind of neat, but then I noticed that every one of them had a pin sticking right through its body. They'd been mounted to look like they were in flight, but they were stabbed, straight through the heart.

Gary emerged from the closet and caught me staring at his collection. "My uncle got me started a couple of years ago."

"Got you started?" Cricket asked. "He gave you his whole collection!"

"So?" He turned back to me. "I've traded up a lot. Some of them are pretty valuable."

"They are not," Cricket said with a scowl. "That's just what your Internet buddies say."

Gary blushed, but he came back fighting. "Oh, now you're an expert on my collection? Like you know anything about it?" From the main compartment of his backpack he pulled out a small Super Soaker, a bright red rubbery football, and a pair of Rollerblades. Then he started emptying miscellaneous things from the side pockets, saying, "When I get my hands on a four-eyed viperwing, you'll envy me all the way to the bank."

"A four-eyed viperwing," Cricket said with a snort. "Right."

He threw his sister a pimply-faced sneer, then handed his backpack over to me. "It's sorta thrashed, but . . ." His voice trailed off as he gave a shrug. Like, what can I say?

"Thanks. I'll take good care of it."

"I wouldn't notice if you didn't." He sat back down in

front of his computer. "Not that that's an invitation to thrash it worse . . ." And we were just starting to leave the dungeon when he asked, "Where you guys going, anyway?"

"Vista Ridge."

He turned back to his computer. "Dodo safari, huh?"

Cricket spun to face him. "It is not a dodo safari! Dodos are extinct—condors are on their way *back* from extinction." She frowned at him. "Just because you've given up doesn't mean I have to."

Gary was ignoring her, typing like crazy at his keyboard as he muttered, "I wonder what a dodo would be worth. Can you imagine if you had one of those?"

"You don't live in the real world anymore, Gary."

He opened one of the dodo bird links that had popped up on his monitor and read, " 'The last known stuffed dodo bird was destroyed in a 1755 fire at a museum in Oxford, England, leaving only partial skeletons and drawings—' "

"Hello . . . ? Gary . . . ? You're researching *dodos*? You need to get away from that computer!"

He clicked on a link and said, "You're not my mom," as another page flew open.

Cricket's face went stony for just a second, then she said, "But you know Mom wouldn't want you living like this! She'd want you to—"

"Time for you to go," he said.

"But she—"

"GO!"

Cricket grabbed the backpack from me and muttered, "Fine," and marched out of his bedroom, up the hall, and into her own bedroom, which was not even remotely dungeon-like. It was tidy and sunny and felt like . . . springtime.

Cricket, though, was like a dark cloud, storming around inside it. "Mom would *hate* that he spends all his time like that. We were always outdoors before. Always *together*. We used to go up to Vista Ridge all the time—to camp, or just to picnic and watch for condors." The storm cloud started to cry. "Now he lives on the Internet, Dad is always at work. . . . It's like the whole family died when she did."

I felt so helpless. I mean, what can you say to that? And maybe my own home situation isn't the greatest—I have an absentee mom and an unknown dad—but neither of them's *dead*.

Well, maybe my dad is, but from the way my mom and Grams won't discuss him, I don't think so.

But *anyway*. I barely knew this girl, and all of a sudden I'm in her house, borrowing her stuff, finding out all sorts of painful things about her life. And I am feeling totally sorry for her, but I also have a killer urge to get *out* of there.

"I'm sorry," she says, flinging tears off her cheeks and trying to smile. "You probably think I'm a total dysfunctional loser."

"No, I—"

"And now you probably don't even want to go camping with me."

"Well, I haven't even asked my—"

"But tough!" she says, laughing. "You're coming

'cause I really, really want you to, and I know you'll have a great time." She took a deep breath. "Now let's get you some boots and let's get packing!"

"I don't know about boots," I told her. "I think I'll just stick with my high-tops."

She eyed my feet. "Those are really worn out, and they have no support, Sammy. You'll feel rocks right through them. If you had some trail shoes or even cross-trainers, you'd be okay. But those?" She looked at me and pulled a face. "You'll die out there in those."

So I tried on her backup boots, and they seemed to fit fine. And I could tell what she meant by support. The boots had a tank for a toe and some really serious tread.

"They feel good," I said with a shrug.

"Great!"

So we moved on to packing, which should have been easier than it was, but there was the whole complication of me not wanting to tell Cricket about my living situation. See, kids aren't allowed to live in my grams' apartment building, and if people find out I am, Grams and I'll both get kicked out. So I had to practically ditch Cricket, then do what I always do—sneak up the fire escape and tiptoe down the hall and into the apartment.

When I told Grams what was going on and that I'd be gone for four days, part of me was hoping she'd say, "No, Samantha. I don't know these people, it's too dangerous, you cannot go."

But another part of me was thinking that if I went camping with Cricket, I'd be able to tell Casey how cool it had been and how I'd seen deer drinking from the rivers and condors swooping through the air.

And a secret, very *stupid* part of me was thinking that maybe I'd run into Casey while I was camping. I mean, what if he was hiking in the same area? It'd be a blast to hang out a little with him and Billy in the wilderness.

So the smart part of me didn't really want to go, and the dumb part of me did.

Grams, though, settled the whole thing. "You're going to see condors?" Her whole face lit up. "That's wonderful!"

I squinted at her. This was very un-Grams-like, and I don't know . . . it made me kind of defensive. Normally she worries about *everything,* and now it was suddenly A-OK that I'd be hiking in the wilderness with strangers?

Wasn't she worried?

Didn't she *care?*

She must have read my mind because she scoffed and said, "They're *Girl* Scouts, Samantha. And this is a wonderful opportunity! Why, I would love to see a condor!"

"Since when do you know anything about condors?"

She patted her hair in an oh-so-superior fashion. "If you would watch the local news with me . . ."

I scooped up my cat, Dorito, and flopped into a chair. "Oh, please, Grams." But then I sat up. "They covered *condors?*"

Grams nodded. "A few weeks ago Grayson Mann did a series for KSMY."

"A *series?*"

"Well. Several two-minute segments spread out over the week. You know how they do."

I stroked Dorito and grunted.

"He went up to a condor watchtower in a helicopter. It's probably the same place you're going. I thought the whole topic was fascinating."

I gave her a wicked grin and said, "I'll bet you did," because anything Grayson Mann reports on she finds fascinating. Not that she has a granny crush on him or anything—she'd better not. He's only about forty and she's . . . well, she wouldn't want me to say. But anyway, I'm sure it's not him—I think it's his hair. It's all feathery and sort of permanently swooped back. Like the wind is his stylist.

Anyway, so Grams had no problem signing the papers. But by the time I'd collected everything I needed, trudged back over to Cricket's, and had Gary's backpack fully loaded, it was nine-thirty and I was exhausted. And since we had to be back at Robin's early in the morning, and since there was no way I wanted to try sneaking into the Senior Highrise with a load of camping gear, the only thing that made sense was for me to spend the night at Cricket's.

Gary never came out of his room. Not that I saw, anyway. Cricket's dad came home from work around eight, poked his head in to say hello, then disappeared to his own corner of the house. There were no pets, no sounds, no music . . . but Cricket gave the house life. She chattered about everything and seemed so excited to have me there. Like I was her first sleepover or something.

Finally I said, "Cricket, I'm so tired. Where can I crash?"

"Oh! Right there!" she said, pointing to her bed.

"No way," I told her. Then I asked, "Is there a couch?" because that's exactly what I sleep on at home.

"No, really, Sammy. I never use the bed." She slid her closet door open about two feet, crawled inside, then peeked out at me and smiled. "This is where I sleep!"

At first I thought she was joking, but then I saw that she was totally set up inside her closet. She had a thin mattress that bowed up against the wall and the sliding doors, a sleeping bag, a big flashlight, a small stack of books, an alarm clock, a hugged-to-death stuffed deer, and a bottle of water. The only thing that didn't seem to belong was a pair of Rollerblades crammed in a corner at the foot of her mattress.

"Wow," I said, truly amazed. "You really do like camping, don't you?"

"I even have *stars* in here. Check it out!"

"Stars?" This I had to see. So I crawled in beside her, and after she closed the door, I could see glow-in-the-dark stars and moons shining faintly from the inside of the door.

"Cool, huh?" she said, opening the door again. "So see? You get the bed." She grinned. "Sorry."

So I slept in a bed for the first time in ages. It was a *great* bed, too, with soft, fluffy covers and pillows and the faint scent of bleach. And flowers . . .

And I was in the middle of having this great dream about floating through the air on a current of puffy white dandelions . . . just drifting up, down, gliding gently through the air . . . when suddenly *clingidy-cling-cling-clang* Cricket's alarm blew the closet door open and booted Cricket into the room.

"Huh?" I said, totally disoriented.

Cricket flicked on the light. "Let's go camping!"

THREE

Cricket's "troop" turned out to be the most un-Girl-Scoutish group of girls I'd ever seen. Not a patch or merit badge in sight. And their uniform? T-shirts, hiking boots, jeans, ball caps . . . no sashes or vests or, you know, *neckerchiefs*.

Also, when you think of a Girl Scout troop, you think of a big *group*. But this troop consisted of Robin's daughter, Bella—who speaks with very precise diction and has dark curly hair that springs out in all directions—Bella's best friend, Gabby—who has big ears and a little mouth—and Cricket, and me. That was it. I was one-fourth of a "troop," and I wasn't even officially in the group!

We all piled into a well-worn van and were on the road by six-forty-five, with Robin driving, Cricket and me in the seats behind Robin, and Gabby and Bella in the seats behind us. And by the time we'd been on the road about an hour, I knew exactly why Cricket was so excited to have me come along. In this troop of three, she was odd girl out. See, Bella and Gabby are best-friends-forever kind of friends. Bella leads, and Gabby's the adoring copycatter, agreeing with Bella about everything, sticking up for her about anything.

It got old in a hurry.

And the *trouble* is, Cricket was trying to act like best-friends-forever with *me*, which became really embarrassing. She wasn't being an adoring copycatter, but it was almost worse—she kept telling Gabby and Bella stories about things I'd done to Heather during the year. At first Bella laughed, but then she started getting annoyed, and before long she was rolling her eyes and pulling faces like she flat-out disliked me. Which of course made Gabby do the same.

"Stop it!" I whispered to Cricket for about the fiftieth time. "Don't say another word!"

If I could have turned around and gone back to the boredom of living in an apartment building with a bunch of old people, believe me, I would have. But I was stuck. And by the time we were bumping along the potholes of a narrow mountain road, I was in a serious frump. How had I let myself get suckered into this?

It wasn't just that the people were driving me crazy. It was the scenery. Everything was so brown. So dry. There were no pine trees, no picturesque mountain streams, no twittering wildlife. And the farther up the mountain we climbed, the more it seemed that this "forest" we were in was really just a wasteland of rejects. Like all the plants and animals that hadn't made the cut for *real* forests were collected and put into this place. Crows and flies, scrub oaks and dusty dirt, dried grass and tumbleweeds . . . who wants those in their forest?

Not me.

Robin seemed to pick up on my mood because I caught her watching me in the rearview mirror. "So, Sammy," she called. "Has Cricket told you about the Vista Ridge Lookout project?"

"A little . . ."

"A *little*? Cricket . . . !" Robin scolded, but she was grinning. "Whatever you've been bending her ear about couldn't have been as important as the Lookout project!"

Cricket blushed.

Robin made a careful turn of the wheel as she negotiated a switchback in the road. "We've been helping with the Lookout project for"—she glanced back at Bella and Gabby in the mirror—"how many years, girls?"

"Since fourth grade!" they answered in harmony.

"Since sixth for me," Cricket said quietly.

Like I cared? I didn't want to hear about condors or some goody-goody Lookout project. I'd been promised camping, but instead I was trapped with a bunch of condor fanatics who'd probably spend the whole time talking about "environmental issues."

And any secret hope of running into Casey and Billy was gone. Why would they waste their vacation in this desert of a forest? They were probably someplace with *real* trees, having a great time actually *camping*.

"Are you okay, Sammy?" Robin asked. "You look a little green."

If I'd have been *thinking*, I'd have said I was sick and had to go home. But I was a *moron* and said, "I just don't really get it, that's all."

"Get what?"

"Well, how you track condors, for one thing. Is the Lookout like a radio control tower? Like at an airport?"

"Good analogy. Only it's not nearly as sophisticated."

"Or as tall!" Bella called from the backseat.

"Or as easy to get to!" Gabby groaned as we thumped and bumped over a really bad pothole.

"But *how* do you track them? Do they have a chip implanted in them?"

Robin took another careful turn. "Again, the same idea, but not as sophisticated. The condors have a transmitter and numbered tags attached to their wings; they don't bother them a bit."

"But *why* do you track them? What good does it do?"

"In the Pleistocene age there were thousands of condors in the wild. By 1890 that number was down to six hundred, and it continued to dwindle until 1983, when the population was a paltry twenty-two."

"Were people hunting them?"

"People weren't hunting them, but hunting *is* what caused part of the problem. Condors are nature's cleanup crew. They eat animals that have died of natural causes, as well as gut piles left behind by hunters. They *also* eat carcasses of animals that have been poisoned by people who considered them to be pests. And if a condor eats poisonous lead from bullets or poison that was in a dead animal's system, it kills the condor, too.

"There was also a problem with pesticides like DDT, which made condor eggs so thin-shelled that they were easily crushed. And since condors breed slowly—one chick every two years, or thereabouts—and since they don't reproduce until they're about six years old, the population fell dramatically. By the late 1980s there were *no* condors left in the wild. The few birds remaining were in captivity." She glanced at me in the rearview mirror. "They were really, *really* close to extinction."

I thought about all of this, then said, "I don't even know what one looks like."

"You *don't?*" everyone cried. Like *I* was the dumb one.

So I scowled around the van and said, "How am I supposed to know what a condor looks like? There are only twenty-two of them, and we don't exactly have a *zoo* in Santa Martina. . . ."

"There's more than twenty-two now," Bella said.

"Yeah!" Gabby chimed in. "And there's pictures all over the Web."

Bella nodded. "And there's one hanging at the Natural History Museum."

"Yeah! It's been up for a year. Didn't your school go there on a field trip?"

God, they were driving me crazy. And then Robin says, "Here," and hands me a pamphlet from the front seat. Can you believe that? They're handing out *pamphlets* like they want to convert me to their birdbrain religion.

Join the Condor Cult!

Sacrifice your summer!

Worship the Mighty Feathered Ones!

Man, was I stuck or what?

But really, what could I do?

I took the stupid pamphlet, and when I turned it face-up, what did I see?

The single *ugliest* bird imaginable. Big hunchy black body, bald, bloated red head and face, and what looks like a little black feather boa around its blotchy red neck.

"That's a condor?" I choke out.

"It's got an almost ten-foot wingspan," Robin says. "An eagle can have up to a seven-foot wingspan, so that gives you some idea of how magnificent the condor is."

My eyes were bugging out at the brochure. How could she think this bird was *magnificent*? That was like calling a barracuda beautiful. So what if it had big wings? I couldn't believe that *this* was what all the fuss was about. That *this* was worth building tracking stations for.

What was *wrong* with these people?

Then Robin said, "Vista Ridge Lookout was originally a Forest Service watchtower for spotting fires, but they stopped using it years ago, and then vandals wrecked it. But with the hard work of lots of volunteers—"

"Like us!" Bella said.

"Yeah, us!" Gabby chimed.

Robin laughed. "—it's become a useful tracking facility."

"You wouldn't believe everything we've done," Bella said.

"Yeah! We painted!"

"And cleared brush!"

"And hung shelves!" Cricket tossed in.

"And helped install windows!"

"And shutters!"

Robin snickered. "You girls make it sound like we did everything!" She glanced at me again. "We're actually just a small part of a large and varied group of people who feel really passionate about saving the condor. The Forest Service, the Audubon Society, Fish and Wildlife, the Wilderness Society, university students—"

"Who only do it for a good grade!" Bella said.

"Yeah!" Gabby added. "Or so they can come up here and drink beer!"

Robin raised an eyebrow. "Hey, now. Those kids would not go into environmental studies if they didn't care about the environment."

"But *you* said they were snot-nosed partyers who had too much attitude and not enough aptitude!" Bella called from the back.

Robin shot her daughter a dark look via the rearview mirror. "I *muttered* it, Bella. And I only said it about one *particular* student."

"Oh, right—that Vargus guy."

"Vargus Mayfield!" Gabby giggled, bouncing in her seat. "He was *cute*."

Bella gave Gabby a pained look. "Cute?"

"They're all cute at that age, girls," Robin warned.

"Like Quinn." Gabby giggled again.

Cricket jolted a little, and Bella backhanded Gabby, saying, "What's up with you? Quinn's twenty-two, he's got a girlfriend, and he's my *cousin*."

"He's got a girlfriend?" Gabby asked, her voice suddenly small. "Since when?"

"Since a few weeks ago!" Then Bella ran down the stats: "Her name's Janey Griffin, and she's new in town. She's super-pretty and smart and athletic—you should see her ride her mountain bike! She works at the Natural History Museum and is really into the outdoors." And as if she hadn't already rubbed it in hard enough, she smiled at Gabby and said, "She is *perfect* for Quinn."

Robin dropped the van into a lower gear. "We are *way* off topic, girls. What I was trying to explain to Sammy is that a lot of people have donated a great deal of time, money, and energy to build a research facility so we can track the flight patterns and roosting habits of condors."

I still didn't get it. So what if they tracked them? How did *that* help?

Then Bella announced, "I have a really good feeling that this is going to be *the* trip, Mom!"

"Me too," Gabby said halfheartedly.

"Let's hope so, girls!" Robin said.

"Wait a minute." I looked back at Bella. "You've been doing this since fourth grade and *none* of you has ever seen a condor?"

Bella shook her head. "Not in the wild."

For a second it was really quiet in the van. Then Gabby said, "But Quinn has. Lots of times. Right now he's monitoring a juvenile and its mother out at Chumash Caves." She gave a dreamy sigh. "He's so devoted. He practically *lives* up here."

So there I am, stuck in a van on a dusty, bumpy mountain road with a bunch of condor *nuts* who obviously have mad crushes on other, older, more *extreme* condor nuts, when all of a sudden, a black jeep comes flying around the corner toward us.

Robin slams on the brakes.

Bella screams.

Gabby screams louder.

Cricket and I hold on tight while our eyes bug out, because the jeep is now totally out of control, sliding and swerving and kicking up clouds of dust as the driver tries frantically to skid to a stop.

But he's *not* stopping, and there's just no place for him to go.

No place but off the cliff.

Or right into us.

FOUR

"Hold on, girls!" Robin shouts as she throws the van into reverse and guns it. She's craned around backward, we're thrust forward, and the jeep is skidding toward us sideways. Then, like it's hit a patch of ice, the jeep's back end swings around and slams into the side of the mountain.

"He crashed!" Bella shouts.

Robin puts on the brakes, then just sits there clutching the wheel, panting for air as she looks through the windshield.

Outside, everything is still. Everything but dust, drifting up through the air.

Finally Robin loosens her grip on the wheel and asks, "Is everyone all right?"

As a yes, we all start talking at once. "Man, that was close!" "Good driving, Mom!" "What's the *matter* with that guy?" "He could have killed us!" "Do you think he's hurt?"

Then the driver steps out of the jeep and Bella gasps. "That's Vargus Mayfield!"

Gabby gasps, too. "It *is* . . . !"

I turn to Cricket. "Who's Vargus Mayfield again?"

"That college student they were talking about earlier . . . ?"

"Yeah," Bella says, scowling at Gabby. "The one with more attitude than aptitude."

Robin gets out of the van saying, "You girls should probably stay put."

We give it a second, look at each other, then all pile out.

Vargus Mayfield's mouth is busy four-wheeling through some rough verbal terrain as he looks over the damage to his jeep.

"The only person you should be mad at is yourself, Vargus," Robin tells him. "There's no *way* you should have been driving that fast on this road!"

"Huh?" he says, blinking at her like he can't quite place who she is. One by one he gives each of us a blank look, but when he gets to Bella, it clicks. "Oh, spare me!" he whines, his whole face contorting. "The goody-goody Girl Scouts?"

Bella steps forward. "Don't make fun of *us*, buddy! We're not the ones with more attitude than aptitude! We're not the ones trying to run innocent people off the road! We're not the ones—"

"Hey, hey, hey!" Robin pulls her back and whispers, "Let me handle this."

But Vargus is already going off. "Like this is *my* fault? I wouldn't be up here at all if it wasn't for that pigheaded Professor Prag! I left messages on his machine, like, twenty times, I taped notes to his office door, but does he bother to call me back? No!"

Robin squints at him. "So you came clear out here to, what, *find* him?"

"I was desperate, man! One of the other teachers told me he was probably at the Lookout, so I got up real early to catch him, but he's not there! Nobody's there."

"What are you desperate about? What can possibly be so urgent?"

"He *flunked* me! He stopped me from graduating! I *so* did not deserve to flunk his stupid class and he knows it! I worked up at that miserable Lookout six weekends. Six weekends! I could have been home having a good time, partying with my friends, but instead I came up here. And for this I get a no credit? It's just not fair! It's not right! It's—"

Vargus had gotten all red in the face and looked like he was going to bust a gasket, so Robin grabbed his arm and said, "Hey, calm down." But he kept right on ranting, so Robin grabbed him by *both* arms and shouted, "Vargus! Vargus, look at me. Look . . . at . . . me . . . !"

Vargus looked at her.

"Take a deep breath."

Vargus took a deep breath.

"I know it seems like the end of the world now, but it's going to be okay."

Vargus just stood there, holding his breath.

We waited.

And waited.

His face turned redder.

And redder.

His eyes started bulging.

"What is he doing?" Bella whispered.

"I don't know," I whispered back.

Finally Robin told him, "It's okay to let it out, Vargus."

A great burst of air shot out of him, straight into Robin's face, then he panted like crazy, looked at his jeep, and wailed, "I'm not gonna graduate, I wrecked my jeep . . . my dad is gonna kill me!"

Robin took a deep breath herself, and after she watched him sob for a few minutes, she headed for the jeep, saying, "I'm going to see if it'll drive or if we have to get you a tow."

"Hey!" he said, charging for the driver's door. "I'll do it!"

She stuck her arm between him and the door. "I really don't think you're in any condition to drive, Vargus."

"I'm *fine*," he said, edging her aside.

Robin shrugged and backed off, and we all watched from a safe distance as Vargus revved up the jeep and maneuvered it away from the mountain until it was facing downhill.

"He's so lucky it was the back end that crunched and not the front end," Cricket said.

"He's lucky he didn't go off the cliff!" Robin muttered.

"Hey!" Vargus shouted, hanging out his window. "Move your van, would you?!"

So we all piled into the van and Robin backed up until there was enough room for Vargus to get his jeep past her easily. She watched him in the mirror until he'd disappeared in a cloud of dust, then shook her head and said, "Well, that was exciting," and headed up the mountain.

It was only another five or ten minutes before Robin pulled off the road, parking alongside a handful of other cars. "Here we are," she said, tossing us a grin. "And in one piece!"

I slid open the van door and nodded at the other cars. "Do a lot of people hike up to the Lookout?"

"Sometimes," Bella said, climbing out after Cricket. "But mostly people park here because it's the trailhead for a bunch of other hikes."

"Yeah," Gabby said. Then she pointed around, saying, "There's an awesome loop that takes you from here along Sky Ridge, down to Rocky Ravine, through Hoghead Valley, beneath Chumash Caves, and around that way to Deer Creek, Devil's Horn, Coldwater Pass, and the Bluffs. Then you can either cut off to go to the Lookout or loop around back to here."

"Takes about a week," Cricket said.

Bella opened the van's back doors and pulled out her backpack. "I wouldn't want to do it in the summer, though."

Gabby nodded, strapping on her pack. "Too many ticks."

"And rattlesnakes."

"And scorpions."

My eyes bugged. "Scorpions?" I turned to Cricket. "Rattlesnakes at least give you a little warning. But scorpions? And ticks? You didn't say anything about scorpions and ticks!"

Cricket threw Gabby and Bella a withering look, then said, "Don't listen to them. I've only ever seen one scorpion, and that was way off in Hoghead Valley."

"One is plenty!"

Boy, was I sounding like a sissy. So what if I saw a scorpion? Like I couldn't just squash it with my tank-toed boot?

But . . . what if one got inside our tent and jabbed me in the middle of the night?

Or snuck up behind me as I was, you know, relieving myself in the wilderness?

Cricket unloaded my backpack, saying, "Don't freak out, Sammy. They're just bugs."

Yeah. Bugs that'll kill you. Or give you Lyme disease. Or suck your veins dry of blood. Or . . .

"Take your backpack!" Cricket said, and she sounded kinda irritated 'cause I was just standing there like a moron while she held it out to me.

So I took it, and I strapped it on like I knew what I was doing. And after Robin had the van locked up tight, we hit the road, them happy, me hoping we weren't headed for Ticksville.

The first thing we did was cross over a bouldery gully, which was not a good way to get used to a backpack. I felt like I was going to topple over and wind up on my back like a potato bug, kicking and flailing, helplessly trying to get back on my feet.

But after we'd crossed the gully and had been going for a while, I got the hang of hiking with a backpack and actually started liking it. It wasn't a big burden like carrying a backpack of schoolbooks is. A hiking backpack is way bigger, and even though it's heavier, it *feels* lighter because it doesn't really hang from your shoulders. The hip belt hoists the weight and sort of suspends it. There is some weight on your shoulders, but it's mostly braced by your hips.

So the first half hour was great. I even forgot about ticks and scorpions and just hiked, keeping up with Cricket no problem. I think she was pushing herself kind of hard, too, because she wiped some sweat off her brow and panted, "I knew you'd be good at this!"

"Thanks!" The sun was starting to really beat down and I was pretty thirsty, so I said, "Can you see which pocket my canteen is in?" because I didn't remember, and the frame of the pack made it so I couldn't really tell.

She patted the side of my backpack. "Right here."

We both took a break for water, but after two little sips she put hers away. "Don't drink so much, Sammy. Only a few swallows."

I lowered my bottle "Isn't there water at the Lookout?"

"Sort of."

"Sort of?"

"It's collected runoff. It needs to be filtered before you drink it." She pointed to my water bottle. "That's got to last you all the way to the top, and it gets steeper."

So I started to put the bottle away, but when Cricket began hiking again, I couldn't resist—I took a couple more sips. And a couple more. We'd put the canteens in the freezer the night before, so the water was icy cold and *so* refreshing. And really, how much farther could the Lookout be?

An hour later I understood that hiking five miles with a thirty-pound pack is nothing like walking five miles with a backpack of books. I was *dying*. The road was steep and dusty, the sun was blazing hot, and I had blisters.

Really *painful* blisters.

About the tenth time the group waited up for me, I finally broke down and said, "I need to put some Band-Aids on my feet. I've got blisters on my heels that are killing me."

So everyone had to wait while I dumped my backpack, unlaced my boots, and got a little lesson in moleskin.

It's not *real* skin from a mole. It's this pink fuzzy stuff that you cut into a doughnut shape and put around your blister. At least that's what they told me worked best. Robin said, "You absolutely don't want to pop blisters— they'll hurt worse, maybe bleed, and probably get infected. The moleskin doughnut keeps the pressure off the blister and will keep the shoe from rubbing that spot." When she was done helping me apply it, she smiled at me and said, "There. You're all set!"

Meaning get up and get hiking.

Which I did.

But I've got news for you—moleskin doughnuts work about as good as they'd taste.

The last thing I wanted was to be a whiner, though, so I just cringed and shuffled along, trying to keep up.

"How you doing?" Robin kept asking me, 'cause obviously I was lagging.

"Fine," I kept lying, 'cause I'm not *used* to lagging. I'm used to being the one going, "Come on! Keep up!

Can't you move a little faster?" But while the others were climbing up the trail like mountain goats, my feet were in pain, my thighs were aching, and I was so thirsty that all I wanted to do was stop and drink water.

"You've just got to keep moving," Robin finally told me. "Stopping all the time makes hiking hard. Just go at a steady pace and don't quit—you'll find that it's actually easier." Then she added, "And go easy on the water. You'll want some left for the last mile. It's steep."

"Steeper than this?" I choked out. And I wanted to kick myself for sounding like such a baby, but I just couldn't help it. On top of everything else, it felt like someone had slipped big ol' boulders into my pack. My hips were aching, but loosening the hip belt so the weight was on my shoulders just made things worse.

Robin smiled at me. "Quite an undertaking for your first hike, especially in somebody else's shoes. But you'll make it." She handed me a piece of gum and said, "This'll help." Then she started hiking again and called, "When you get to the top, you'll feel great!"

As I trudged along, the others kept me in sight. I could tell they were annoyed that I was holding them back, and I *hated* that. Why didn't they just go on ahead instead of following their stupid *safety* rule that was making me feel like a complete loser.

Hmm. Maybe they were worried that I'd spot a condor without them.

Ha.

Like I'd even care?

Also, I didn't want them to know, but I'd run out of

water. My lips were flaky and cracking, my face was scorched and dry. . . . I felt like I'd been hiking up an endless sand dune in the Sahara Desert. *Water,* my mind kept saying, *water. . . .*

Then Cricket called, "We can see the Lookout, Sammy! You're almost to the top!"

Thank God.

I plodded along, and when I finally reached the top, I felt like shouting "Robin Terrane is a liar!" because I did *not* feel great.

I felt *destroyed.*

The others were already heading up the stairs to the Lookout, so I twisted out of my backpack and dumped it alongside the lineup of other packs.

But as I started up the stairs, Bella, Gabby, and Cricket came pounding *down,* and I could see from the look on their faces that something was wrong.

Very wrong.

FIVE

Vista Ridge Lookout is a one-room, square metal building on stilts. It has a set of metal stairs leading up to a green door and windows all the way around that are protected by brick-colored shutters. The top half of each shutter swings up and attaches to the roof awning, and the bottom half swings down, practically touching a deck that goes clear around the building. The deck has a chain-link "wall" to keep you from falling over, but it makes the Lookout seem like a prison guard tower instead of a bird-watcher's playhouse. A little barbed wire, a few guns . . . you'd be all set.

Anyway, there I am, parched and in pain, dying to get inside the Lookout for some water and shade, only the other girls are charging *down* the steps. Bella sees me and cries, "Someone broke in! Mom thinks they might still be inside!"

It didn't seem very smart for Robin to stay up there alone, but less than a minute later she came through the doorway and called, "Nobody home. But the place is turned upside down."

"But why?" Bella cried, heading back up the steps. "Why would somebody do that?"

"Is anything missing?" Cricket called as we followed Bella.

"It's hard to tell."

Inside, we all just stood around for a minute, trying to absorb the mess that surrounded us. There was broken glass from a window next to the door. You couldn't tell from the outside because the shutter concealed it, but it had been busted so somebody could reach inside and unlock the door. There was enough light flooding in through the open door for us to see that desks and chairs had been flipped over and that cups and books and pictures and binoculars and *beer* cans were strewn everywhere. But the corners of the room were in shadows, and the whole place felt really eerie.

Gabby made a sort of hiccupy sound, and when I looked at her, I saw that she was crying.

Crying.

And then Bella broke down and wailed, "I can't believe someone *did* this!"

"So what do we do?" Cricket asked.

Robin took a deep breath. "I guess the best course of action is to see if we can find the shortwave radio. If we can, I'll get in touch with the sheriff and try to reach Quinn. He told me he was coming up last night, so I don't know where he is. It's not like him to be late."

"There's no cell service?" I asked, because Robin had a cell phone clipped to her pocket.

Robin shook her head. "But we'll be able to radio down to the base station."

"The base station?"

"The main fire station in Santa Luisa." Then she added, "We can also reach the sheriff or Professor Prag at the college."

Robin handed Cricket a small ring of keys and said, "Would you and Sammy go outside and open all the shutters?"

"Sure."

The padlock of the broken window's shutter had been put back through its latch so the shutter still *looked* locked, but the loop part of the lock had been cut near the base.

"Did they *saw* through it?" Cricket asked, studying it, too.

"I don't think so. See how the metal looks pinched? I think they used bolt cutters."

"What are bolt cutters?"

"My friend Hudson has a pair. They've got long handles for torque and a curved pincer-looking blade. I saw him cut open a rusted lock in his garage once—snapped right through it."

Cricket moved to the next window and unlocked it, her lips tight, her nostrils flared.

"You okay?" I asked as I helped her hook open the top shutter.

"No," she said, "I'm *mad*." She went on to the next window. "You have no idea how upsetting this is. A lot of people work really hard to fix up this place and then some *moron* comes along and trashes it. Why? Why would anyone want to *do* this?"

I helped her with the next shutter. "Maybe because they're mad at someone?"

At first she didn't get it, but then her eyes got really wide. She dropped the shutter she'd been lifting and ran inside the Lookout crying, "Robin! It was Vargus! It had to be Vargus!"

"Calm down, Cricket. I know. You're probably right." Robin was collecting beer cans, potato chip bags, and other trash in a plastic bag. "But he's long gone and will deny it, so we need to find the radio." She took a deep breath and looked from Cricket to me and back. "It would help a lot if you could open the rest of the shutters."

Gabby and Bella had filtered some water, so after I downed as much as they'd let me have, I made a quick stop at the area around the broken window. I didn't see a thing. No snagged hairs, no clothes fragments, no blood . . .

Too bad for us, this was real life, not the movies.

So I went back outside and helped Cricket open the rest of the shutters. "Wow," I said when we were all done and I finally noticed the view.

"Amazing, isn't it?"

I nodded. It wasn't that it was so beautiful, it was that you could see so *far*. The hills just seemed to roll away, getting soft and fuzzy in the hazy distance.

"Here, do this," she said, grabbing my arm. "Walk around the whole thing. Don't look down, just out."

When we'd made it halfway around, I said, "Wow," again, and it came out all breathy. Like I really meant it.

"Doesn't it feel like you're on top of the world?" she whispered.

I nodded and watched a hawk riding a thermal along

the canyon. It didn't flap, didn't seem to put in any effort at all. It just glided along, tipping slightly from side to side as it circled and swooped and rode the wind.

"You see hawks up here all the time," she whispered. "Them and crows." She laughed. "I hate crows."

I laughed, too, because I'm no fan of crows myself. They're big and ugly and oily and scary, and they *caw*. Like it isn't bad enough to be big and ugly and oily and scary? You also have to *caw*?

But anyway, there we are, having a laugh about crows, when all of a sudden I see a little flash of light down in the canyon. Like someone signaling with a mirror. And then I notice a trail of dust rising into the air. "What's that?" I ask, pointing.

Cricket squints, then runs inside the Lookout. "Someone's coming up the back road!"

"There's a back road?" I ask, following her.

Cricket grabs a pair of monster binoculars and races outside again, the rest of us right behind her. She studies the flashing puff of dust a minute, then squeals, "It's Quinn!"

"Really?" Gabby says, grabbing the binoculars away. But before she can even get focused, Bella pulls them from *her*, saying, "Let me see!"

"How can you tell it's him?" I ask Cricket.

She grins at me. "Red truck, condor flag . . . it's him!"

Robin heaves a sigh of relief and says, "Thank you, Lord," then goes back inside the Lookout.

It took about twenty minutes for Quinn's truck to finally reach the Lookout. There was a blue and orange mountain bike in the bed of the truck, and he had a passenger with him—a woman with amazingly long honey blond hair.

Gabby and the other girls raced down to greet Quinn, but I stayed upstairs with Robin. She'd cleaned up the room a lot but was still very firm-lipped.

"Do you think it was Vargus?" I asked.

She nodded.

I shook my head. "But you know what? He didn't seem drunk, and he didn't *smell* drunk. Did you smell anything? Like when he blew that breath in your face?"

She stopped and stared at me, then frowned. "And I got a good whiff, too."

I went over to her trash bag and pawed through it. "There are at least ten cans in here. And all these chip bags? It's like there was a party up here." I took a leftover chip and bit into it. "These are totally stale."

Just then the girls came in and announced, "Quinn's here!" and then in strode . . . a samurai.

Wearing hiking boots.

And jeans.

And a T-shirt.

Okay, so it was just his *head* that looked samurai-ish. Dark hair held in place by a tattered strip of black fabric tied around his forehead, deep brown eyes . . . But the way he carried himself was very fluid. Very *light*. Like he was walking on a stream of air.

He got directly to the point. "The girls think it was Vargus. Do you agree?"

"I don't know who else. *But*"—Robin showed him the

trash sack—"not even Vargus could down a case of beer and not be drunk."

"Maybe he came up last night?"

"He said he came up this morning to talk to Dennis about not passing his course, but he could have been lying. He was in a hurry and very agitated."

Quinn nodded. "I'll radio the sheriff."

"But we can't find the radio!" Robin said.

"It's in my truck."

"Oh, *you've* got it . . . !" Then she asked, "Were you up here at all yesterday? Was Dennis?"

He shook his head. "I was running behind all day, and I'm pretty sure Dennis had meetings." He glided toward the door. "I'll call the sheriff. We need to have Vargus questioned."

So Quinn went down to his truck. His long-haired friend was leaning against the tailgate and looked really outdoorsy—tan skin, good muscles—like she was ready for anything.

She hung out with him as he used the shortwave radio, but she didn't come up to the Lookout afterward, which Gabby and Cricket sure didn't mind. They sort of melted at Quinn's feet when he returned, and Gabby said, "We're *really* hoping to see a condor this time, Quinn. Do you think we will?"

"Pretty good chance, I'd say!" He smiled at her. "I checked on JC-10 and AC-34 last week. They're doing great."

"Who are JC-10 and AC-34?" I whispered to Cricket.

"Juvenile Condor Number Ten and Adult Condor Number Thirty-four," she whispered back.

"You saw them?" Gabby squealed. "At their cave?"

Quinn nodded.

They were all so excited. And not only did the switch in mood feel weird to me, it also seemed strange that all of them were so attached to birds that didn't even have real names. I mean, ugly or not, if they'd named them something like Swooper or Flygirl or Buzzilla, that would be one thing. But AC-34? How could anyone care about a big ugly bird named AC-34?

"Can you take us to the cave?" Gabby was asking. "Can you *please?*"

Quinn hesitated, then gave her a bit of a samurai squint. "Too much human contact is not a good idea. I've been up there twice in the last month, but that's because I wanted to make sure their roost was still free of glass and bottle caps."

"Glass and bottle caps?" I whispered to Cricket.

Cricket whispered back, "Condors feed that stuff to their young." She shrugged. "Nobody really knows why."

"Wouldn't that kill them?"

"Exactly," Quinn said, extending a hand as he did a samurai glide over to me. "Quinn Terrane. And you are . . . ?"

I put out my hand, and all of a sudden I understood what made Cricket and Gabby so . . . *buttery* over this guy. He was like a black hole of magnetism, his eyes sucking you in, not letting you go.

"S-Samantha," I stammered. "Samantha Keyes."

My own voice kind of snapped me free of his magnetic pull. Samantha? *Samantha*? I never introduce myself as Samantha. That's how my *grandmother* introduces me. Did I think it made me sound older? More sophisticated? *Smarter*?

What kind of embarrassing moron was I?

I pulled my hand away and said, "But I go by Sammy."

"Well, Sammy," he said, "Cricket is right. Why condors feed their young dangerous shards and bottle caps is unclear. What *is* clear is that human influences have compromised the condor's safety for over a century." He flashed a glistening white smile. "I take it you've joined the ranks of those committed to fighting back these influences?"

Now I was mad at *him*. What did he take me for? Some gooey-eyed teen who'd swoon at his eco-happy feet?

Please.

So inside I'm going, Yeah, dude. I'm here to help save that rare, intelligent species that feeds *glass* and *bottle caps* to their young. I can't think of a more worthwhile cause to devote myself to. . . .

But outside I nodded.

Like a hypnotized idiot, I nodded.

SIX

Robin shooed us outside to set up our tents. I think she wanted to discuss the break-in with Quinn without a gaggle of girls interfering. So Cricket and I picked a spot near a big fire ring on the back side of the Lookout, while Gabby and Bella set up their tent about twenty feet away.

We started by kicking away rocks and big pebbles, then unrolled the tent so the doorway faced the fire ring. After that we popped together sections of lightweight tubes that were connected by a long elastic cord running inside them. Very ingenious. Imagine a little bundle of metal tubes that turns into one long, sort of bendy tube that you then thread through cloth tabs on the top of your flat tent. You do that twice, so you have a big metal X lying on top of your tent. At this point it just looks like a mega-mess spread across the dirt, but all you have to do is put the ends of the long, bendy tubes over pegs built into the corners of the tent and voila! The mega-mess magically transforms into your home away from home.

"That's amazing!" I said when it had sprung to life.

"And look," Cricket said, lifting the whole tent by the tubes. "If you don't like the spot you picked, you can move it anywhere you want."

I laughed. "Wow."

She put it back where it had been. "The bad thing is that the wind can upend it, too, so we do have to stake it down."

So we found some rocks, used them to drive in stakes at the corners, then started moving in. We rolled out our pads, unstuffed our sleeping bags, and unpacked our clothes.

"Ah," I said, diving onto my "bed." "This feels so nice!"

"You shouldn't be half in and half out," Cricket said. "You should always click the dirt off your boots like this, then get inside." Then she added, "And close the screen. Always close the screen. All the way."

The way she said it sounded very . . . ominous. So I clicked the dirt off my boots, pulled my feet inside the tent, and said, "Or what?"

"Or flies get in."

But it wasn't just flies, I could tell.

She saw the way I was looking at her and said, "Or mosquitoes. One little mosquito in the tent can make you itch for a week."

But it wasn't just mosquitoes, either.

"Look," she said, because she could see my mind was coming to its own conclusions, "just don't leave the screen open or bugs get in."

"Bugs like ticks and scorpions?"

"All bugs." She started scooting out of the tent. "Hey, I'm starved, aren't you?"

I scooted out of the tent behind her and zipped the

door closed tight. "Are you kidding? I'm in an eat-a-cow-*now* mood."

Unfortunately, there were no double cheeseburgers up at the Lookout. And since it was roasting hot out, none of us really wanted to collect wood, start a fire, and *cook* lunch. So Bella, Gabby, Cricket, and I sat on an outcropping of rocks that overlooked the canyon and ate trail mix, beef jerky, and dried bananas.

Now, while we'd been setting up our tents, Quinn's long-haired friend had sort of made the rounds, saying hello to everyone and checking out the views. She seemed nice enough, but she'd put Gabby into a serious frump.

"Why'd he bring her up here?"

"Why not?" Bella asked.

"Because she doesn't care. It's obvious she doesn't care! Is she working right now? Is she doing anything but walking around?"

Bella rolled her eyes. "What do you want her to do? Give her a chance, would you?"

But Gabby didn't want to give her a chance. She wanted her *gone*. So even though we were eating lunch on a big outcropping of rocks with a really spectacular view, none of us were actually *appreciating* the view. Gabby kept glancing over her shoulder at the Lookout, jealousy just radiating off her. Bella and Cricket kept glancing at Gabby, *annoyance* radiating off them. And I was too bugged by the pesky little flies buzzing around my head to pay attention to anything else. You wouldn't believe these flies. They're *weird*. Little and kind of gray, all body and not much wings. And they *buzz*. But what makes them unbearable is that they try to fly into your ears and up your nose. Seriously. They're little buzzy kamikaze flies that dive-bomb your ears and eyes and nose.

And as if I didn't hate them enough already, there I am, in the middle of ripping off a bite of jerky with my teeth, when one of those pesky little flies shoots right up my nose.

"Oh!" I squeal, jumping up and snorting out like crazy.

Everyone looks at me.

"Oh!" I squeal again, dancing around. "There's a fly!" I snort out hard. "Up my nose!" *Snort.* "It's stuck!" *Snort-snort-snort-snort-snort-snort-snort!*

"Did you get it?" Cricket asks.

"I don't know!" I stop snorting out and inhale through my nose, and sure enough, there's still a buzzy booger up there. "No!" I squeal, snorting again like crazy.

Cricket stands up and plays fly ejection coach. "Take a deep breath through your mouth, close off your good side, and *blow*."

So I do that and . . .

I've *still* got a fluttery fly booger.

"Do it again!"

So I do it again and . . .

The fly does not eject.

Then Bella says, "Maybe it's just a phantom fly."

"A phantom fly? A *phantom* fly? This is no phantom fly!"

"No, no. You *had* a fly, you got *rid* of the fly, but it still *feels* like one's up there." She shrugs. "You've got a phantom fly."

"IT'S NOT A PHANTOM FLY!" I shout, and I shout it so loud that "FLY . . . FLY . . . FLY . . ." echoes through the canyon.

Cricket's and Bella's eyebrows go up like, "Wow!" and then Bella stands up and shouts, "HELLO!" into the canyon.

Gabby, though, totally ignores everything that's going on around her and says, "I don't get what's taking them so long. And why won't Quinn let us see the nest? What does he think we are? *Children?*"

"Will you shut up about Quinn? Can't you see I've got a fly up my nose?" I let out a sinus-shaking, face-quaking *snoooooort.*

"BELLA!" Bella shouts into the canyon, but when the echo dies out, she turns to Gabby and says, "You're acting like an idiot, Gabrielle."

"Why? Because I want to see a condor?"

"CONDOR!" Bella hollers into the canyon.

"CONDOR . . . CONDOR . . . CONDOR . . . ," echoes the canyon as I go, *"Snoooort!"* trying to clear the fly, and Cricket says to Gabby, "No, because you're so hot for Quinn!"

"QUINN!" Bella hollers.

The canyon echoes, "QUINN . . . QUINN . . . QUINN . . ."

"Shut up!" Gabby snaps at Cricket.

"You shut up!" Cricket snaps back.

"Snoooort!" goes my nose.

"SHUT UP!" Bella hollers into the canyon.

"SHUT UP . . . SHUT UP . . . SHUT UP . . . ," goes the canyon.

"And quit it, Sammy, would you?" Cricket snaps. "It's just a little *fly*."

"But it's wedged up there!" I wail. "It's practically in my *sinuses*."

Gabby turns on me. "Then suck it up and spit it *out* already!"

"Ooooh!" I squeal. "That's gross!"

"GROSS!" Bella hollers.

"GROSS . . . GROSS . . . GROSS . . ."

And I'm sorry, but I just couldn't stand being around *any* of them anymore. I got off the rock and shuffled away as fast as I could, thinking, I don't care if it's a million miles away, I don't care if I have blisters screaming and a fly up my nose, I'm going *home*.

But Cricket catches up to me and says, "Sammy, I'm sorry I yelled at you. Gabby was driving me crazy." She swings around in front of me. "Is it still buzzing?"

I shake my head. "But it *is* still up there! This is no 'phantom fly'!"

"I'm really sorry, okay?" She walks with me as I storm along. "I guess you don't like camping after all. I . . . I really thought you would. I always thought you were, you know, *tough*."

Great. Now I've got screaming blisters, a fly up my nose, and a totally destroyed ego.

I throw her a look that would've singed steel.

"I didn't mean anything *bad* by that. I just—"

"Never *mind*!" I snap. "I just want to be left alone, okay?"

"Sorry," she says, hurrying off like a dog with its tail between its legs.

"Cricket!" I shout after her, because who wants to be a blistery fly-up-her-nose whiny *meanie*?

She turns around.

I shuffle over to her, saying, "Look. I'm sorry to let you down, but I'm just not used to this. I don't know how it all works. I've got blisters and a fly up my nose, and I feel like a wimp." I turn to the side, snort again, but nothing comes out.

"Try what Gabby said."

I pull a face. "That is just too gross!"

She shrugs. "Worse than having a fly up your nose?"

So I let out all my air, then suck up hard, and *fwap*, the fly shoots up, back, and down into my mouth. "Eeew!" I wail, kind of prancing in place. "Eeeew!"

"Spit it out! Spit it out!"

Like I'm gonna swallow it?

So I rasp it forward and hock a big ol' fly loogie onto the ground, which we both immediately squat to look at.

"See!" I shout. "You call that a phantom fly???"

"Nooooo," she says. "And it's big! It's like the condor of all flies!"

It was actually just a little black wad in a puddle of snot, but the fact that she'd called it the condor of all flies was so nice. And so funny! So before I can remember how mad and miserable I am, I start laughing, which makes Cricket start laughing, too, and pretty soon we're both hysterical.

Finally she brushes away a tear and says, "It will get better, Sammy. I promise."

I'm still kind of hiccuping with laughter. "Oh, yeah? When? After condor *scorpions* attack?" And I guess I was kinda over the edge, because I thought that was the funniest darn thing I'd ever heard.

Anyway, we wound up going back over to Bella and Gabby, who were now *both* hollering stupid stuff across the canyon.

"Eat!"

"EAT . . . EAT . . . EAT . . ."

"At!"

"AT . . . AT . . . AT . . ."

"Joe's!"

"JOE'S . . . JOE'S . . . JOE'S . . ."

Then Gabby said, "I know, I know, I know! Let's all say our own names at the same time!"

Cricket frowned. "It'll just be noise."

"So what! Let's try it!"

So on the count of three we all shouted our names at the same time.

Now, going out, it sure sounded like a big wall of noise, but the weird thing is that coming back, it didn't. It sounded like four voices calling four names. You couldn't really *understand* the names, but it was still kind of haunting as they bounced across the canyon.

"Cool," I whispered.

"Yeah," Cricket added.

"I know, I know, I know!" Bella said. "Let's say our names in succession." She pointed around. "I'll go first, then you, then you, then you!"

So we went, "BELLA, GABBY, CRICKET, SAMMY!" but it was too long, and the only thing that echoed was, "SAMMY . . . AMMY . . . AMMY . . ."

"Well, that stank," Bella said.

Gabby started going, "I know, I know, I know!" but Cricket stopped her. "Shhh!" She turned to me. "Did you hear that?"

I had, but I'd thought it was just a re-echo. You know, an extra-*long* echo.

"That was your name!" Cricket whispered.

Gabby and Bella squinted at her. "What are you *talking* about?"

But then it came again. "SAMMY . . . AMMY . . . AMMY . . . ?"

It was like my name was stuck in the canyon. Only it wasn't my voice. And it wasn't just a call.

It was a *question.*

"HELLO?" I called down, and when the echo was done, there was a moment of silence and then a reply.

"SAMMY? . . . AMMY? . . . AMMY?"

"Oh my God," Cricket whispered. "Do you know anyone else who's backpacking?"

"Can't be," I said, looking into the canyon. "There's just no way."

But while my head was trying hard to be rational about the impossibility of it all, my heart was skipping around happily in my chest.

"CASEY?" I called. But when the echo died out, it was quiet.

"Casey?" I called again, but there was no answer.

Cricket grabbed my arm and squealed, "Casey's out here? Wait till Heather hears about this—she is going to *die.*"

Bella was all over me, scolding, "What are you *doing*? We can't have *boys* finding us out here! It's against the rules!" Then her face smoothed back and her jaw dropped and she said, "*That's* why you wanted to come with us? So you could hook up with some *guy*?"

Cricket scowled at her. "Oh, lighten up, Bella. That had nothing to—"

Bella spun on her. "You expect me to believe she *likes* camping? She fell apart on the hike, she freaks out about a little fly up her nose—"

"Stop it!" Cricket snapped. "This is her first time and she got really bad blisters and it's all just new to her. She didn't come so she could meet up with Casey! That's ridiculous." She turned to me. "Right, Sammy?"

I used to be such a good liar. I could talk my way out of jaywalking tickets or off buses that didn't have stops where I needed them. I could fake my way into private parties or out of near arrests. I could put ketchup on an arm and make everyone believe I was dying. I lied, I lied a lot, and it didn't bother me a bit.

But somewhere along the line I started feeling bad

about it, and as soon as that happened, I became terrible at it.

Especially around people who are nice to me.

Who stick up for me.

Who *look* up to me.

Or, at least, *used* to.

So I didn't jump in and say, "Of course not!" No, I hesitated. And hesitating when you're *supposed* to be lying is a dead giveaway that you *are* lying.

Or about to, anyway.

And in that moment of hesitation, Cricket's eyes got bigger and bigger and I could see hurt springing up all over the place inside her.

"No!" I said. "I knew he was going camping, but I didn't know *where* or even when."

Bella snorted. "Yeah, likely story. Wait until my mom hears about this." She pointed at me and said, "Boys are not welcome, you got it? It's inappropriate and against the *rules*."

I put my hands up like her finger was a gun and I didn't want to get shot. "I have no problem with that, Bella. Besides, I don't even think it was him. He didn't answer, and it didn't *sound* like him. It was probably somebody who heard us shouting our names and was just playing around."

And I should lie and say I really believed that it couldn't be Casey and that even if it was, the wilderness was too huge for him to ever find me.

But the truth is, inside I had this hope.

This stupid little hope.

SEVEN

About two minutes after Bella got done scolding me about boys being against the *rules,* Quinn's truck fired up. "Hey!" Gabby cried, charging off the rocks. "He can't be *leaving. . . .*"

Cricket scrambled to catch up to Gabby while Bella threw me a disgusted look and muttered, "This troop is a boy-crazy joke," and headed for the truck, too.

"Quinn, stop! Where are you going?" Gabby shouted.

"Sorry, sweetheart," Quinn called, "but we've really got to get going."

"But we were really, really, *really* hoping you'd take us to see JC-10."

"I'm afraid—"

"Pleeease?"

"Knock it off!" Bella said through her teeth. "You're embarrassing all of us."

Then *Janey* kinda leaned across the seats and said, "We'd love to take you out there, but we have work to do and—"

"You've been out there?" Gabby gasped. She looked at Quinn like he'd totally betrayed her. "You took *her* out there and you haven't taken us? After all the work we've

done around here? After all the *time* we've spent waiting and watching?"

Janey eyed Quinn like, Uh-oh, then pulled back as Quinn said, "Sorry to disappoint you, Gabrielle, but we've got work to do." And with that, he drove off, his condor flag flapping in the air behind him.

Bella scowled at Gabby. "You're a total embarrassment." Then she headed for the Lookout, saying, "Excuse me while I go do something constructive."

"Me too," Cricket said, trying to cover up the fact that she'd also been swooning over Quinn, even if she'd been more discreet about it.

I followed, too, but Gabby just stood there, squawking, "Why are you being so mean to me, Bella? I didn't do anything wrong! Don't you want to see a condor before you *die*? We've been coming up here since fourth grade! Why does she get to see them and we don't? I'm sick of doing all this and never seeing a stupid condor!"

"*They're* not stupid!" Bella shouted back as she stormed up the stairs. "*You* are!"

Cricket and I both cringed.

"You're *mean*," Gabby screeched.

"And you're a good-for-nothing tagalong who doesn't know two half hitches from a square knot!"

"I DO SO!"

"What's going on?" Robin asked, poking her head out through the Lookout doorway.

"This troop is a disaster," Bella grumbled.

"What?"

So Cricket and I sort of held our breath, waiting for

her to tattle on us, but she just frowned and said, "Never mind," and pushed past her mother and into the Lookout.

We went in after her like a little litter of naughty puppies, which was stupid, but that's how she was making us feel.

Bella looked around the room, which was now clean and tidy. "Anything stolen?"

"'Unaccounted for' is what we're calling it for the time being," Robin said.

"So what's 'unaccounted for'?"

"A receiver, a shooting net, and the most recent record log. But Quinn thinks Dr. Prag or one of his interns might have them." She shook her head. "And I can't really see why Vargus would want to steal them."

"Are they expensive?" I asked.

"Moderately. But even if he listed them on the Internet, I don't think he'd be able to get much money for them."

"So what's happening with Vargus?" Bella asked, picking up a pair of binoculars, putting them down, picking up a pad of paper, putting it down.

"Quinn thinks it must have been him. The sheriff's going to bring him in for questioning, so I guess we'll go from there." She brightened. "The good news is there's still a receiver here, so we'll be able to monitor condor activity and . . ." She looked around. "Where's Gabby?"

"Who cares?" Bella snapped.

"You two are *fighting*?"

"She's an airhead, Mom."

"Bella!"

"Well, she is. She's head over heels for Quinn, and it's the most embarrassing thing I've ever seen."

Robin put her arm around her daughter. "It's a crush, Bella. Don't be so hard on her. You'll have one soon enough."

Bella snorted. "Well, *I'll* never act like an *idiot*"—she shot me a look—"or do something as sappy as shout someone's *name* across a canyon."

In theory, Bella was someone I might really have liked. She seemed spunky and competent, curious and smart. And even though her impression of me and her reaction to me were my own stupid fault, I *didn't* like her. Not one little bit. Maybe she was spunky and competent and curious and smart, but she was also a condescending tattletaling campaholic.

Robin took a deep breath and said, "Well," and looked at her daughter like she didn't really know what to do with her. Then she sighed and said, "Bella, it's been an intense day, and I haven't even set up my tent yet. We need to gather firewood, purify water. . . ."

"I'm on it," Bella said, marching past us and out the door.

So once again the naughty little puppies followed her. Down the steps we went, then across the clearing, past the tents, and toward a grove of oaks. Gabby was sitting on one of the big logs by the fire ring looking really dejected, so Cricket waved her over, calling, "Come on, Gabby! We're collecting firewood!"

It took a little while for her to join us, but it didn't take long for her to figure out that Bella wasn't talking to her.

Cricket pulled me aside and whispered, "I'm so sorry Bella's acting like this! She likes to be the center of attention, but she's never done *this* before!"

"This is worse than school," I said with a smirk.

Cricket laughed. "At least she's not Heather."

I laughed, too, because it was true. A condescending tattletaling campaholic has got nothing on Heather Acosta.

Nothing at all.

Anyway, after we'd spent a long time gathering what seemed like a ton of wood, Gabby went up to Bella and said, "Why are you acting like this? I didn't do anything to you."

Bella finally quit the mute act and said, "Because you're an idiot," which made Gabby burst into tears and run back to camp.

So Cricket faced off with Bella. "Quit being like that! Talk about embarrassing!"

"Oh, and you're not? You're hot for Quinn just like Gabby! You think no one can tell?" She gathered a huge load of wood in her arms and muttered, "You're *all* idiots."

For the next hour, we hauled the wood back to camp in silence, replaced missing boulders in the fire ring in silence, and got a fire going. In silence.

Then after we'd dug a latrine behind some bushes, we walked about a quarter of a mile to a spring and filled our canteens with water. It looked like clean, fresh water, but we still had to purify it, because in the wonderful Phony

Forest there are even bugs in the *water*. They may be microscopic, but they can make you really sick.

Anyway, after that we boiled a pot of water and ate rehydrated Chicken à la King Noodle Dinner with rehydrated bread pudding for dessert. Everything we did seemed to take forever to do, so by the time we finally sat down to eat, it was seven o'clock and I was famished.

Now, it's hard to say if something's tasty or gross when you're inhaling it, but I *can* tell you that I was looking around for seconds and there weren't any.

Through all this, Gabby was weepy, and Bella was Mute Girl to everyone but her mother. And even though Robin tried to get them to make up, Bella'd have none of it, so the tension at dinner was thicker than rehydrated pudding. And then, as we were washing the dishes, a sharp sound cracked through the canyon like a whip, the echoes slapping one side, then the other. And before the echoes had even died out, it happened again.

My heart froze for a second because there was no doubt in my mind what it was.

Gunshots.

Now, I don't know if my fear of guns comes from just not knowing anything about them or from the times I've had one stuck in my face.

Probably more to do with having them stuck in my face.

But according to Grams, her *father* used his rifle to bring dinner home from the wilderness. "It's a way of life, Samantha. When you've done something your whole life, you don't think it's cruel or revolting or heart-wrenching. You don't analyze it. You just do it."

I said something about her eating Bambi and Thumper as a girl, but she just harrumphed and said, "And now you eat Bessie and Nemo, only you won't look them in the eye."

I didn't touch any kind of meat for a month after that.

But anyway, standing there in camp, I don't know what unnerved me more—the cracking sound of a gun echoing through the canyon or the chilling silence afterward. Every creature seemed to be holding its breath, every plant held stock-still. Even the air had stopped moving.

I choked out, "Is it hunting season?" and I was trying to be calm and reasonable, but this whole place, this whole Phony Forest, felt like one of those computer games where when you finally master one level, you get moved to the *next* level, where new and deadlier things try to kill you.

Robin shook her head. "There's not supposed to be hunting of any kind here. It's a restricted area because of the condors."

We were all uneasy for a little while. But the shots had been a long ways off, and since we were safely up at the Lookout, why worry? Before long Gabby and Bella went back to feuding, and Cricket and I finished the dishes and stored all our food in the Lookout so Creatures of the Phony Forest Night couldn't get it.

Robin tried to mend the fence between Bella and Gabby by bringing out a receiving gizmo that tracked condors, but Bella just stormed down the Lookout stairs saying, "I'm not falling for that, Mom!"

Robin handed the receiver to Gabby. "Why don't you show Sammy how it works? I'll have a talk with Bella."

So Gabby took it and folded out the receiver, transforming it into something that looked like an old-fashioned TV antenna, only smaller and flatter. She plugged a cable from the antenna into a power pack, slung the power pack over her shoulder, and started scanning the skies with the antenna for a signal.

"What are we listening for?" I finally asked, because it didn't seem to be picking up anything.

"A *beep-beep-beep*," Cricket whispered.

"Or a loud clicking," Gabby said, playing with the power pack controls. "Which would mean it's really close."

But after a while of hearing no beeps or clicks, Cricket grabbed me by the arm and whispered, "Let's go."

So we left Gabby to scan the dusky skies alone while I learned how to brush my teeth using only about two tablespoons of water and how to set things up for the night—flashlight and boots at the ready, tomorrow's clothes in the sleeping bag to preheat against the chill of morning, today's clothes in the sleeping bag stuff sack to use as a pillow.

"We'll air out today's clothes tomorrow and keep rotating them," she told me. "Sleep only in your tank top and undies. No socks, no sweatshirt, no—"

"What if I have to get up in the middle of the night? What if bears attack?"

Then I remembered that we were in the Phony Forest.

Scorpions, yes.

Bears, not likely.

Cricket chuckled. "Look, you can wear your gym shorts if you want to, but not much more. You'll overheat."

"Really?"

She nodded. "That bag's rated to subzero, and it won't get anywhere close to that tonight."

So we got ourselves into bed, but we didn't go to sleep. First we listened to Bella stomping around, saying stuff like, "There's no way I'm sleeping in the same tent as her, Mom! I'd rather sleep outside and get attacked by coyotes!"

"Coyotes attack *people*?" I whispered.

"Bella's just trying to worm her way into her mother's tent."

Bella shouted, "I'd rather die the slow, painful death of a hundred scorpion stings than sleep in the same tent as her!"

"Oh, Bella," Robin said with obvious fatigue. "There are no scorpions up here."

"There are, too!"

Bella kept at it, and finally Robin gave up. "Just get in here and get to bed. I've got a splitting headache and need some sleep!" Then she called, "I'm sorry, Gabby. I think we're all just exhausted. Everything will be better in the morning!"

Cricket whispered, "I don't know why Bella's being so bratty."

"Do you think she's jealous of Quinn?" I asked. "Maybe she's used to getting all Gabby's attention and now some of it's going to Quinn?"

I guess I forgot to whisper, because Bella shouted, "I'M NOT JEALOUS OF QUINN!"

I looked at Cricket like, Wow, and she nodded and whispered, "Voices carry."

"She's right, Bella!" Gabby shouted. "You're just JEALOUS!"

"YOU'RE AN IDIOT!" Bella shouted back.

"BOTH OF YOU STOP IT!" Robin screamed. "I NEED SOME SLEEP!"

Cricket covered her mouth, trying to stifle a giggle, then whispered, "I shouldn't think it's funny, but I do. Normally I'm the one who's left out." She smiled at me. "I'm glad you came. I hope it hasn't been too much torture." Then she pointed up at the sky through the screen. "Look at the stars."

You always hear about the billions of stars in the sky, but only a few of them seem to shine down on Santa Martina. For one thing, there's a lot of fog at night. But also I guess just being in a city with electricity stops you from really noticing them. Oh, you see stars, and on a clear night you see what seems like a *lot* of stars, but looking through the tent screen, I realized that what I'd seen in Santa Martina was barely a twinkle in the huge night light of the galaxy.

"Wow . . . !" I said, and it came out all breathy and awestruck.

"*This* is why I go camping," Cricket whispered. "My mom loved this place." Then she added, "My family used to come up here a lot, but they don't want to now without my mom."

I snuggled deeper into my sleeping bag and looked up at the sky. "I'm sure she'd be glad to know you still come," I said softly. And after a long quiet time of just gazing at the stars, my eyes began to close. The cool breeze was so nice on my face. The warm bag so cozy around me. And the truth is, I was exhausted.

And I was almost asleep when Cricket whispered, "Good night, Mom."

At first I thought she'd forgotten it was me in the tent, but when I opened my eyes, she was still gazing up at the stars.

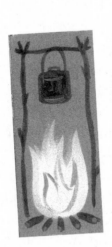

EIGHT

I did not want to get up in the morning. I'd taken a quick little 2 a.m. trip to the bushes and knew—it was chilly outside! So Cricket and I stayed in our bags and played a few hands of rummy with the mini-deck of cards she'd packed, and I discovered that not only is Cricket not quiet, she's a poker-faced shark! That girl remembers every card that's been played, and she's ruthless.

So she was having a great time, and even though she was chewing me up and spitting me out, I was having a great time, too. I could have sat in the tent playing cards all day. But Bella was outside getting the fire going, and Cricket started feeling guilty. "We should probably go help."

I felt like saying, "Aw, do we have to?" but I'd promised myself I wasn't going to whine about *anything* anymore. So instead I said, "Sure," and pulled on the army pants that Cricket had lent me.

Robin was talking quietly with Bella when we emerged from the tent, and when she saw us coming their way, she seemed to give Bella some final advice, then headed up to the Lookout calling, "Good morning, girls! I'm going to see if I can catch some flight activity. Let me know when the water's hot!"

We waved, and Cricket called, "Tell us if you get any signals. I want to show Sammy!"

"Will do!"

When we reached Bella, she grumbled, "Sorry about last night. I was a jerk and I know it and I'm sorry."

I was pretty impressed. I mean, she *had* been a jerk, but that's not an easy thing for anyone to admit. It's a whole lot easier to just go on being a jerk and blame other people for the way you act.

I know all about that.

Anyway, Cricket sort of grinned and said, "But the real question is, are you an idiot?"

Bella gave her a tired smile. "Yeah, I'm an idiot. I'm a *huge* idiot." Then her eyes came to life and her smile got brighter. "Just not about *boys* like *some* people."

Cricket and I both laughed, and then Cricket lowered her voice and asked Bella, "Have you talked to Gabby yet?"

Bella shook her head. "I started to, but she's still asleep."

Cricket whispered, "She can't still be asleep. She probably just doesn't want to come out. You should go in and talk to her!"

Bella looked over at Gabby's tent. "Will you guys get the water going?"

We both nodded. "Sure."

So we grabbed the pail and headed off toward the spring, only we'd barely made it through camp when Robin came onto the Lookout deck and called, "Do any of you know where the receiver is? I thought I left it on the desk last night."

But before we could answer, Bella comes scrambling out of the tent, crying, "She's gone! Mom! Gabby's gone!"

"What do you mean, she's gone?"

"She stuffed her sleeping bag to make it look like she's here, but her boots are gone, her flashlight's gone . . . *she's* gone!"

"Calm down, calm down," Robin said, walking toward the tent. "Maybe she's out taking care of business," which is Robin-speak for going pee.

"Why would she stuff her sleeping bag? Why would she take her flashlight? She's been gone since before daybreak!"

Robin checked out the tent, and when she emerged, she looked very sober. "Gabby!" she called. "Gabrielle!"

So we all started calling, "Gabby!" and after searching around the latrine and the spring and everywhere else in the general vicinity, Bella, Cricket, and I went to the rocks and shouted, "GABBY," into the canyon.

No response.

We did it again and again, but all we got back was the lonely echo of the canyon.

"Where did she *go*?" Bella wailed. "Do you think she started walking home?"

I shook my head. "I think she's out tracking down a condor."

Bella turned to face me. "You can't just hike into the canyon and find a condor!"

I shrugged. It didn't seem so crazy to me. "She knows about where they are, right?"

Cricket cut in, saying, "She's talking about AC-34 and JC-10, Bella. Gabby knows they roost in the Chumash Caves area."

"That place is huge!"

"Not if you have the receiver," I said.

Bella's eyes bugged, and without a word to us, she charged off the rocks shouting, "Mom! Mom! Gabby's got the receiver! Mom!"

Robin didn't want to believe that Gabby had actually taken off to track down a condor, braving scorpions and ticks and rattlesnakes and coyotes—not to mention scarce and buggy water. "But why?" she finally asked. "It makes a lot more sense that she started for home."

"Tell her," Cricket whispered to Bella, but Bella just stood there. So we both said, "Tell her!"

"Bel-la," her mother warned.

So Bella looked down and mumbled, "I told her that she didn't care about condors, that she only cared about Quinn, and that she was a good-for-nothing tag-along who didn't know two half hitches from a square knot."

"Bella!" Robin's faced morphed from shock through disbelief clear over to anger. "You of all people should know what it's like to have cruel things thrown in your face! Gabrielle *adores* you. You're the sibling she never had. The one she looks up to, the one she admires. How could you be so cruel?"

Bella started crying. "I'm sorry, Mom. I'm so sorry! She was just being so stupid about Quinn, and I thought—"

"You thought you could manipulate her into submission by cutting her down? Doesn't this remind you of somebody?"

"I'm so, so sorry!" Bella wailed.

Robin held the sides of her head. "Well, what are we going to do? We have to go after her. She can't be out there *alone*. What if she gets bitten by a rattlesnake? What if she gets lost? What if she runs out of water?"

"She's a good Scout," Cricket said, trying to be reassuring. But her eyes were kind of watery, and the way she said it was more like, She *was* a good Scout.

Like she was reading her epitaph.

Robin's hands moved around to cover her face as she muttered, "Why did Quinn have to take the radio?" She took a deep breath and held it for a long time, then finally dropped her hands, let out the breath, and said, "Okay. The best scenario is for us to all go after Gabby together"—she turned to me—"but Sammy, I'm afraid your blisters would prevent you from keeping up. *So*"—she took another deep breath—"Sammy and Cricket, you stay here while Bella and I try to track Gabrielle down. Quinn said he'd be back this morning, but I don't want to wait around. When he does show up, though, tell him what's happened and get him to drive out to the caves, keeping his eye out for us *and* Gabby. Hopefully he'll be able to give us all a ride back to camp."

"What if Quinn doesn't show up at all?" I asked. "Can you make it out to the caves and back in one day?"

"One very long day, yes." She turned to Bella. "We're going to have to hustle. Get your daypack. Bring water, purifying tablets, enough food for the whole day, matches, and your emergency kit." She started for her tent. "I'll do the same."

It took them all of seven minutes to get ready. And as they hurried down the back road, Cricket and I were both feeling really left out. Really *helpless*.

I hate feeling helpless. I'd rather be angry or hurt or *tortured*.

Anything but helpless.

Bella waved as they started running down the back road. "See you soon, I hope!"

"Call us on the echo phone if you need anything!" Cricket shouted.

Bella laughed and waved. "Will do!"

After they were out of sight, Cricket and I tried to be useful. We cleaned up camp, gathered firewood, aired out everyone's clothes and sleeping bags, and hiked to the spring for water. Cricket kept checking her watch, and finally she said what I knew she'd been thinking: "I wish we could have gone with them."

"You should've just gone."

"No way! This is your first time camping *and* it's against the rules."

I rolled my eyes.

"It's a good rule, Sammy. The buddy system is not something you play around with. Besides, someone had to stay behind to tell Quinn. He's our real hope of finding her."

We'd done everything we could think to do, so we went up to the Lookout and used the high-powered binoculars to scout the area for Quinn's red truck.

No sign of it anywhere.

"What does he do all day, anyway?" I asked.

I meant that as where-else-might-he-*be,* but Cricket lowered the binoculars and said, "You wouldn't believe all the things he does! He coordinates everything around here."

Everything?

I looked around at the craggy nothingness of the Phony Forest. So far, I was not impressed.

But Cricket was just warming up. "He's a zone biologist, and he's made lists of the birds, mammals, reptiles, and insects that live in this biome. He can tell all about any animal up here! He knows the phylum and genus and species and"—she laughed—"and whatever else zone biologists know."

"But what good does that do? Why not just let the bugs and snakes live happily ever after? Why make lists and categorize them?" I squinted at her. "And who *pays* him to do this?"

"The more you study something, the better you understand it, the more you can protect it from human interference." Then she added, "And the government pays him. He got a grant."

"But I still don't get it. Why not just *not* come up here? Wouldn't the best thing be to leave everything alone?"

81

She shrugged. "People are going to come. People like to camp and backpack and be part of nature. We *are* part of nature. What Quinn does helps people understand how to share the forest with the rest of nature." All of a sudden she got really excited. "See? *Not* knowing how to share the forest with the rest of nature is exactly how humans drove condors to near extinction. It's a perfect example! That's why Quinn makes lists! To protect the biggest and littlest creatures of the forest."

I scowled at her. "Creatures like ticks and scorpions and rattlesnakes?"

"They're all part of the balance of nature, Sammy. Birds eat bugs, snakes eat rodents . . . it all balances out."

I sighed and muttered, "I still can't believe he gets *paid* to make lists of bugs."

Cricket held the binoculars to her eyes and muttered, "And I wish he would just show up."

I let her scan the area for a minute, then asked, "So where else could he be? Or maybe he already ran into them on the way up?"

She shook her head. "He went down that way," she said, pointing toward the road we'd hiked the day before.

"The roads don't connect?"

"It's a long way around."

"But it is possible?"

She nodded, then said, "I guess so."

After another minute, I said, "You want to go to Echo Rock and make a call?"

She laughed. "Sure."

So we got down to the outcropping of rocks and called, "HELLO!" and waited through the echoes.

There was no answer. The wind was gusting upward, out of the canyon. It was warm and dry and didn't seem to know where it wanted to go. First it gusted to the left, then the right.

"HELLO!" we shouted again.

Again, no answer.

"NO . . . QUINN," we yelled, hoping that Robin and Bella might hear us and that they'd understand.

After that we took turns scouring the canyon with the binoculars for signs of life, but all we saw were a few birds flapping by.

"Hey, look!" I said. "There goes a condor!"

"That's a *crow*."

I laughed. "No, it's not! It's a condor!"

She tossed me a grin. "Very funny."

Then all of a sudden we looked at each other, our eyes wide.

"Did you hear that?" Cricket whispered.

I put up a finger, and we both held our breath and waited. And there it was again, riding the winds up, out of the canyon, "Help!"

Cricket shouted, "GABBY?"

There was no answer.

"BELLA?" we both shouted into the canyon.

We waited, but again, all we heard was the wind.

Finally Cricket said, "We did hear 'help' . . . didn't we? Maybe we imagined it?"

"We both imagined the same word?"

"Maybe it was just the wind?"

I shook my head. "It was someone calling for help."

"Do you think it was Gabby?"

"I have no idea."

"What if it was Bella or Robin? What if something happened to them? What if . . ." She was looking really panicky. "I hate this feeling. And I hate doing nothing! Why isn't Quinn showing up?"

We scoured the area with binoculars some more but saw no sign of Quinn. And even though it didn't make any sense, even though I knew I shouldn't say it, it was nearly noon and I was sick of standing around in the dusty heat doing nothing. "You want to go try to find her?"

Cricket's eyebrows flew up. "And leave you here? No way!"

"I meant both of us. My blisters don't hurt *that* bad anymore."

"So why do you shuffle around like you do?"

"I'm thinking I could put another level of moleskin on. You know, build it up? Pad it more?"

Cricket hesitated, balancing what we should do against what she wanted to do.

"Get me some moleskin," I said, plonking down on the ground to unlace my boots.

"It makes more sense to st—"

"Get me some moleskin."

Ten minutes later I was patched up, and we both had food, water, and emergency supplies in our daypacks.

Then we left a note for Quinn inside the Lookout, locked the windows and the door, and took off. We didn't even bother to think through the reasons we were going. Neither of us tried to talk the other one out of it. After all, what was there to discuss?

It was a mistake, and we both knew it.

NINE

We'd been hiking all of five minutes when I knew that the extra moleskin wasn't going to do much good. And after a while, the pressure from it pushed my feet forward and started giving me blisters on my little toes. But I decided, Forget it! What's a little pain in the foot?

Better than a pain elsewhere, which is what I would be to Cricket if I complained or slowed her down.

So I played with new ways of walking and just toughed it out.

I also took it easy on the water.

It helped that we were going downhill and that there were stretches of shade. It also helped that Cricket stopped every twenty minutes to look through the binoculars. And the fact that we weren't just standing around twiddling our thumbs made us feel better, which got us to thinking more positively. "That was probably Gabby calling for help," Cricket said at one point. "And that's a good thing! Bella and Robin have probably found her and they're all fine." She turned to me. "Right?"

"Right!" I said, like I believed it. But in my head I'm going, So *why* am I torturing my feet, hiking into this canyon?

In a lot of places the road seemed more like a deer path than something trucks could drive on. There were scrub oaks and prickly bushes everywhere, and sometimes the road was so overgrown that Cricket and I had to walk single file to avoid the wicked poison oak plants that were everywhere. Cricket gave me an education on how to identify the stuff, then instructed me not to touch it, burn it, or *eat* it.

Like I would want to?

Anyway, we continued hiking along, and after a while Cricket said, "Up here a little ways you're going to have to decide how adventurous you want to be."

She seemed to be in such a good mood. Like being out in the woods hiking had made her forget all about that cry for help. I shuffled faster to catch up with her. "This seems pretty ding-dang adventurous to me!"

She laughed, and when we rounded the next bend, she swung off her daypack and came to a halt. "How do you feel about taking a shortcut?"

"A . . . a shortcut?" I blinked at her. And all of a sudden I realized what this was.

It was cosmic revenge.

I mean, I'm always dragging Marissa on shortcuts, over fences, through dangerous territory. . . . I'm always making her *follow* people she doesn't know and go places she hates being. And lots of times we wind up in situations where there are creepy-crawly *bugs*. She freaks out and I always tell her to chill out—that they're just bugs. One time we were trapped in a basement with evil, dangling black widow spiders and I told her she was overreacting!

Yes, this was definitely payback. Marissa had prayed to the Gods of Revenge and said, "Please, please, *please* teach Sammy what it's like to be me!" and they had listened!

Man, had they listened.

"Sammy?" Cricket said, sort of cocking her head at me.

"Huh?"

She had smoothed out a strange-looking map on the ground and was on her knees in front of it with a compass in her hand. "I asked you how you feel about taking a shortcut."

I wasn't really ready to answer the question, so instead I pointed to the map and asked, "What's that?"

"A topo map. You've never seen one?"

I rearranged my ball cap, anchoring all the hairs that had escaped. "Not like that." The map was mostly tan and olive green, and it looked like someone had drawn a bunch of squiggles and peanut-shaped designs, then traced larger and larger circles and peanut-shaped designs around them. Some of the lines were close together, some were farther apart . . . and the tracings were kind of sloppy. Like whoever had done it wasn't very *good* at it.

"It shows the topography of the area," she said, twisting the outside part of her compass and positioning it on the map. "You know, the lay of the land. Hills, valleys, elevations, distances. . . . Once you figure out what everything means, it's really easy to read." She smiled up at me. "And it's very handy for taking shortcuts."

"Why are we taking shortcuts?"

She laughed. "Because shortcuts are shorter."

I squatted beside her and muttered, "Not always."

"Well, in this case, they are." She adjusted the map a little, then pointed to places on it as she said, "This is where we are, right here. And this area over here is Chumash Caves. We could follow the trail clear around this way—which is how Quinn gets near it in his truck and the way Bella and Robin are most likely hiking. Or we can cut down through the valley this way, shortcutting over to Miner's Camp here, then take the trail south through Hog Heaven."

I squinted at her. "Hog Heaven?"

"The real name is Hoghead Valley, but I call it Hog Heaven." She smiled at me. "Better, don't you think?"

"Because hogs love it?"

She laughed. "They're actually wild boars, and they're mean."

I rolled my eyes. "Oh, great."

She folded the map so our location was still showing, then wiped the sweat off her brow. "So? What do you think? It'll save us at least an hour. Maybe two."

"Which means it'll save us two hours, maybe four round-trip?"

She nodded.

My feet were all for that. "Then sure."

She pointed across the valley. "See that outcropping of rocks near that big dead oak?"

"Yeah."

"That's our site point. Once we reach it, we'll take out the compass again and pick another site point. If all goes well," she said, cutting off the trail and down the mountainside, "we may even beat Bella and Robin to Chumash Caves!"

Now, maybe in her mind this was a race, or maybe she was trying to prove something, I don't know. But she was in a great mood, so I just tagged along, trying to adopt some of her positive vibe.

In the process I discovered some interesting things about hiking cross-country. For one thing, what you see clearly as a big dead oak with an outcropping of rocks from the trail above becomes almost invisible as you drop down the hillside. And the little scrubby oaks between you and the big dead oak become enormous trees that block your view. Nothing actually changes size, but it sure *seems* like it does.

Also, what *looks* like a straight shot to a big, dead oak with an outcropping of rocks winds up being a series of zigzagging steps around shrubs and trees and conspiring arms of poison oak.

Much tougher than sticking to the beaten path.

But when we finally reached the big dead oak, Cricket seemed pleased. "We made good time. You're doing great!"

She didn't ask about my feet, and I was glad. They felt like bloody stumps of pain.

We took a few swigs of water, found a new site point, and took off again. This time we were on fairly flat terrain, and except for my feet screaming at me, things were going pretty smoothly. That is, until I heard this deep, kinda rough *cracking* sound.

I stopped short. "What was that?"

Crrraaaack!

Cricket looked around, her eyes wide. "I don't know."

CRRRRRAAAACKKKK!

We both screamed and charged forward as the oak tree we'd been standing beside suddenly split near the base and thundered to the ground.

My heart was pounding and we were both shaking as we looked back at the enormous heap of shattered oak, which was still quivering from the fall. "Holy smokes! That coulda *killed* us!"

Cricket was holding her heart, panting for air. "Sudden oak death," she gasped.

"Sudden oak death?"

She nodded. "Must be. It's a disease. Kills trees. I've heard about it, but I've never actually seen it happen." She shook her head. "Wow."

I looked around. We were *surrounded* by oaks. "Can you tell which ones have that disease?"

She looked around, too. "The ones with brown leaves . . . ?"

"These *all* have brown leaves!"

We got out of there quick, steering as clear of oaks as we could. But no other trees came crashing down, and after we reached the next site point, it was only about ten minutes more before we found Miner's Camp.

Now, you'd *think* that finding an official campground would have been a relief, but we were in the Phony Forest, and the definition of "camp" in the Phony Forest is a place where they post a sign. They don't have picnic tables or outhouses or faucets or water pumps . . . just a sign.

Miner's Camp.

I was dying to sit down and take off my boots, change the moleskin or add some more, then maybe have a snack and, you know, *rest*. But before I could present this decadent little scenario to Cricket, she nodded toward a grove of oaks about fifty feet away and whispered, "Let's get out of here."

I hadn't noticed the three men or their camp, because they blended into the scenery perfectly. Their tents were tan, their backpacks were tan, and the men looked like trees in their green-and-tan camouflage shirts, pants, and hats. They were sitting on tree stumps around a fire ring, stock-still, studying us. I felt like a deer being watched through the scope of a rifle.

"Right," I whispered.

Cricket pretended not to see them, keeping her eyes locked on the trail as we moved through Miner's Camp. I pretended to do the same, only I had my eyes cranked to the side, trying to see if they had guns.

"That was so scary," Cricket whispered when we were a safe distance down the trail. "Three of them, two of us, no one else around . . ."

I nodded. All of a sudden ticks and scorpions and rattlesnakes seemed like little-kid fears.

Cricket glanced over her shoulder, then yanked me off the trail and behind some trees. She squatted and whispered, "Let's wait here for a minute and make sure they're not following us."

So we waited and watched.

And waited and watched.

And again, I was reminded of Marissa.

How many times had I done the same thing to her?

Finally I whispered, "Do you think they're the ones who fired those shots last night?"

"I wouldn't be surprised." Cricket stood up like she was getting ready to go, then did a quick double take at my shirt. I looked, too, as she flicked a little bug off my shoulder. It was small—maybe a quarter of an inch— almost round and smooth, with a teeny-tiny head and short little legs.

"What was that?" I asked.

"Just a bug," she said, but she was checking out her own shoulders, moving away from the tree we'd been hiding behind.

I caught up to her. "What kind of bug?"

She laughed, but it was a forced laugh. "You worry too much—it was just a bug." Then she tried to change the subject. "Are you thirsty?"

"It was a tick, wasn't it?"

She looked away. "Yeah. I just didn't want to freak you out."

All of a sudden I itched all over. I started swatting at myself and inspecting my clothes, and finally she said, "Sammy, I want to get farther away from those men, okay?"

Oh, yeah. The men.

So I trudged along after her, feet screaming, itching from imaginary ticks, dying of thirst because it was hot and dusty and I was running out of water. And just when I thought I couldn't get any more miserable, the trail took us through a meadowy area that was swarming with those stupid kamikaze flies.

I pinched my nose safely closed with one hand and swatted around my face like crazy with the other. "What's with these flies?"

"Cow pies," Cricket answered.

And sure enough, there were big dried splots of cow plops dotting the meadows. "There are *cows* down here?"

She laughed. "Yup."

Then I practically stepped in some nuggets of fresh, grassy poop that were right in the middle of the trail. "And *horses?*"

"Pack animals, not wild ones." She swatted away some flies. "But that would be so cool, wouldn't it? To see wild mustangs race through the valley?"

Right. Like wild mustangs would come anywhere *near* a tick-infested, gnatty-flied forest of scorpions, rattlesnakes, and scary men with guns pretending to be trees?

I made it through the meadow without getting any flies up my nose, but even in the luxury of fly-reduced air, I guess I started lagging. Cricket had to keep waiting for me, and finally she asked, "Are you doing okay?"

I made myself not complain. "Where's the next water?"

She said, "It's coming up soon," but when she saw me start to guzzle from my canteen, she pulled it away from my lips. "Not *that* soon! And after we get there, we'll have to treat it, which takes about twenty minutes."

I moaned and broke down, saying, "My blisters are

killing me. I've been trying so hard not to complain, but I need to change the moleskin or *something*."

"Uh-oh."

Something about that uh-oh really tweaked my beak. I mean, here I'd been toughing it out for hours, and my reward was an uh-oh? An *Uh-oh, you're slowing me down* uh-oh?

I plopped down on a big rock that was in the shade and said, "Don't worry. I'm not going to *strand* you down here. And I won't hold you to your *buddy* system. I just need to do something about my blisters. They *hurt*."

So off came the first boot. And I literally had to *peel* off the sock because it had sort of rolled together with the second layer of moleskin on my back blister and was *cemented* to my little toe, where a blister had ruptured and oozed and bled all over the place.

"Eew. Eew-eew-eew!" Cricket said when she saw my foot. "That's bad . . . !"

No kidding.

It was the same story with my other foot, only worse. I shook my head and said, "I don't know how I let you talk me out of my high-tops."

Cricket's face was all contorted as she looked at my feet. "I don't know how you've been *walking* on those!"

I rested my feet on top of my boots and looked up at her. "With great pain."

"I'm sorry." She sat down on a rock next to me. "I'm so, so sorry! I had no idea they were this bad! We should never have left camp . . . !"

I lifted my left foot onto my right thigh and started peeling off the old moleskin. "I'll patch them up, don't worry."

"Quinn'll come," she said softly. "Quinn'll find us and give us all a ride back to camp."

I cocked my head at her. "Is that what you want? For Quinn to rescue us? Because you know what? I think I'd rather walk."

Her eyes popped wide. "Why in the world do you say that?"

I grimaced as I pulled off the bottom doughnut of moleskin. "He bugs me."

"You're kidding!" Then she snorted and said, "Well, at least you're not falling all over him like *someone* we know."

I snorted back. "Someone who's probably hoping Quinn'll rescue *her*, too."

Cricket gasped. Like the thought had never even occurred to her. "Do you think that's why she did this? So Quinn would rescue her?"

I started peeling moleskin off my other foot. "No, I think she did it because Bella's a brat." I swatted away a fly. "What's her deal, anyway? And what did Robin mean about her of all people knowing what it's like to have people say cruel things?"

Cricket took a deep breath and thought a minute, then really fast she said, "Bella's adopted. Her mom was in and out of jail all the time and had some loser boyfriend who didn't want Bella around. So Robin adopted her. Robin was the mom's social worker."

I blinked at her. "Holy smokes."

"Yup. Holy smokes is right."

I thought a minute and said, "So I guess that's why Bella has to be the center of attention. Childhood scars or whatever?"

Cricket nodded. "Probably so."

"And maybe Gabby crushing on Quinn makes Bella feel like she's getting abandoned for some guy again?"

Cricket's jaw dropped. "Wow. That's *deep*."

"I don't know about *that*. . . ."

"No, I'm serious. That makes perfect sense."

I sighed. "It does. And it makes it hard to stay mad at someone when you understand them, huh?"

Cricket nodded, then shook her head at my feet. "I was never mad at you about hiking slow, but I sure do understand now why you were."

I pushed at the blister on my heel. It was huge. So was the one on my other foot. They were at least an inch and a half across and full of fluid. "This is ridiculous. I'm going to pop them."

"No! You're not supposed to. They'll get infected."

"Well, I'm gonna."

"But—"

Just then we heard voices. Voices and footsteps and . . . laughing.

"Oh, no!" Cricket whispered, because the sounds were coming from the direction of Miner's Camp. The direction of the Camo Creeps. "Come on! We've got to hide!"

I looked at her and then at my feet, like, How am I supposed to go *anywhere*?

"Just put your feet in your boots and come on!" she whispered frantically.

So I shoved them in and shuffled after her, laces dragging, until we were safely behind some scrubby oaks.

Safely, ha! For one thing, it was kind of a lame hiding place. We were only about twenty feet off the trail, so if the Camo Creeps had heard us crunching through dead oak leaves, they could have found us, no problem.

But also, as the footsteps and talking and laughing got closer, I noticed that the little plants all around us had shiny green leaves. Shiny green leaves with a tinge of red.

And while I was looking at the plants, I saw something move in the sandy dirt in front of me. At first it looked like the sand itself was moving, but then I realized that something sand-*colored* was moving toward me, a thin layer of sand half covering it.

It was only about two inches long, but it had pincers. And a tail.

A tail that was now curving up and aiming at *me*.

"Cricket!" I whispered, pointing at it.

"That's a scorpion!" Cricket gasped, backing up like crazy.

I scrambled back, too, and that's when I noticed the little brown things crawling up my pants, landing on my shoulders, coming at me from everywhere!

"Ticks!" I cried, and that was it. I lost my mind. I charged back to the trail in my stupid loose boots, doing a total freak-out dance as I twisted out of my daypack, threw off my cap, then ripped off my shirt and slapped myself like crazy, crying, "Aaaaaahhhh! Aaaaaahhhh!"

I didn't care if I died at the hands of Camo Creeps!
I didn't care who saw me in my underwear!
I just wanted those bugs off me!

But when I freak-danced my way smack-dab into the Voices on the Trail, I changed my mind.

And I changed it quick.

TEN

Thank God I had underwear on, because in running away from scorpions and ticks, I barreled right into two back-packers.

Two backpackers with a six-foot *rattle*snake.

All I really saw was the snake. "Aaaaaahhhh!" I cried again, doing a U-turn back toward Cricket.

Cricket's eyes popped wide when she saw the back-packers. She snatched my shirt off the ground and held it out to me, while a voice behind me called, *"Sammy?"*

I went from full-throttle freak-out to internal melt-down.

I knew that voice.

I knew it very well.

Oh, why hadn't I let the scorpion kill me?

Why hadn't I let the ticks suck me dry?

Why hadn't I eaten poison oak and suffered a slow, agonizing death by suffocation?

Anything was better than dying of mortification!

I ripped the shirt away from Cricket, held it to me, and turned around. "Casey?" I choked out.

"I *told* you I heard her calling your name!" Billy said to

Casey. "I told you!" Then he grinned at Cricket. "And she's with Mo-jo Kuo-jo!"

Cricket blushed beet red.

"But . . . ," Casey said, still not believing it was me. "Why are you . . . ?"

"Ticks!" I said, sputtering like a madman. "I was covered in ticks!"

Cricket tried to come to my rescue. "And there was a scorpion!" She held her fingers at least eight inches apart. "It was this big!"

"No way!" Billy said. He shoved the lifeless rattlesnake on Casey and cut off the trail toward where we'd been. "Where? Where was it?"

Casey just stood there, the rattlesnake U-ing from one hand to the other. He looked at my shoes with the laces all dragging in the dirt. He looked at my face, at my filthy, singed skin and cracked, flaky lips. And he did his best to politely *not* look at the rest of me. "What are you *doing* down here?" he finally asked.

I cringed. "Uh . . . backpacking?"

"WHERE'S THAT SCORPION, MO-JO?" Billy shouted from behind us.

"BY THE TICKS AND THE POISON OAK!" she shouted back.

Casey was still staring. "But . . . where's your backpack?"

Cricket stepped between me and Casey and whispered to me, "Put yourself together! I'll explain it to him."

So I dashed for cover as fast as I could in my blistery

feet and clunky, dangly-laced boots. Then I checked over my shirt, pulled it on quick, picked up my hat and day-pack, and reemerged before the ticks could attack again.

"I DON'T SEE IT!" Billy shouted.

"IT'S BACK THERE!" Cricket called, then continued talking to Casey. ". . . So we decided to cut cross-country and try to find them. But Sammy's feet are just raw with blisters and we had to stop to fix them, and then we heard people coming and thought it was those creeps we saw back at Miner's Camp and got scared—no! We didn't get *scared,* we decided to be *smart* and play it safe and hide from them. . . ."

"But then the ticks and scorpions attacked and I totally freaked out," I said, finishing the story.

"Okaaaaay," Casey said, still looking confused and un-comfortable.

But I didn't want to explain any more. Or apologize for being a wilderness wimp. It seemed like it would just make things more . . . pathetic. And since Coach Rothhammer is always telling us that the best defense is a good offense, I forced a little smirk and said, "So what are you guys doing with a rattlesnake, huh? Jumping rope down the trail?"

"Uh, no . . . ," he said, but it made him sorta grin. Like he was on his way back into a universe he understood. He shook the rattler's head and said, "This monster and Billy got into a little spat. Fortunately for Billy, Billy won." He pulled a face. "But not by much."

"MO-JO! WHERE'S THAT SCORPION?"

"IT'S PROBABLY IN MINER'S CAMP BY NOW!" Cricket shouted back. "It was moving fast."

"So why are you carrying it around?" I asked Casey. "Why didn't you just leave it for the birds to eat?"

Casey shrugged. "'Cause *Billy* wants to eat it."

"No way!"

Billy was back. "I can't believe you guys let an eight-inch scorpion get away!"

I looked at him. "What were you going to do, *eat* it?"

Billy grinned at Casey. "You told her about my battle with the beast?" He took the rattler from Casey. "It was intense!" He started dancing around with the snake like they were boxers in the ring. "He jabbed, I dodged. He jabbed, I dodged. He jabbed, I dodged—"

"Did you shoot it?" Cricket asked. "We heard two shots last night. Was that you killing the snake?"

Billy looked shocked. And kinda hurt. "No, I didn't *shoot* him! I went at him *man-o a snake-o*! Serpent against human! Ancient biblical enemies colliding again in the New World!" He quit dancing around and shrugged. "I used a rock."

"A *big* rock," Casey added.

"I was gonna roast him at Miner's Camp, but those pig poachers chased us off."

"Pig poachers?" I asked, picturing a big vat of water with a pig in it. You know, like you'd poach an egg. "Those guys dressed like trees are *pig* poachers? How do you poach a pig?"

"You kill 'em!" Billy said. "When you're not supposed to!"

"They're boar hunters," Casey said, dropping his voice. "It's illegal down here, but that doesn't stop people."

My mind scrambled around, adjusting to the fact that there were no vats of water involved in this sort of poaching. "But how do you know they're boar hunters?"

He snickered. "Just look at them."

Billy jumped in, shifting his eyes side to side and making his voice all breathy as he said, "They track 'em. They use their keen wits to uncover signs of piggy activity. They look for hoofprints. And broken twigs. And . . . and piggy poop. *Especially* piggy poop. And when they've tracked one down, they stalk it until it's in a place where they can face off with it. Then they throw little rocks at it until it's all angry and pawing at the earth and snorting through its big, ugly, hairy snout. That's when they get their bows ready. They get their bows ready, and when the boar charges, *pa-choom, pa-ching*! They let those arrows fly!"

Casey grinned at Billy. "And if they miss . . ."

Billy laughed. "They *run*."

"Wait," I said. "They don't use guns?"

They both shook their heads, and Casey added, "Guns are not sporty enough for boar hunters. They're into the hunt. It's a *game* to them—"

"Like paintball!" Billy said. "With wild pigs!"

"Only they use arrows and they *kill* them?" I asked.

Casey smirked at Billy. "Yeah. Minor differences." He turned back to me. "They don't use twangy kid arrows, either. They use compound bows."

Billy nodded. "Which is like using a high-powered rifle instead of a BB gun."

"But they don't use guns. At all? Ever?"

Casey shrugged. "Hard to say. And I'm not into hunting, but if one of those boars was charging at me, I might shoot it. They're big and hairy and have tusks. They can kill you."

"Like this sucker!" Billy said, shaking the head of his snake.

"So wait," I said. "Does this mean you're a snake poacher?"

"No way!" he said. "This beast attacked *me.*"

Casey eyed me. "Which is how boar hunters get around the no-hunting laws. They say they shot in self-defense."

"Even though they provoked them?"

Casey nodded. "Exactly."

Cricket checked her watch. "Which way are you guys going? Because we really need to get moving."

Casey looked at Billy.

Billy shrugged and gave a little grin.

Casey gave a little grin back, then looked at us and said, "Wherever you're going, that's where we're going."

Billy wagged his rattler at us. "We've got enough food to share."

Cricket scowled. "You need to cut the head off that thing before you inject yourself with venom, Billy."

Billy's eyes got wide. "How stupid do you think I am?"

We all looked at each other and laughed. Then I said, "Not stupid, Billy. Just wild."

"Hmm." He looked at the snake. "Time for the guillotine, you goliath serpentine!"

So while he went to hack off the head, I got busy trying to fix my feet. And the minute Casey saw the blister on my heel, he said, "Holy . . . uh . . ."

"Smokes?" I said, thinking it was really cute that he didn't want to cuss around me.

"Yeah—holy smokes! You walked from *where* with those?"

All of a sudden I felt really good. Like, no, I wasn't a wimp. I was just stupid for ever giving up my high-tops.

He saw me getting some moleskin ready and said, "You can't do the whole doughnut thing on those. You've got to *pop* those."

"See?" I said to Cricket.

And before she could say anything about infection leading to future amputation or whatever, Casey had swung his pack off and had a first aid kit out. He sterilized the tip of a needle with a match, then got down on one knee in front of me. "May I?"

I tried to banish insane thoughts about him being down on one knee and stuck out my foot, which was embarrassingly filthy. "Go for it."

"Cute feet," he said with a grin.

"You're a real comedian."

He cleaned the heel with some sort of wet wipe, then held the needle above the blister and said, "Ready?"

I nodded. "Hours ago."

He eased the point of the needle through the skin, and when he pulled it out, a *geyser* of clear liquid shot out. "Wow!" I laughed, then pushed on the skin, keeping the geyser flowing until the blister was empty. "That feels better already!"

"And now," Casey said, "forget Band-Aids, forget moleskin. . . ." He produced a roll of athletic tape. "We tape it closed and leave it that way the whole time you're out here. It's like a second layer of skin, but it won't move, so you won't get a blister." He finished wrapping it up, then said, "And yeah, it'll hurt when you pull it off, but you'll be back home, where you can deal."

He did the same operation to my other foot, then cleaned up the blood-crusted blisters on my little toes and taped them up, too.

Now, while all this foot repair business was going on, Cricket had sort of eased away from us, supposedly to watch Billy behead the snake. And in between trying not to giggle because my feet were ticklish, I was trying really hard not to blush, because the way Casey was handling my feet wasn't analytical or medicinal . . . it was really tender.

"There," he said, sort of patting the tops of both my feet when he was all done. "You're good to go." He packed his first aid kit up, saying, "If it still hurts too much to walk, we can try putting a doughnut of moleskin on top of the tape, but tape by itself works best for me."

I started shaking out my filthy socks, but he snagged them away and handed me a clean pair out of his backpack. "Fair trade."

"Oh, right," I said, but his socks had nice soft padding around the heel and toe, so I didn't argue. And when I laced my boots back up, the heels did still hurt some, but it was nothing like before.

"Well?" Cricket asked when she saw me standing.

"I think I'm good." And after testing them out a little I said, "Let's go!"

So Cricket and Billy and the beheaded snake led the way, while Casey and I brought up the rear. And the four of us talked about the goofiest things as we hiked along, munching on trail mix and energy bars—what would go good on a rattlesnake sandwich, how a hogshead is an actual unit of measure, how cows' eyes are on the sides of their heads and mountain lions' are in front . . . stuff like that.

But we also talked about more serious things. Like hunters and hunting and the gunshots we'd heard. And Cricket got to give both the guys a huge earful about condors and their reentry into the wild and how important it was to educate hunters about burying gut piles and using lead-free ammunition and all of that.

"Have you ever actually seen a condor?" Casey finally asked. "Because rumor is, they're butt-ugly birds."

I tried not to, but I couldn't help it—I busted up.

Cricket spun on me. "That doesn't mean they don't have the right to live!" She scowled at Casey. "And no, I haven't."

"Sorry!" he said. "Sor-ry!" Then he snuck me a look, which cracked me up all over again.

I did actually feel a little bad about laughing. Cricket had been so nice to me. But with Casey and Billy around, it was hard *not* to keep on laughing as we hiked down the trail. They're just fun to be around, and of course Billy being Billy, the entertainment is never-ending.

Fifteen minutes later, though, Cricket was *still* kind of pouty, but Billy fixed that. "Yo! Yo! Listen up! I got me a rhyme!" He turned around and walked backward so he was facing Casey and me as he said,

"I got big ol' wings and I love to fly,
I get up in da air and I block da sky!
I'm lookin' for a carcass, a pile o' guts,
And if you think *I'm* ugly, you should see *your butts*!"

He pointed at Casey and me when he said the bit about the butts, and that was it—Cricket busted up.

After that, we were all having a good time, and I have to admit that I'd kinda forgotten what our mission was. I wasn't thinking about condors or Gabby or intercepting Quinn or the cry for help. I was just hiking along with my friends, having a good time.

But then I heard something. Something off in the distance. And at first I thought it was a cat, but a *cat*?

Mewing?

Out *here*?

So I stopped short and said, "Shhh!" and there it was again.

Through the brush.

Off the trail.

Somewhere in the distance.

A voice crying, "Help!"

ELEVEN

"Help! Somebody, help!"

"That's her!" Cricket cried. "That's Gabby!"

We cut off the trail toward the voice, calling, "Gabby! Gabby, where are you?"

She didn't seem to hear us, though. And it felt like we were chasing a voice mirage. "This way!" one of us would say, and we'd go that way for a bit, then hear, "Help! Somebody, help!" coming from a different direction.

"Maybe she's not here at all!" Cricket finally said, sort of panicked. "Maybe we're hearing an echo!"

"We're too low for that to be an echo." I looked around at the others. "Aren't we?"

"Help! Somebody, help!"

"On the count of three," I said, "everybody shout, 'Gabby,' as loud as you can."

So I counted off, and we all shouted, "GABBYYY!"

There was a moment of silence and then, "Over here!"

"It's her!" Cricket squealed. Then she shouted, "Over where?"

"Here!"

Whole lot of help that was. But we kept shouting back

and forth, and finally Casey pointed and said, "There!" as the back end of her disappeared behind some trees about fifty yards away.

"What are you *doing*?" Cricket shouted. "Hold still!"

"I can't!" Gabby called. "He'll get away!"

We all looked at each other like, Huh? then charged on.

"You think she's chasing a condor?" I asked Cricket.

"You can't chase a condor . . . it would fly away!" Then she called, "Gabby! Where are you?" because we'd lost her again.

No answer.

"Gabby!"

Still no answer.

"GABBY!"

"Shhh! Over here!" came a hoarse whisper.

We hurried around a group of scrub oaks and ground to a halt right beside Gabby. She looked bedraggled and ruddy-faced and was holding the transmission receiver she'd taken from the Lookout across her chest like a shotgun. It was a strange sight. She looked like a warrior who'd lost her mind and thought she could blast her way to freedom with an old-fashioned TV antenna.

But then, across a small clearing, we saw what she'd been tracking.

It was big.

Black.

Hunchy.

But the head wasn't red, it was black, and honestly,

there was nothing magnificent about it. It looked like some sort of oversized turkey vulture with a big number tag on its wing. So I asked, "Is that a *condor*?"

Gabby whispered, "It's JC-10."

"But why isn't his head red?"

"'Cause he's a juvenile. They don't turn red until they're full grown." Then she added, "He's hurt."

"What's wrong with him?" Cricket whispered.

"I'm not sure, but he can't really fly. And he's separated from his mother, which is not good."

"Why's a bird that big need to be with its mother?" I asked.

"Offspring stay with their parents for about two years," Gabby whispered. "They don't become mature until *six* years. They learn how to survive from their parents, so it's *real* important to keep them together."

"So where's the dad?" I asked.

This time Cricket answered. "Dead. They found him about six months ago—some kind of poisoning." She turned to Gabby. "Are you sure he's hurt?"

"Watch."

Just then the bird whooshed out his wings, making a *roadblock* of feathers. My jaw dropped, and Billy whispered, "That baby is *huge*."

The bird tried to fly, but it didn't really go anywhere.

"See?" Gabby whispered. "I think it's the right wing."

"It doesn't look broken," Cricket whispered. "But you're right—something's wrong with him."

"And he's not going to survive very long if he can't fly."

Cricket nodded. "The coyotes will get him."

"Or the mountain lions."

"Or the—"

"Stop!" I whispered. Like I needed to hear about more ways the Phony Forest could kill you?

Gabby blinked at me like she hadn't realized I was there. "Oh, hi, Sammy." Then she saw the boys. "Who are *you*?"

Cricket hurried to make introductions. "Billy, Casey, Gabby. And a formerly fierce rattlesnake."

Gabby's eyes lit up. "Hey! We can use the snake as bait!"

"No way!" Billy said, pulling back. "This sucker's my dinner!"

We all scowled at Billy like, C'mon . . . !

"And so what if you bait it," Billy said. "You may get close, but he's not going to let you catch him. Look at that beak!"

The bird did have a fierce-looking beak. Not quite as big or as curvy as a parrot's, but still, not something you'd want to mess with.

Then all of a sudden runny white stuff came shooting out of his backside, right onto its legs and feet. I pulled a face. "Oh, man. Something really *is* wrong with him."

Cricket kinda eyed Gabby, who kinda eyed Cricket.

"What?" I said, because they were obviously both thinking *something*.

Finally Gabby said, "That's nothing to worry about."

"Really?"

Cricket nodded. "He's just cooling himself off."

I blinked at her. "With *poop?*"

She gave a little shrug. "Gross, but that's what they do."

I eyed Casey, who kinda smiled and said, "Guess he's just cooling his heels."

Apparently the bird was all through cooling his heels because he hippity-hoppity-flippity-flapped away from us, making surprising time for a cripped-up bird.

"I wish we had that shooting net," Gabby grumbled.

"I wish we had the radio," Cricket muttered.

"And I wish we knew where the trail was," Casey said, looking around. "Billy and I could hike out and get some help, but I have no idea which way to go."

"I've got a topo map, so I'm sure we can find it," Cricket said. "But I really think we should all stick together." She looked at the sun and then checked her watch. "It's a good thing it's summer—we've got about four hours to figure this out and get back to the Lookout."

Half an hour later we were still just following that behemoth bird. So I finally said, "We've got to either *do* something or let him go."

"We can't just let him go!" Gabby snapped.

"So let's *do* something."

"Like what?"

I shrugged. "I don't know. Tackle him."

"*Tackle* him?" Cricket and Gabby cried together.

"Look. He's just a big bird. There are *five* of us! Billy can bait him with some snake meat, then we can grab him."

"It'll *hurt* him!" Gabby cried.

"He's already hurt . . . !" I said back.

"We might kill him!"

I rolled my eyes. "Oh, please. You said he's going to die out here if we don't do something, and I'm sorry, but I don't consider following him around the forest *doing* anything. Let's just tackle him and bring him in!"

"No!"

Now, if it had just been Gabby saying no that would have been one thing. But it was Cricket, too. So I rolled my eyes again and said, "Whatever," and followed them as they followed the bird.

After another fifteen senseless minutes, I got a little flash of an idea. "How's a shooting net work? Is it just a net that shoots out of a barrel and holds down the wings so the bird can't fly?"

"Yeah," Gabby snapped. "And we don't happen to have one."

"But we do happen to have a tent." I looked at Casey. "Right?"

Casey nodded. "Actually, we have two."

"Two?" Cricket asked, looking from Billy to Casey. "Why two?"

Casey snorted and looked at Billy. "He crawls around at night. And he punches."

"In his sleep?" I asked.

Billy gave me a goofy grin. "I sleepwalk at home, but there's not enough clearance in a tent."

"Which confuses him," Casey said. "So he turns into the Sleep Zombie and tries to kill me."

Billy put his arms in front of him like Frankenstein. "Sleep Zombie . . . wants . . . out!"

Even Gabby was losing her bird-stalking concentration. "You're a Sleep Zombie?"

Billy wiggled his eyebrows. "Only at night."

"Which *means*," I said, "that we *really* want to get back to the Lookout before dark. And since these guys have tents, I've got an idea."

"Yeah?" Casey asked. "What's that?"

"Billy baits the bird with the snake—"

"Hey—that's *my* dinner!"

I turned to him. "Listen, Mr. Sleep Zombie, I don't want to play chase-the-condor all night! We're out of water, Cricket, Gabby, and I don't have much food. . . ."

"Dude," Casey said to him, "let's hear her idea, okay?" He turned to me. "All right. Billy baits the condor, and we . . . ?"

"We each take a corner of your tent and use it like a net."

"You mean drop it over the bird while it's eating?"

"Right. It can't spread its wings, it can't *go* anywhere. . . . We wrap it up and carry it out."

Everyone looked at everyone else, and finally Cricket said, "It might actually work."

We were chasing after the bird again, and this time it seemed to take forever for it to stop, so when it finally did, I said, "Okay. Billy, get some of that snake ready. Casey, get your tent out. Cricket, stick with Gabby if the bird starts moving again."

"His name's JC-10," Gabby snipped.

"JC-10 is *not* a name," I snipped back. "It's an alpha-numeric designation."

Billy had produced a knife from his pocket and was starting to slit the snake. "So let's name the beast!"

I hesitated. "Which beast? The snake or the bird?"

"JC-10 is not a beast!" Gabby said.

Billy looked over his shoulder at the condor. "Oh, yes, he is. And I think his real name's Bubba."

"Bubba?" we all cried. "No way!"

"How about Flyboy?" Casey said.

I said, "Or Birdzilla?"

"Meathead!" Billy cried. "Meathead is a perfect name because—"

"Shut up!" Gabby snapped. "Don't *even* go there!" Then very quietly she said, "I think we should name him Marvin."

"Marvin?" We all kind of looked at her, then looked around at each other like, Why not?

So JC-10 became Marvin, Billy got a hunk of snake ready, and the rest of us worked fast to prepare the tent, tying lengths of rope through the corner grommets so we'd be able to stand as far away as possible. And when we were all in position, holding the tent up as high as we could, Billy put the chunk of snake on the ground underneath it.

Then we held very, very still and waited.

And waited.

And *waited*.

Marvin didn't budge.

For ten minutes we stood there. And watching Marvin, I figured out that the little black box near the number tag on his wing was the transmitter. It was only about the size of a nine-volt battery, and it had a little tail on it, which was probably the antenna.

My arms were starting to ache. Cricket and Gabby were shifting around a little, and I could tell they were really tired, too. And just when I was thinking we wouldn't be able to hold the tent up much longer, Marvin did a little hop-flap forward.

We all held our breath.

He did it again. And that was it—he gave in to the mouthwatering aroma of dead snake.

We all looked at Cricket, and when she nodded, the four of us pulled down on the tent, blanketing Marvin beneath it.

"You got him! You got him!" Billy cried, hopping around. But Cricket had left her daypack in the way, and in all the commotion of catching the bird, she managed to step on it and fall over.

Quicker than I could've cried, Help! Billy grabbed her end of the tent and pinned Marvin down. And when we'd wrapped him up and knew he couldn't get away, we took a minute to be ecstatic and relieved and amazed that we'd actually done it.

But then Cricket and Gabby started worrying that we were suffocating him. And then when we tried to give him some air, he *attacked* us with his beak. Man, what a weapon! He hammered around like crazy, so we just covered him back up.

After that I said, "Okay. Let's pack him up and go. We're running out of daylight."

Trouble is, Cricket first had to figure out where the heck we were. And because there were no obvious peaks or valleys or, you know, *site* points in our vicinity, she was having trouble placing us on the topo map.

But since we all knew it would be stupid to start walking aimlessly through scrub oaks and scorpions, the guys and I just paced around for half an hour waiting for her to figure it out, while Gabby cooed at Marvin through the tent.

Finally Cricket threw her hands in the air and said, "I don't know. I can't tell, I don't know." She pointed behind us. "That's north, and I *think* the trail's to the west . . . but I'm not sure." Then she snapped at Gabby. "Stop talking to him! He's supposed to have limited human contact!"

"It's a little late for that!" Gabby snapped back. "And we've got to do something. He's going to suffocate in this tent!"

Casey went over and rearranged the tent so Marvin could breathe through the screening, then picked up the bird bundle and said, "Lead on, Cricket. We're burning daylight."

So we walked and we walked and we walked, and we stopped twice to let Cricket try to figure out where we were, but it didn't help. All we could see in every direction were thorny bushes, weeds, and scrub oaks.

Then the sky got dusky and the air cooled off, and finally Casey stopped and said, "I hate to be the one to say it, but we're down here for the night. We need to pick a spot and set up camp."

"But we don't have our sleeping bags," Gabby said. "Or water!"

Casey scratched the back of his neck. "The five of us can fit in the tent and we've got two bags. We'll survive."

"But . . ." Gabby's eyes got huge. "Oh, Robin's not going to like this! She's not going to like this at all!"

"What are we going to do with Marvin?" Cricket asked. "He can't stay in the tent with us—he won't fit!"

"And he's a *stinker*," Billy said. "Man, he's rank!"

I looked at the others. "What if we set up the second tent and put him *inside* it?"

Casey nodded. "That should work."

"If he doesn't claw his way out," Billy said.

"They don't have *talons*," Gabby said like a know-it-all. "They're not *predators*. They're *scavengers*."

"Yeah. They've got to eat *other* people's snakes," Billy grumbled. He was still hauling his stupid snake around, only now it was about five feet long, with about a foot of skin dangling. "And maybe that thing doesn't have *talons*, but I bet it hammerheads out of the tent in five minutes."

Cricket took a deep breath. "Let's not fight." She turned to Gabby. "We're lucky we ran into these guys, okay? They helped us catch Marvin, they're sharing their supplies . . . they're being really nice. We need to just set up camp and make the best of it."

"I agree," I said. "And if anyone's got a better idea, let's hear it."

No one did. So we put Gabby in charge of Marvin, while Billy made a fire ring, Cricket gathered wood, and Casey and I put up the second tent.

When everything was set, we all worked together to get Marvin inside the tent. He *was* really stinky, but it was actually easier than it might have been because he was pretty subdued. And after we unwrapped him and closed the screen, he just sort of stood there while we crouched in front of the tent and looked at him with a flashlight.

Now, maybe we shouldn't have been using a flashlight on him at all, but it's not like we were putting it in his eyes or anything. And Cricket and Gabby were in obvious awe over the fact that right there, right through the mesh, was a real, live *condor*. And I don't know, it was sort of contagious.

Then Billy said, all matter-of-factly, "What if he's sick from the bird flu?"

We all pulled a face at him like, Oh, *nice*, and right then Marvin tried opening his wings. He couldn't raise them very far, but I was close enough now where I could see that he had some kind of rash that ran under one wing and along part of his chest.

I took the flashlight from Gabby and shined it directly on the rash. "What's *that*?"

"What's what?" Cricket asked.

"Those spots." Marvin's wing was down now, but I could still see some of the spots along his chest. "They're brown."

Almost like he was trying to show her what I was talking about, Marvin turned and raised his wing again. And that's when I saw that it wasn't just spots. There was a whole area of patchy, crusty brown.

It wasn't some weird bird rash.

It was blood.

And in the pit of my stomach I knew—Marvin had been shot.

TWELVE

Casey confirmed it. "It looks like he was hit with birdshot."

"Somebody *shot* him?" Gabby gasped. "What kind of idiot would shoot a condor?"

Cricket's eyes were huge. "They must've seen him and thought he was something else. Like maybe a turkey vulture sitting in a tree? Nobody would shoot a condor on *purpose*."

We were all quiet a minute, then I asked Casey, "Is birdshot meant specifically for birds?"

He kinda grinned. "That's why they call it birdshot."

"But you wouldn't go hunting, say, rabbits with it?"

"Oh, I think people do."

"People like Elmer Fudd!" Billy said.

Billy said it all goofy-like, which made Gabby glare at him and say, "This is serious, okay?"

"I wewize dat!" he said, sounding just like Elmer Fudd.

"Then act like it!" Gabby snapped.

He put his finger to his lips and whispered, "Pweaze, wady! I'm twying to wisten!" Then he turned to Casey. "Gow won, den."

"I don't even know what I was saying," Casey grumbled.

"Sowwey."

"How about boar?" I asked Casey, trying to get things back on track. "Would you use birdshot if you were trying to kill a boar?"

"*Buck*shot, maybe. Birdshot would probably just make it mad. And shot's messy. If you're hunting for game, you have to get all the little pellets out before you eat it." He hesitated. "You know how shot works, right?"

I shook my head. "And how come you do? You're scaring me, you know."

He laughed. "I'm not into guns, but there's this guy in our neighborhood who's a skeet-shooting fanatic."

"Skeet? Is that some kind of bird?"

"Sort of. It's a clay pigeon."

"A *clay* pigeon?"

"It's a little Frisbee of clay that everyone calls a pigeon. Don't ask me."

"*You* know," Billy said, pretending to aim a shotgun in the air. He cried, "Pull!" then tracked who-knows-what with the imaginary barrel of his gun. "Phuuugh! *Crack-crack*, phuuugh!" He lowered the "gun" and blew on the end of the imaginary barrel.

Casey eyed Billy with a scowl. "*Anyway*, shotguns use fat cartridges with a bunch of pellets in them. When you fire a shotgun, the cartridge opens up and the pellets spray. The size of the pellets depends on what you're hunting, but any size shot starts out in a tight wad, then spreads out. So the closer you are to something, the more concentrated the damage."

"Can you tell how far away someone was when they shot Marvin?"

He looked at Marvin and shook his head. "I have no idea. But I do think Marvin's lucky to be alive."

Ever since I'd seen the blood on Marvin's chest, I'd had the eerie feeling that this hadn't been an accident. But who wants to believe that someone had come out to the woods to hunt and kill an endangered species? Now, though, that eerie feeling had become the creeping shivers. Like an army of ticks doing a speedy march up my spine. So I finally just came out and said it. "I think someone shot him on purpose."

Cricket looked at me like there wasn't enough combined insanity in the world to make someone actually believe that. "Why would anyone shoot a condor on purpose?"

"I don't know, but shot pellets hit him under his wing and on the inside of his chest. He must've been in flight when someone fired at him."

"I still say they thought he was a turkey vulture," Cricket said.

"Or maybe he startled them," Gabby added.

I shook my head. "Is it so hard to believe someone would shoot a condor?"

"Yes!" Cricket and Gabby both cried.

I poofed out a breath of air, then said, "What about AC-what's-his-name? Were you able to track him?"

"It's AC-34, and it's a *female*," Gabby said like a nature girl smarty-pants. "She's Marvin's *mom*, remember?"

"Oh, right," I said, "like I was so reminded by the *name*."

"Shut up," Nature Girl snapped back.

"Look. I'm just thinking maybe the mom got shot, too. We heard two shots. Two distinct shots, remember?"

"AC-34's fine," Gabby said.

"How do you know that?"

"Because I tracked her signal, that's how. I tracked both of them. AC-34 was headed west. It was *Marvin's* signal pattern that was weird. And when I tracked him down about an hour later and saw that he was hurt, I started following him and calling for help."

"How long did you follow him?" Cricket asked.

"All day. Forever. *Hours.*"

I scratched my head. "Well, I tell you what, my gut tells me that him being hurt was no accident."

Casey and Billy had been hanging around listening to all of this, but now Billy broke away from the group, saying, "You go ahead and listen to your gut and I'll listen to mine. It's snake time!"

"Aren't you afraid it's rancid by now?" I asked.

"Or poisoned?" Gabby said. "What if it bit itself?"

Billy laughed. "You just want me to give it all to Marvin! Well, forget it! I conked him, I'm eatin' him!"

Cricket's face pinched up as she whispered, "Do you think someone was wanting to *eat* Marvin? Like what if they're stuck down here and starving and—"

"You don't go shooting a rare, endangered species for dinner!" Gabby snapped. "It's just not done!"

Cricket gave a helpless shrug. "But if they didn't know . . ."

"How could they not know?" I asked. "It was in flight and it's huge!"

Gabby spun on me. "How could they not know? If it wasn't for us, *you* wouldn't have known!"

Oh. Good point. So I shut up about it and helped Billy get a fire going while the others got the people tent ready. I was starving. We all were. Which is probably half the reason we were all snapping at each other. I mean, it's bad enough to be lost and tired, but lost and tired and hungry and thirsty and in charge of a shot-up condor?

We were all totally stressed.

Well, everyone except Billy. He was having a blast getting his snake ready for roasting. "Check out this skin!" he said after he'd gutted the snake and peeled the skin off whole. "This is the most bitchen snakeskin ever!"

We all looked at him like, Bitchen? 'cause who actually *uses* that word? Sure, I'd heard it in old movies and stuff, but in real life?

"And check out the rattle! I'm gonna tie a piece of leather to it and wear it around my neck. You know—like those surfer dudes wear a shark's tooth?"

"Like cannibals wear shrunken heads?" Gabby muttered.

Billy's eyes got big. "The head! I should have kept the head! I could have—"

"Billy!" we all shouted. "Enough!"

He scowled and grumbled, "You guys are no fun," then dug through his backpack for some spices.

I went up to Cricket and Gabby, who were searching their daypacks for food. "What's left?"

"Not much," Cricket said. "Gabby's down to one smashed energy bar."

"How about water?"

Cricket checked her canteen. "About an inch left."

It was the same story with Gabby, and I had even less.

"We'll survive," Cricket whispered. "It's just for one night."

"What are you guys whispering about?"

Casey's voice startled me, so I spun around. "Uh, nothing."

"Food," Gabby said. "We're talking about food and water and how we don't have any."

"Don't say it like it's his fault," Cricket said through her teeth. "Do I have to remind you that all of this is *your* fault?"

"My fault? Like it's my fault somebody shot a condor? What was I supposed to do? Let it *die*?"

"Whoa. Take it easy," Casey said. "I've got plenty of food; the problem is water."

I pulled a little face, which I shouldn't have because it made my bottom lip crack. I tried to lick the pain away and said, "You don't have much, either?"

He shook his head. "Maybe a cup. Not enough to

cook dinner, that's for sure. And most of my stuff has to be rehydrated."

Just then I smelled something wonderful. Something smoky, roasty, mouthwatering wonderful. And before it dawned on me what it was, my stomach grumbled like, Let-me-at-it!

"Oh, wow . . ." Gabby gasped, her nostrils flaring as she inhaled the smell. "That can't be . . . *snake*?"

One by one we stumbled over to the fire ring. It was like Billy had cast out lines of aroma and was now reeling us in by the nose. He had the snake lashed to a stick and was roasting it like the biggest hot dog ever.

"I've never tried snake before," Gabby said, still in a trance.

"Me either," Cricket said, all snake-charmed.

I didn't say anything. I just drooled.

"Ah-ah-ah," Billy said, in slow rotisserie mode. "I saved a chunk for our wounded phoenix, but the rest is mine."

"Our wounded phoenix?" Casey asked.

Billy rotated his snake-kabob. "From the ash shall rise a magnificent beast, and all shall gaze in wonder at its glory!"

Casey shook his head. "Where do you *get* this stuff?"

Billy grinned. "From the Book of Billy Pratt." He looked around at us. "So what are *you* guys eating?"

"Trail mix," we grumbled.

"Mm-mmm," he said, slowly turning the snake. "Sounds delish."

So we all sat around the fire choking down nuts and raisins while Billy roasted his snake. And it was looking pretty done to me, when all of a sudden the lashings that held the snake caught on fire.

Billy started dancing around, blowing on the snake, crying, "Out, you heathen flame! This is my snake! Mine!" But all that did was make the snake fall off the stick and into the dirt.

Billy stood there a minute, smoky stick in one hand, charred and dusty snake at his feet. But then he chucked the stick into the fire, dusted off the snake, and declared, "Chow time!"

We watched him scarf for about five minutes before I finally chuckled and said, "What a caveman you are, Billy."

He showed me his snaky teeth. "Ug."

"What's it taste like?" I asked. "Besides dirt."

"Chicken," he teased. Then he added, "Actually, it does." And *then*, because Billy doesn't know when to quit, he said, "Hmm. I wonder if condor tastes like chicken."

"That's it," Gabby said, standing up and heading for the tent. "I'm going to sleep."

"Be there in a minute, honey!" Billy called.

"You're weird!" she called back.

Billy blew her a squeaky kiss. Then he grinned at Casey and said, "I believe the wench has a thing for me."

"In your dreams," Casey snorted.

"Which I'll get to soon enough! But for now, somebody tell us a scary story!"

I deadpanned, "Deep in the forest, between the

darkness of time lost and souls betrayed, roamed a dreadful beast known as Billy Pratt. . . ."

"*Aar-ooooo!*" Billy howled.

Casey laughed, but Cricket stood up and said, "I'm sorry, but I'm going to sleep, too. I'm just beat."

Which left me and Casey sitting around the fire watching Billy eat snake. "That looks like it's all bone," I said as he chucked another section of snake ribs into the fire.

"It is," he admitted. "This sucker's one big tunnel of bones."

"Does it really taste like chicken?" Casey asked.

"Here, bro. Be my guest." He broke off a piece and handed it to Casey, then broke off another and handed it to me. "Don't tell the wenches," he whispered. "Wouldn't want them to get jealous."

So I took the snake, and yes, I ate it.

And you know what?

Rattlesnake tastes like chicken.

Kinda *stringy* chicken, kinda *tough* chicken, but still, chicken.

After we were all done picking the bones clean, we poked at the embers for a while and just laughed about stupid stuff.

Which basically means that Billy did all the talking.

And since the fire was dying down and Billy and Casey had jackets but I didn't, I wound up sitting with Casey, his jacket draped across both of us.

And really, I didn't know what we were doing up so late. I was dead tired, I was sore and parched and filthy and chapped, but I didn't want to go to sleep. I just wanted to sit under the stars with Casey and watch the fire burn down to embers, while Billy prattled on about the "snake floss" between his teeth and whatever else happened to ping-pong through his head.

But finally the fire was out, and Billy actually seemed to be running out of energy, too. So I said, "How *is* this sleep business going to work?" I looked back at the tent. "That is not a five-person tent."

Billy stood. "Those wenches are just going to have to scootch. No way I'm staying out here so the centipedes can get me."

"Centipedes?" I looked at Casey. *"Centipedes?"*

He sort of shrug-nodded. "Little, but deadly. They come out at night."

"Oh, great . . . !"

He laughed. "Yeah, they're pretty creepy." He stood up. "So it's either let the bird go or cram into one tent."

Obviously we couldn't let the bird go.

Which left the tent.

He shot Billy a look. "No Sleep Zombie tonight, all right, man? I have a feeling we're in for a killer day tomorrow."

Aar-ooooo!

THIRTEEN

It's not something I like to broadcast, but when I sleep, I drool. Not always, but when I'm really tired, big puddles of saliva seem to just drain out of my mouth. Some mornings it's so bad you could row a boat from one side of my pillow to the other.

Seriously.

And it's not like having a boy-girl slumber party in a tiny tent with only two sleeping bags wasn't awkward enough or that being crusted in dust with a sunburned nose, cracked lips, and little bits of snake between my teeth wasn't *revolting* enough, I also had to worry about drooling.

So I parked myself on the opposite side of the tent from Casey, grabbed a corner of one of the sleeping bags, and turned my back. And I must've been really, *really* tired, because I don't remember a thing after that. I just conked out.

In the *morning*, though, I got woken up by a little tickle on my chin. So I open my eyes, and there's Billy Pratt, kneeling over me, seeing how far he can make a stream of my drool stretch.

"Grab a life jacket!" he says when he sees my eyes open. "We're gonna drown!"

Gabby and Cricket giggle while I wipe my mouth and bolt upright.

And that's when I see that what I've been half hugging and drooling all over is the calf part of Casey's leg.

"Oh!" I try to wipe his pant leg dry. "Oh, I'm so sorry!" And for the second time in two days, I wanted to shrivel up and die. I mean, *I'd* been the Sleep Zombie. I'd migrated over, used his leg as a pillow . . . and drooled!!

It was beyond embarrassing or humiliating or even mortifying.

It was ego-slaying!

And really, when your ego's been slain, there's only one thing to do.

Run!

So I bolted from the tent and went around in circles doing nothing for a minute, my ego-free mind frozen in my thick, drooly skull. Then I went over and checked on Marvin. Somehow I felt connected to him. Injured and ugly, we were birds of a feather.

He was pretty subdued, just sitting in the tent. I talked to him a little, but he just looked at me with sort of blank brown eyes. "We'll get you some help," I told him, then muttered, "Wish the same was true for me."

Billy squatted beside me and slipped the last chunk of rattlesnake into the tent. "Don't swallow it whole, big guy. I don't know how to Heimlich a bird."

"Do you know how to Heimlich a human?" Gabby asked, coming up from behind.

Billy grinned at her. "Choke on something and I'll demonstrate."

She huffed off, and since Casey was on his way over, I rushed away to help Cricket clean out the tent.

"Hey," Casey said, catching up to me. "It was just a little drool—don't be so embarrassed."

"It was a *lake*." I covered my face and took a deep breath. "My nose is fried, my lips are cracked, I'm a terrible camper, and I drool!"

He peeled my hands away and smiled at me. That's all, just smiled. But that smile said more than any words between us could have. He didn't care that I was uglier than a sunburned warthog. He didn't care that I was a miserable camper. He didn't care that I drooled. So all of a sudden I *didn't* feel uglier than a sunburned warthog. I didn't feel like a miserable camper. Okay, the drool would always be embarrassing, but still . . . I just felt happy to be standing there with Casey's hands wrapped around mine.

Happy to be soaking in his beautiful brown eyes.

His smile.

His . . .

"Would you two get over here and help us!" Gabby snapped.

We looked at her and Cricket, tearing down the people tent. "I think she's talking to us," Casey said with a grin.

"Yeah," I said, grinning back. "Must be."

After that I felt a lot better. And after we'd torn down camp, I decided to focus on helping Cricket get us back to the trail. So while she laid out the map and tried to figure out where we were, I used the binoculars to scout out the landscape. I climbed to the top of a big, crumbly rock formation and found out that I could see a lot farther. A lot *more*.

"You know what?" Cricket called up to me. "I think my compass is broken."

"You're kidding!" Gabby said, hovering over her. "How can your compass be broken?"

"Maybe when I stepped on my pack yesterday . . . ?" She handed it to her. "It's telling me everywhere's north."

"Oh, *great*," Gabby said after playing with it for a minute. "Just *great*."

Now, the way she said it was really snotty. Really *mean*. So I called down, "Just use yours, Gabby."

"I didn't *bring* mine," she snapped.

"Oh," I said, looking at her through the binoculars. "So I guess this is all Cricket's fault."

It took her a minute, but when she got it, she screeched, "Shut up!"

"Sure," I called back. "If you'll quit *snapping* at everyone all the time."

Without missing a beat she called back, "At least I don't *drool* on people."

I lowered the binoculars, studied her for a minute, then raised them again, muttering, "I definitely need to get out of here."

Then I spotted something on the canyon wall behind where we'd made camp. Not directly behind—to the right a ways. It was an area of white rock with some shrubs and trees and stuff, but the trees were sparse compared to everywhere else. And the rock had strange formations. They were sort of long, flat openings. Like a bunch of fat-guy bellybuttons.

"Hey!" I called down to Cricket. "What do those Chumash Caves look like?"

"Can you see them?" she called back, already charging up the rock to join me.

"Do they look like fat-guy bellybuttons?"

She stopped, then raced up the rest of the way. "Yeah!"

I handed over the binoculars when she reached me and pointed. "Over there."

"That's them!" she squealed. Then she lowered the binoculars and said, "We *passed* them?"

"What do you mean, we passed them?" Gabby asked, coming up the rock. "How could we have passed them?"

Cricket didn't answer. She just handed her the binoculars, saying, "Wow, were we ever lost!" She jumped up and down a little. "But *now* I can figure out where we are!"

"Without a compass?" I asked.

She nodded. "I've done plenty of hiking down here. I just needed a bearing!" She started pointing around. "The trail's somewhere over that way, but Deer Creek winds around *that* way, and we really need water!" She took her binoculars back from Gabby and started down the rock, crying, "Deer Creek, here we come!!!"

Billy and Casey had been taking care of the behemoth bird and were looking kind of worried when we joined them. "I don't think he's doing too well," Casey said. "He's really lethargic."

"Water!" Cricket said. "We'll get him water and get him out of here!" She was acting all hyper. All *happy.*

"Huh?" Billy and Casey said.

"Sammy spotted Chumash Caves. I know exactly where we are! Well, not *exactly,* but close enough! Come on! Let's go!"

So Casey and Billy strapped on their packs, and since my daypack was practically empty, I went up to Billy and said, "Hand over the bird."

He eyed me.

"I'm serious, Billy. You've got a full pack; I've got next to nothing."

"Is this a stickup?" he asked, one eyebrow arched high. Then his eyes popped and he said, "Aaagh! She's got drool!" and shoved Marvin into my arms.

"Yeah, I've got *major* drool," I told him across the top of the wadded-up tent. "And I'm not afraid to use it!"

After that, everyone seemed to be feeling better. Even Gabby. She started apologizing to Cricket as we were hiking along, so I dropped back and let them have some privacy. I think I heard Gabby crying some, and I think she also gave Cricket a hug, but it was hard to tell with a big ol' bird in my arms.

Casey offered to carry Marvin a couple of times, but I told him, "Back off, buddy, or I'll hose you down!"

The truth is, though, Marvin was heavy. He felt like fifty pounds, but that was partly because the combination of him and tent was so bulky and hard to handle. I was wishing someone else would carry him, but I wasn't about to ask.

I was through being the weak link.

By the time we found Deer Creek, I was exhausted, sweating, and *parched*. I put Marvin down and I was about to throw myself into the creek, but Cricket held me back.

"What? I'm going to drown in *that*?" It was all of a foot deep. *Maybe*.

"Wet feet will give you big blisters. Just splash some on your face and neck. You'll feel a lot better."

So that's what I did. That's what we *all* did. And it turns out that Billy and Casey had a portable water-purifying pump, so we didn't have to wait twenty minutes for the purifying tablets to work before drinking. They just pumped it through their purifying gizmo and passed it around. And you know what?

Water is wonderful.

It's the nectar of the clouds!

Man, is it good.

Anyway, after we were done splashing in water and eating a bit, we gathered our stuff and followed Cricket "thataway!" We hadn't found the trail yet, but she seemed really confident about where it was.

And I was really hoping she did know, because Marvin wasn't doing well. We'd tried to get him to drink at the creek, but he'd barely taken in any water. And he was feeling heavier by the minute.

Not that I was going to *complain* . . .

Anyway, there we are, just hiking along in a file—Cricket, Gabby, me, then Casey and Billy—hoping that we'll find the trail, when Cricket points and calls out, "Chumash Caves, on your left!"

Casey says over my shoulder, "Hard to believe Indians used to grind their acorns up there, huh?"

I nod and keep looking at the caves. "You know, before this trip I never thought of myself as being even remotely wimplike, but after the two days I've had out here, I can't imagine living like they did. It must've been so hard. What's there to gather around here besides acorns? I haven't seen a single berry. And what did they hunt? Venomous snakes? Boars with killer tusks?"

"Condors!" Billy calls from behind us. "Hey, *they* could tell ya they taste like chicken!"

Gabby shouts, "They didn't even know what chicken was!"

Cricket stops and turns around. "They did not eat condors, Billy. They *revered* condors. They saw them as a symbol of power. They painted them on their cave walls and on their pottery, and they wove them into their blankets." She takes a deep breath, then says, "Native Americans believed that the beating of the condor's wings brought thunder to the skies. Which is why they call it the thunderbird!"

My jaw dropped. The *thunderbird*?

All of a sudden the bundle in my arms felt radically different.

I was hauling around a *thunderbird*?

I told myself I was being stupid. What difference did it make what you called it?

It was still a big ugly bird.

But . . . a *thunderbird*?

Cricket had started hiking again, so we all fell in line behind her. And we'd only been hiking another five minutes or so, when all of a sudden she cries, "Trail!"

At that point she's probably forty feet ahead of me, and believe me, no one's more anxious to get a glimpse of the long-lost trail than I am. But as I'm hurrying along, the toe of my boot kicks into a little pile of horse poop.

Now, I may not know piggy poop from coyote poop, but horsey poop is a different story. If you've ever been to a parade, you know what it looks like and you know what it smells like. It's just processed grass, usually done up in tidy nuggets.

Like barbecue briquettes, only bigger.

And made out of grass.

Or hay.

Or, in this case, Phony Forest foliage.

Anyway, at first I'm like, Horse poop, so what? But then something clicks.

Hard.

I screech to a halt, do a U-turn, and bumper-car Marvin right into Casey.

"What's up?" Casey asks as Billy bumper-cars him from behind.

"Uh, I'm not sure." I kick over a few horsey briquettes,

scout around a little, and hand him the bird. "Could you hold Marvin for a sec?"

But when he sees me following a faint trail of crushed grass toward a ring of trees *away* from everyone else, he passes the bird over to Billy and calls, "Hey, Cricket! Wait up!" as he hurries to join me. "What's going on?" he asks me.

I keep on walking. "That horse poop's not very old."

He doesn't say it right away, but eventually it comes out: "So . . . ?"

"So I saw some on the trail yesterday."

Another pause. "And . . . ?"

"And there are no wild mustangs around here."

We're at the ring of trees now, and when we step inside it, I see that, sure enough, someone's used the camouflaged area as a camp. There's a crude fire ring with a pile of ash and a small area of flattened dry grass where a tent used to be.

"Where are you guys *going*?" Cricket calls. "The trail's over here!"

Casey calls back, "We'll be there in a minute! Sammy's found a campsite!"

"We don't need a campsite!" Gabby shouts. "We need to get back to the Lookout!"

"Give us just a couple minutes, okay?" Casey calls. "We'll be right there!"

I poke through the ashes in the fire ring with a stick. No smoldering embers or heat at all. And I unearth two burnt-clean cans, a wad of aluminum foil, part of a protein bar wrapper . . . and no bones.

So I give up on that and pace off the size of the flat-tened area where the tent used to be. Four feet by six feet. About. Then I find more horse poop near one of the trees. Quite a bit more. And there's poison oak galore. I'm do-ing my best to avoid it, but it's under every tree, popping up everywhere, lovin' life.

A crow caws at us from the top of a tree, then flaps kind of awkwardly as it takes off. And that's when I see something long and black on the ground across the camp area. I rush over, and what I find is the biggest feather I have ever seen. "Casey!" I gasp. "Look."

"Sammy, I don't get it. Why are you so spun up?"

"They don't make crows this big—this is a condor feather!"

"But . . . *we've* got the condor! And they do lose feath-ers, right? Like any other bird? And we're right near Chumash Caves . . . which is where they roost, right?"

I nod because he *is* right.

But still, something *feels* wrong.

Casey follows me as I wander along the outskirts of the campground. There are hoofprints in the sandy dirt in a lot of places, but they get more concentrated as we near an opening between two large oaks on the far side of the camp.

I point at the dirt and say, "I think they came in and out through here. Quite a few times."

"You part Indian?" Casey asks.

I almost tell him, "No," but then it hits me that I don't know—seeing how my mom won't tell me who my dad is. Then I get distracted by a large patch of flattened grass on the back side of one of the trees we've just passed, and when I check it out, I discover a large, dark brown spot on the ground. I squat down to get a closer look, then ask Casey, "Is this blood?"

He inspects it, and says, "That would be my guess."

"Hey, you guys! Where are you?" It's Cricket's voice, and it seems more worried than irritated.

Casey waves across the clearing at her and calls, "Back here!" while I start to follow a sort of choppy streak of flattened dirt and grass that's leading away from the camp. "See these hoofprints?" I whisper to Casey. "And this flattened path? It's like something got dragged along through here."

"Must've been heavy," he says.

And that's when I hear a buzzing sound in the air. It's not loud or scary or weird. It's just one of nature's sounds. Like a bee buzzing. Only it's not just one, it's several. No, not just several, *bunches*. Like a big ol' *swarm* of buzzy bees.

I look up and around, suddenly worried that this forest also has beehive bombs hanging from trees. "You hear that?" I ask Casey.

Just then Gabby calls, "Where are you guys *going*?" and when we turn around, all three of them are coming toward us, Billy waddling along with his backpack *and* Marvin.

"I just want to check something out!" I call back. "It'll only take a minute!"

So I hurry along, following the choppy streak of flattened dirt and grass between shrubs and trees and nasty prickery plants pretending to be flowers. I'm still dodging poison oak because it's still everywhere, and the buzzy sound is getting louder.

"You think it's a beehive?" I ask Casey.

"If that's bees," he says, "we're outta here."

But then we come to a large clearing beneath the steep white face of Chumash Caves and discover that it's not a beehive.

It's something much bigger.

Much weirder.

Much *grosser*.

FOURTEEN

Casey and I just stare at what looks like a giant *fly*hive that's dropped out of the sky. It's big and black and buzzy and just *nasty*. And what flashes through my mind is that we've discovered the mother ship of gnatty flies. You know, like a giant flying cow pie from space! But then I realize that this giant flying cow pie has cloven hooves.

And *tusks*.

"What *is* that?" Gabby asks as the others join us.

"It's a bug blitz!" Billy cries. "Those buzzy boogers brought down a boar!" Then he grins and adds, "Cool."

I pick up a rock and chuck it at the mother ship, and we all watch as the invasion of flies lifts off and swarms noisily above it.

The ship has hooves and tusks, all right. Plus a wiry-haired body with a big hairy head, pointy hairy ears, and a huge round snout. It's like a cross between the Big Bad Wolf and one of the Three Pigs.

The flies come back in for a landing, so Casey moves a few steps closer to the dead boar and chucks another rock at it. "The stomach's been slit open and the guts are pulled out, which is what's making these flies so crazy."

"Any arrows?" I ask.

He chucks another rock, takes a few steps in, and swats flies from around his face. "Not that I see."

"Was it shot?"

"I can't tell!"

"No little pellets?"

He kicks the carcass, shooing flies away and waving them from around his head. "Don't see any!"

"Why are we *doing* this?" Gabby asks. "Can we please just *go?*"

Casey hurries back toward us as Cricket says, "We really do need to get going. Robin and Bella are probably worried sick about us."

So we move away from the mother ship, and as I relieve Billy of his bird burden, I say to Gabby, "Can you try to get a reading on Marvin's mom while we're hiking?"

"Why? What's that got to do with anything?"

But Cricket grabs her by the arm and says, "Yes, she can do that. Now let's get *moving.*"

So we fall in line, and as we're hiking back toward the trail, Billy starts chanting:

"Hup, two, three, four!
Hup, two, three, four!
Keep an eye out for the flies,
They will eat you up alive,
Watch your face, dude, watch your back,
Buzzy boogers will attack!"

When he starts on the second verse, Casey moves up next to me and says, "Tell me what you're thinking."

I take a deep breath. "Okay. Yesterday when we were walking through some meadow covered in cow pies and swarming flies, I saw horse poop. Fresh horse poop."

"Still steaming?"

I laugh. "Not *that* fresh, but you know . . . still moist."

"Yum."

I laugh again. "The point is, I didn't see a guy on a horse, did you?"

He shakes his head.

"But the person who camped back there had a horse. And I think he used the horse to drag that boar from the place where he shot it to that clearing." I look at him. "What do bow-and-arrow hunters do with a boar when they kill it?"

"Butcher it for meat. Or mount the head on their wall."

"But this one was killed, slit open, and left behind. I think it was used as condor bait. The campsite was near the caves where Marvin and his mother were roosting, and I'm sure that's not a coincidence. I think someone camped there so they could catch or kill a condor. Marvin got away, but I have a bad feeling about his mom. Especially since there was a condor feather *in* that camp." I sort of scowl and say, "What's bugging me is the shots. We only heard two shots, and they were in a row. I'm guessing those shots killed the boar. Then it would take time to drag a boar into a clearing and gut it, and even more time after that for it to attract a condor, right? But we didn't hear shots after those first two." I look at him. "So when did Marvin get shot?"

Casey scratches the side of his head. "Maybe you just

couldn't hear it? Maybe they used a rifle on the boar and something smaller on Marvin? Or maybe the person who killed the boar didn't have anything to do with Marvin getting shot. The feather in the camp could just be a coincidence. Or maybe the boar was killed before you even got here and one shot was for Marvin and the other was for his mom?" He sort of frowns and says, "But why would anyone bait and shoot a condor?"

"It doesn't make sense to me, either."

"And how would they know there were condors living in those caves? I sure didn't."

"You don't watch the local news?"

His eyebrows shoot up. "You *do*? And what's the local news got to do with this?"

"Actually, I try not to, but you know that reporter with the swoopy hair? Grayson Mann?"

"I know who you're talking about. My dad calls him Pretty Vegas."

I laugh because somehow the name is perfect. "Exactly! Well, apparently he did a whole series of spots on the condor for KSMY. So anyone who saw the show knows that there were condors living in those caves!"

"But I still can't believe someone would go through all this trouble to *kill* one."

Billy had gone through about five verses of his fly march but had finally quit. And I guess Casey and I had raised our voices, because Gabby calls out, "You're paranoid, you know that? And you're flat-out wrong!" She turns to face us. "I've got a signal on AC-34 right now! She's actually pretty close by!"

"Really?" Cricket says, hurrying over to check the receiver.

I look at Casey.

He looks at me.

We both shrug and I call, "I'm glad, Gabby!" but inside I feel kinda weird. I mean, I *want* to be wrong, I just can't quite believe that I am.

We headed back toward the Lookout the same way we'd come, only everyone agreed that without a compass, we wouldn't be taking any shortcuts.

We did try shouting up to the Lookout a few times, but since we couldn't see it or hear our voices echo, we quit. What was the use?

When we got to Miner's Camp, the Camo Creeps were still there. It was like they hadn't budged since we'd been there the day before. I took one look at them and kept on trucking, but Casey called, "You guys see anyone on horseback come through here yesterday?"

They just stared.

So Casey stepped off the trail toward them and said, "It's important. Did you see a guy on a horse come through here yesterday?"

They all glowered at him, and the biggest one growled, "This is our camp, kid—get out."

And I couldn't believe it, but Casey went even *closer.* "Look, man. Someone's been taking potshots at condors." He pointed toward me. "We've got a wounded one right here. We think it was a guy on horseback. Can you help us?"

Slowly they all stood up and started coming toward me. "Are you serious?" "You got a *condor* there?" "A *thunderbird*?" "You joshin' me?"

So we showed them Marvin and they showed us a lot of dirty teeth as they smiled and took turns looking at what was apparently the eighth wonder of the world.

"Yeah, we saw a fella on horseback," one of them finally said. "Yesterday. Around suppertime. He was riding a chestnut mare, blue and tan blanket under the saddle."

The other two looked at him, then started chiming in.

"That poor horse was overloaded."

"Saddlebags out to here."

"And the cat riding her was wearin' shades *and* a hat."

"That's just not right. You wear one or the other."

They all nodded. "Not both."

"Unless you've been city-fied."

"Or *sissy*-fied," the biggest one said with a laugh.

I was hanging on their every word. "Did the guy *say* anything?"

"Not a word."

"Just rode on through."

"Yeah. And he switched that poor filly every step of the way."

I thought about this a minute, then asked, "What about clothes, hair color, anything else . . . ?"

"Well, he had on that *hat*," the big one said, looking at the others.

"So it's hard to know about the *hair*."

"He coulda been *bald* fer all we know. . . ."

"But he *was* wearing ridin' gloves."

"And cowboy boots."

"And, a-course, jeans. . . ."

"And a T-shirt. It was green, wasn't it, boys?"

The other men nodded. "Olive green."

Then they all glanced at each other. "That's about it."

A crow cawed at us from the branch of a tree. The big man gave it a disgusted look and muttered, "Outta this campsite, ya oversized flyin' cockroach."

I snickered, which made him grin at me and say, "Bottom of the bird barrel in my book." He shot a look at the crow again and told it, "Go back to the rest of your murder, why don'tcha?"

"Back to your *murder*?" Gabby whispered, her eyes wide.

Cricket told her, "Flock of seagulls, murder of crows . . . ?"

The big guy nodded. "Perfect description of their kind, too, if you ask me." He turned back to me. "Any more we can do for you, missy?"

I shifted Marvin to my left side. "You said the horse was really loaded. Could he have been packing something as big as this?"

"You tellin' me he was packin' out a *thunderbird*?"

"We don't know that!" Gabby said. "We don't know any of that!"

I looked the guy square in the eye. "That's what I'm saying."

"Let me at that sucker! Let me at that sucker and I'll—"

"*And*," I throw in, "they used a boar to bait it."

They all fell quiet until one of them finally asked, "How do you know that?"

I held his gaze. "We found the campsite. We found the boar. Big hairy beast with tusks and a big ol' snout."

"Look," Cricket said, pulling on my arm. "We've *really* got to get this condor some help." She gave me a stern look. "So if we could get *moving . . .*"

Just then we heard frantic honking in the distance, and when we looked up, we could see a spot of red on the ridge above us.

"Quinn!" Gabby squealed. "It's *Quinn*."

Cricket and Gabby jumped all around, *hugging* each other in between waving up at the ridge. One of the Camo Guys scowled. "Nature Ninja to the rescue."

I busted up. "Not a fan, huh?"

He shrugged. "He's just a little too by-the-book. Likes to nose in other folks' business."

"Was he nosing in your business yesterday?" I don't even really know why I asked. It's not like I thought Quinn was roaming around the canyon with a shotgun or anything.

"Day before," he said. "Gave us the third degree." He sort of frowned. "But what else is new? We get that from everybody."

I wanted to say, Well, maybe if you didn't dress like trees and give people the evil eye when they came through camp, they wouldn't think you were boar-hunting wackos. But were they boar-hunting wackos? Maybe they were thunderbird-worshiping, tree-hugging wackos. It was really hard to tell.

"Come on, Sammy," Cricket was saying, tugging on my sleeve. "We're going to eat some lunch while we wait for Quinn to show up."

"Snake?" Billy asked, looking around. "Did someone say snake?"

Casey rolled his eyes and yanked him along. "More like sticks and berries, dude."

I laughed, then followed, calling, "Thanks a lot!" to the Camo Campers.

But the minute we were out of earshot, Gabby started hissing in my ear. "I can't believe you were *talking* to them! They're so creepy!"

"But they gave us a lot of valuable information!"

"Couldn't you tell they were making all that stuff up?" She snorted. "A *chestnut* mare, a *blue and tan* blanket, an *olive green* T-shirt, riding gloves, cowboy boots, a hat and sunglasses . . . they were stringing you along!"

I couldn't believe my ears. "Why are you putting me down? I'm just trying to help figure out who shot Marvin. And I thought they were really helpful!"

Gabby smirked. "They played you *bad*. They acted all sincere and helpful so you wouldn't think *they* shot Marvin."

"But—"

"And how convenient that they didn't *talk* to the guy—"

Now I was getting mad. "Did they talk to *us* when we came through? No! They—"

"And how convenient that he was wearing gloves and a

hat and sunglasses so they couldn't tell you any *real* details about him!"

I zeroed in on her. "That's *exactly* what you'd want if you'd just bagged a condor!"

"Nobody just bagged a condor! Marvin's with us, and I got a really strong reading on AC-34. She is *fine*." She leaned in closer. "And get this straight: *I'm* the one who found Marvin, not you! So quit acting like you know everything!"

So that was it.

I screwed my mouth into a little knot and said nothing.

The others had found a place to park and wait for Quinn to arrive and were digging into Billy and Casey's trail mix. I was all for that, but Gabby was more interested in proving that she was right and I was wrong. She fired up her receiver and got busy tuning in the signal for Marvin's mom.

"See?" she said to me, turning the controls so the chirping sound it was making was loud and clear. "That's AC-34's frequency. Nobody packed her out of here. She's fine!" She turned the volume down and murmured, "And close!"

Everyone looked up, checking the skies for a really close condor, but saw nothing. And there was definitely no thundering. All we could find was that same stupid crow, perched near the top of a tree in front of us. It cawed down at us, loud and hard. Like it wanted our food and was mad at us for taking so long to leave.

Billy chucked a rock at it, which made it flap awkwardly

out of the tree. But instead of flying off, it fluttered down to the dirt a few yards in front of us.

"Can that be the same crow that was in that camp you found?" Casey asked me. "Did you notice how gimpy it was flying? This one's doing the same thing."

"You're right. That's weird. . . ."

"Brazen beast," Billy cried. "Quit stalking us!"

But Gabby was staring at the receiver, and her little mouth was shrinking into a teeny-tiny wad of lips, while the tops of her big ears seemed to glow red.

"What's wrong?" I asked.

She picked up a pebble and chucked it at the crow, then played with the controls of the receiver as the crow flapped up into another tree.

She gasped, and now everything except her ears was chalky white.

And that's when I understood what was wrong.

According to Gabby's receiver, Marvin's mother was nothing but an oversized flying cockroach.

FIFTEEN

I whispered, "Cricket, can I have the binoculars?" and when she handed them over, I zeroed in on the crow. "Yup," I said, passing them to Gabby, "he's got a transmitter on his back, which is why he's flying funny."

Gabby took the binoculars and checked it out herself. "But *why?*" she said, lowering the binoculars and looking at me. "Why does he have AC-34's transmitter?"

From the look in her eye, I could tell that she had bubble brain. It didn't mean she was being stupid—it meant that her brain was just having a hard time letting in the truth.

I hate bubble brain. It's an awful feeling. A confused feeling. And when something finally does puncture the bubble, your brain tries like mad to patch it over. Tries to keep the truth out. Eventually, though, the bubble cracks and the truth floods in, and when that happens, you're left feeling completely destroyed.

Like when it finally sank in that my mom was not coming back—that being a movie star was more important to her than being my mom. I wanted so badly to go back to believing what I used to believe, but when the bubble finally bursts, there is no going back. All you can do is hobble forward and eventually learn to deal and accept and even understand. But getting there can take a long, *long* time.

So even though she'd been really hostile about the Camo Guys, when Gabby looked at me and asked, "But *why?*" I didn't think, Man is this girl slow, or, Yeah, Snotty, take that! I just felt bad for her because I could tell there was a bubble around her brain. A bubble that was trying to protect her from the truth.

Quietly I said, "I'm sorry, Gabby. I know these birds are very important to you."

"Crows? I don't give two hoots about crows!"

"No, condors."

"Of course condors are important to me! Would I have come down here if they weren't?" She squinted at me hard. "What I don't understand is why someone would put a condor's transmitter on a crow!"

So I took a deep breath and said, "Because they didn't want anyone to know what happened to the condor."

"What do you mean, what happened to the condor?" She turned to Cricket, who caught my eye, then said to her, "Someone down here was poaching condors, Gabby."

"Poaching condors!? Why would anyone poach a condor!"

Billy had the binoculars now, and from behind them he muttered, "So they could say, Tastes like chicken?"

"Not funny, Billy!" Cricket and I shouted.

"Yeah, it is," he said, still looking through the binoculars. "You guys just don't appreciate death humor."

"Death humor?!" Gabby's eyes were enormous. "Are you telling me AC-34 is *dead*?"

The bubble had been penetrated.

But then her brain tried like crazy to patch up the hole. "I don't believe it!" she said. "There's no way!"

"Gabby," I said gently, "she's either dead or captured. It's the only thing that makes sense."

"To *you* maybe."

Cricket nodded. "To me, too." Then she added, "And I don't know how you'd keep a live condor."

Gabby stared at us for a minute, then turned to Billy and Casey. And when they shrugged like, Yeah, we agree, the bubble finally burst. "But *why*?" she wailed. "We try so hard to get them to live and someone comes along and *kills* them?"

So while she was coming to grips with that, Billy and Casey tried to sneak up on the crow to catch it and remove the transmitter. But even with the two of them working on opposite ends, they couldn't get close.

After watching them for a little while, Cricket said, "I bet they used the shooting net to trap that crow."

"Who did?" Gabby asked.

"Whoever broke into the Lookout." Cricket looked at me. "Don't you think?"

I nodded.

Her voice went up a little with hope. "And if they used it on the crow, maybe they also used it on Marvin's mom."

I looked at Cricket. "But why catch one condor and shoot the other?"

She looked instantly dejected. "I know. It doesn't make sense."

"None of this makes sense!" Gabby wailed. "Why kill a condor? Why *capture* a condor? What are you going to *do* with it?"

None of us could come up with an answer, so we just watched Billy and Casey try to catch the oversized cockroach. It was ridiculous entertainment, and I was just about to get up and join the fun when the crow flapped up to the safety of a tree branch.

Gabby was still struggling with things. "But how do you know that the person who broke into the Lookout is the person who killed the boar? And how do you know that the person who killed the boar is the person who shot Marvin? And how do you know that—"

I wasn't sure how long she was going to go on, so I said, "The person who broke into the Lookout stole three things."

"But you don't know that! Maybe they're just misplaced!"

"Okay. But the three things that are misplaced are a receiver, a shooting net, and an activity log. They used the receiver and the activity log to find Marvin and his mom, and the shooting net to trap a crow to use as a decoy."

"And maybe also to catch a condor," Cricket added.

Just then Quinn's pickup truck came around the bend. The instant it stopped, Bella jumped out, and two seconds later she and Gabby were hugging and crying and saying they were sorry.

Then Quinn and Robin piled out of the cab, followed by a short man with a tidy brown and gray beard, khaki shorts, and little wire-rim glasses on his very long, pointy nose. Immediately he glared at Billy, who was tossing rocks at the crow in the tree. "What do you think you're doing, young man?"

Billy sized him up—or, I should say, *down*—quick. And in true Billy fashion, he put on English airs and said, "I'm flushing out a condor, sir."

The guy's glare became as sharp as his nose. "Flushing out a . . . why, that's no condor!"

"Tut-tut," Billy said. "My mistake." Then he pointed over to where Quinn and the others were tending to Marvin. "*That* lad's the condor." He chucked a rock up at the crow. "This fella's just the wannabe hanger-on derelict ne'er-do-well caw-meister."

Ol' Needle Nose looked at the tent, then the crow, then Billy. "What *are* you babbling about?"

Billy hitched a thumb over at me. "Perhaps she should clarify."

Spectacle Schnoz turned to face me. "You? And who are you?"

"I'm with Robin's group."

His eyebrow arched. "A *name* would be constructive. . . ."

He was being all condescending and hyper-quizzical, so I peered at him down the length of *my* nose as I said, "Yes, it would . . . !" And after we'd stared at each other a minute, I gave an overly exasperated sigh and said, "And you are . . . ?"

"*Me?* I'm Professor Prag. The question is, who are you?"

But just then Cricket comes skidding over, saying, "Get in the truck! Quinn says we need to get Marvin out of here *now*. He's radioed for a helicopter to meet us at the Lookout. They're going to fly Marvin to an animal hospital!"

So I start for the truck, but Professor Pragface actually grabs my arm and says, "First, I demand to know who you are!"

I squint at him. "You *demand*? What are you, the name police? Let go of me!"

He lets go of me, but his eyes don't. And let me tell you, they drill me like he's gonna kill me.

"Come on, Sammy," Cricket whispers. "Billy! Casey!" she calls. "Get in the truck! We've got to go!"

Mr. Pint-sized Name Police gives me the steely eye. "So it's Sammy."

"Yeah," I say, trying to steely-eye him right back.

"Short for Samantha?" he says, like ooooh, isn't he smart.

So I look at him like, Ooooh, aren't you smart.

And yeah, I was being bratty, and no, I didn't care. There was something about his oh-so-superior airs that was totally tweaking my beak. I *hate* oh-so-superior, and I now understood exactly why Vargus Mayfield had hated him as a teacher.

"What about the crow?" Billy called. "Shouldn't we get the transmitter off of him?"

So Quinn produced a mini-bazooka from behind the front seat of his truck, which turned out to be a shooting net.

"I thought that got stolen from the Lookout," I whispered to Cricket.

"It must be another one," Cricket whispered back.

So we all stood back while Quinn took aim at the crow, which was now on the ground under a scrub oak about twenty feet away.

"You're going to have to twinkle him out," Dr. Schnoz whispered.

I pulled a face at Cricket like, Twinkle him out? and she gave a little shrug back like, You got me. . . .

But Quinn said, "Go ahead," so ol' Pragface starts tippy-toeing toward the crow. I'm not kidding. Here's this angry-looking guy with little round-rimmed glasses *tippy*-toeing toward an oversized flying cockroach.

Billy and I look at each other like, Whoa, is he freaky or what? And then Billy starts pretending he's the professor, squishing his face so his nose is all pointy, putting his hands up like bunny paws, and tippy-toeing in place.

And really, I'm doing my best to not crack up, but it's like holding in a sneeze. You can do it for a little while and then *ka-choo*—it busts out whether you want it to or not.

Lucky for me, the laugh escapes just as Quinn shoots the net. And like a sneeze, the net bursts out *fast*. It's big, too. Big enough to catch a handful of *people*.

Anyway, it sails through the air and traps the crow no problem, and then Professor Needle Nose swoops in and says, "Gotcha!" with way too much glee. He turns to Quinn. "And why are you monitoring *Corvus brachy-rhynchos?*"

Which apparently is Oh-So-Superior for *crow*.

"We're not," Quinn says, and starts explaining the situation as he reaches through the netting to remove the transmitter. But even after he's handed Cricket the transmitter and let the crow go, he's *still* having to explain things to the professor because, for such a supposedly smart guy, Mr. Corvus Brachyrhynchos is sure asking a lot of dumb questions. Like, "How did they know the camp was used by someone with a shotgun? Are they sure the hog was slit open? What if it was downed by coyotes? How can they be sure it was a man on a horse?"

He finally shut up when we piled into Quinn's truck. The adults got the cab, while the rest of us *and* the backpacks *and* Marvin crammed into the bed of the truck.

After we'd been driving for a while, I peeked inside the tent to check on Marvin. His eyes were droopy, and I could feel my heart lurch. He was not doing well. Not well at all.

I bit my lip and looked away, thinking that after all this, that big ol' ugly bird had better not die.

SIXTEEN

On the ride back up to the Lookout, Casey sat close beside me and whispered, "You okay? You've got this gutsy girl thing going on the outside, but on the inside you're upset." He caught my eye. "I can tell."

I tried to scowl like, You're full of condor poop, buddy, but my chin kinda quivered and gave me away.

He smiled at me and put his hand on my knee. "He would have died out there on his own, you know."

"It looks like he's going to die anyway," I said, and my voice came out all raspy.

"They're helicoptering him out of here, they've probably got some raptor expert waiting for him at that animal hospital. . . . Your big buddy is gonna pull through."

"He's *not* my big buddy," I said, because I didn't *want* him to be my big buddy. I didn't *want* to care about him at all. I wanted to go back to thinking he was an ugly oversized turkey vulture who ate guts and bottle caps.

"So why wouldn't you let anyone else carry him?"

My eyes popped. "You think I *wanted* to carry him? That bad boy is heavy! I just thought it was fair since I was the one who was carrying the least."

Casey just smirked.

It was strange pulling up to the Lookout. It felt like a week since Cricket and I had left camp, but it had only been a day. Everything was pretty much the way we had left it, except for the blue and orange mountain bike leaning against the steps.

"She's back?" Gabby whined.

This time Bella just let it slide. Then, as we were unloading the truck, Robin perked an ear and said, "Listen! They're already here!"

At first it was a distant, choppy sound, but as the helicopter came around the mountain and into view, the noise became thunderous.

"It'll be safer in the Lookout, girls!" Robin called, tossing Bella the keys. Then she realized that her little group had grown since the last time we'd been there. "And boys!" she added. "Go!"

So the six of us ran up the steps, opened a few shutters quick so we could watch, then dove inside. Janey wasn't inside the Lookout, but wherever she was studying bugs and bones—or whatever people who work at natural history museums do—she couldn't have missed the arrival of the helicopter. It put up a huge dust storm and we felt like the Lookout windows might implode from all the wind it was making.

The blades never stopped turning. Quinn held open the passenger door, and we all watched as Professor Prag got in with Marvin, who was still wrapped in the tent.

"Why is *he* going?" I asked. Something about turning over Marvin to the professor just felt wrong.

"Probably because he knows about birds," Casey said.

Then Billy made me laugh by saying, "Dr. Corvus Brachyrhynchos, at your service." He had one eye open wide and the other squinting like he was wearing a monocle. "I steal your bird, I steal your tent." He got a manic look in his wide-open eye. "I am a *fowl* creature!"

"We'll get your tent back, Billy," Cricket said. "I promise."

After the chopper was out of sight, Bella let out a big sigh. "I can't believe everybody saw a condor before me. I missed out on *everything*. . . ."

Cricket said, "Be glad, Bella. It was no fun."

"But you guys had such an adventure. You found a condor, you got lost, you roasted *rattlesnake*. . . ." She sighed again like it was the dreamiest night imaginable. "All we did was worry."

"How far did you guys hike?" I asked.

"We went over the ravine, through Hoghead Valley, *past* Chumash Caves clear out to Devil's Horn. We didn't get back until dark and we were really hoping everyone was here, but then *nobody* was."

"Did you go through Miner's Camp?"

"Had to."

"Were those boar hunter guys there?"

She sort of cocked her head. "What boar hunter guys?"

"The ones dressed like trees?"

She shrugged. "We didn't see anybody in Miner's Camp."

"Did you *look*?"

"Sure, we looked. We were looking for Gabby, weren't we?"

"But . . . they said Quinn talked to them the day before. So their camp must've been set up. . . ."

"Oh, there was a tent, but no people."

Just then Quinn and Robin came in. "Well," Robin said. "What do you say we make something to eat? From what Gabby told us, you must be famished!"

"We are!" Cricket said, heading for the door. "Come on! Let's get cooking!"

But while everyone else was filing out, I took a little detour over to where Quinn was frantically making notes in a new log book. "Excuse me," I said. "You know those guys dressed in camo gear at Miner's Camp?"

He nodded but didn't look up.

"Are they boar hunters?"

He stopped and looked at me. "Most likely."

"But you've never caught them hunting?"

He shook his head and went back to writing in the log. "And they always have a camping permit, so there's not much—" He suddenly looked at me with a sharpness in his eye that hadn't been there before. "Maybe they're the ones who shot JC-10! Why didn't I think of that before?"

"Wait a minute! The reason I was asking was—"

But he was already charging out the door.

So I'm left standing there with more questions than ever, and then my eye catches the new log that Quinn had written in. His penmanship is blocky and surprisingly precise, considering how fast he'd scribbled, and right above his writing is an entry made at eleven that morning: *Picked up strong signals from both AC-34 and JC-10 at 280° east. D. Prag.*

"Hey, Quinn!" I call as I pound down the Lookout steps.

He's leaning inside his truck talking on the radio, and when he's done, he peels his headband off and wipes his brow with it, then flashes me his samurai smile. "I don't know why I didn't put that together earlier! Thank you so much for the tip, Sammy."

"But . . . wait. So much of this doesn't make sense and I . . ." Between the heat and his blinding smile, I lose my train of thought for a minute. So I jump ahead to "Where'd you guys get another receiver?"

"Another receiver?"

"The log says you guys picked up signals this morning."

"Oh. I borrowed it from Professor Prag yesterday."

"So that's where you were yesterday? At the college?"

He hesitates, then asks, "What's this all about?" Again, that smile. That brain-freezing smile. "Gee, Officer, should I call my lawyer?"

Then someone calls, "Quinn!" from over by the fire ring, and there's Janey, with the others, waving and smiling.

Quinn puts his hand on my shoulder like we're chums and steers me toward the fire ring. "Let's see what's cooking."

Now, okay, (a) I didn't like the way he was treating me like a child, and (b) I wasn't going to waste my time asking him any more questions. First he thought Vargus had broken into the Lookout. Then he jumped all over the idea that the Camo Campers had shot Marvin and switched the transmitter. It was like he wanted to blame someone, *any*one.

Why wasn't the truth more important than the blame?

I let him lead me toward the fire ring, because I've learned that sometimes it's best to just pretend to go along. Besides, I'd already totally alienated Professor Pointy Nose; it probably wouldn't be too smart to do the same with Quinn.

But as we walked, I tried to figure out how all these random scraps of information fit together. Maybe Quinn and the professor were in cahoots. Maybe they'd lured Vargus up to the Lookout and had strewn beer cans around to make it seem like college students had stolen the equipment? After all, Quinn knew when Robin was planning to come up. She'd been surprised that he wasn't there already. So maybe he'd been hanging back, waiting for her to discover Vargus?

And how convenient that the professor had a receiver.

And where'd Quinn get the shooting net?

Where was he yesterday when Cricket and I were waiting and waiting for him to show up?

Anyway, we'd barely made it over to the fire ring when a white four-wheel drive with a giant KSMY emblem on the side comes revving up to the Lookout.

Quinn actually moans, "Oh, no," when out of the cloud of dust surrounding the SUV emerges Pretty Vegas himself—Grayson Mann. With him, there's a kinda heavyset man wearing cargo shorts and a T-shirt, carrying a big video camera.

"Mr. Terrane, Mr. Terrane!" Grayson calls out to

Quinn. "We intercepted some radio traffic about a shot condor. Is it true?"

"I'm afraid so." Quinn sees the guy in the cargo shorts hoist the big camera onto his shoulder and says, "Mr. Mann, I really don't want to turn this into a media event."

"I understand, I understand," Pretty Vegas says to him. Then he nods at the cameraman. "You remember Alton from our earlier coverage, right?"

Quinn and the cameraman give each other familiar nods, and with that formality out of the way, Pretty Vegas asks, "So when did it happen? How's the bird? Is there anything we can do to help you track down the hunter?" He pumps his shirt in and out trying to cool off a little. "Name it and we're on it."

Quinn says, "I know you mean well, but I'm afraid the exposure from your miniseries might be exactly what led someone to the birds in the first place."

Pretty Vegas's jaw drops. "Are you saying this is our fault? We were just trying to inform the public of the plight of the condor and help you get the funding you said you so desperately needed to keep the program going . . . !"

Quinn sighs. "I'm not saying this is your fault. We really appreciate your efforts and support. You and Alton did a terrific job putting that series together." He takes a deep breath and adds, "*But* I think under the circumstances, not turning the situation into a public spectacle would better serve the condor population."

"We're not talking about making it a public spectacle! We're simply interested in helping you track down the hunter so he doesn't strike again! It's been proven time and time again that if the public is on the lookout for a certain criminal, the public *will* find that criminal!" He fans his shirt again, then scratches his forearm, and I'm actually feeling kinda sorry for him 'cause he's obviously dying in his sweaty, itchy work clothes.

"I still don't think it's a good idea," Quinn tells him. "Law enforcement is involved, and we've got the best in the field attending to the injured bird. We're hoping he makes a full recovery."

Pretty Vegas hands him a business card. "Well, if you change your mind . . ." Then he adds, "Just promise me you won't give the story to anyone else. We're the station that's rooting for *you*. . . ."

Quinn nods. "Like I said, we appreciate that."

"I feel for you," he says, with a friendly pat on Quinn's shoulder. "Those birds are your pride and joy." Then he drops his voice and says, "Public outrage is a powerful tool. And your everyday viewer can be very generous. . . . There are all sorts of ways we can help." Then he adds, "And if it was just an accident, public awareness could prevent future injuries." He cocks his sweaty, swoopy-haired head a little. "You think it might have been an accident?"

Quinn nods. "That's certainly a possibility."

I feel like screaming, "*What?* A condor's transmitter got strapped onto a crow by *accident?*" But Quinn shoots me a look, and it hits me that maybe he just doesn't want to give anything away to a reporter. Or maybe he just wants to get rid of the guy.

Then Pretty Vegas's eyes narrow a bit and he says, "What about that group of developers?" He snaps his fingers, trying to remember something. "Luxton Enterprises—that's it!"

"What about them?" Quinn asks.

"They had this grandiose plan for a golf course and estate homes, but their property butts up to the condor sanctuary, so they got denied."

"Right. But that got nixed in the early stages. And it's been over a year."

"But it's still real motivation! Trust me, I've got a nose for this sort of thing." He scratches his arm and fans his shirt. "I'm going to do some checking for you. We'll get to the bottom of this! Come on, man, think about it—if they're the ones behind this, they might not stop until they kill them all!" Then, like he's switching cameras in the newsroom, he turns and flashes his reporter smile around at the rest of us, shaking hands, going, "Grayson Mann, KSMY . . . Grayson Mann, KSMY . . ." Then he hands a *business* card to each and every one of us, saying, "Here's how you can reach me if there's a break in the story. I'm behind you people. Behind you one hundred percent."

When he's gone, Robin takes a deep breath and says, "Media people," and Quinn mutters, "I'm sorry I ever let Dennis talk me into doing that series."

A little alarm goes off in my brain. "Professor Prag wanted TV cameras up here?"

He nods. "He thought it would help raise funds, which it has." Then he kind of eyes me and adds, "I know you and

Dennis didn't hit it off too well, but I can see why—Dennis likes things done his way and you like to buck authority."

"I like to buck *stupidity*."

The minute it came out, I wished I could take it back—even if it was the truth. But the odd thing is, Quinn just sort of pulled back a smile and said, "Dennis is far from stupid, but I do admit he takes some getting used to."

Then Janey pipes up with, "But back to the condors. It sounds like that Luxton Enterprises is worth looking into . . . don't you think?"

Quinn nods, but it's sort of a reluctant nod.

"What's wrong, honey?"

"I don't know," Quinn says. "I guess I don't really want to believe any of this. Some angry developer's going to extinguish an endangered species for a few houses and a golf course?"

Janey shakes her head. "I know, but it's probably worth millions to them."

Robin nods. "She's right, Quinn."

"But this doesn't seem like it was a big-bucks operation," I tell them. "I mean, come on. One guy on a horse? A slaughtered pig? A four-by-six tent? And why put a transmitter on a crow? It sure doesn't sound like someone who's trying to get rid of all the condors."

All the adults just stand there blinking at me. And then Quinn says, "I'm sorry, sweetheart, but maybe you should just let the adults handle this."

So I blink at *him* a minute, then snort and walk off, wondering why I even cared.

SEVENTEEN

When the food was ready, everyone else joked and chatted while they ate, but I scarfed and brooded.

At one point Casey whispered, "*Psst.* What are you thinking about?"

"Huh? Oh . . ." I looked around. Billy was poking at the wood in the fire ring, Robin was cleaning up, and Quinn was busy entertaining Janey and the other girls with some adventure story. I shook my head. "I can't talk about it right now."

I did talk to him for a little while about other stuff, but I must have drifted off to Broodsville again because the next thing I know, Robin's saying, "So we all agree?"

"What?" I whispered to Casey. "What are we agreeing to?"

"Packin' it in. Goin' home. Gettin' out of Dodge." He grinned at me and shook his head. "You have amazing powers of concentration."

"You mean we're going home? All of us?"

He nodded. "Welcome back."

I kinda cringed. Here I'd been sitting right next to him and all I'd really done was think about condor killers.

Did I care about them more than I cared about him?

No!

But my stupid fanatical brain had sure made it seem like I did.

"I'm sorry," I whispered. And for the first time ever I reached out and touched his hand.

Everyone else was standing up, so we did, too, only he held on to my hand and said, "Can you tell me about it on the ride home?"

"You're coming with us?"

"My dad's not scheduled to pick us up at the trailhead for two more days. But Robin's offered us a ride and we're taking it." He eyed the stack of dirty plates that Robin had collected. "You guys kinda ate up all our food." He hesitated. "So can you talk to me about it on the way home?"

I glanced at the other girls, then shook my head. "I want to," I said quietly, "but I can't."

"So I guess that means you'll finally have to give me your phone number?"

"Uh . . ." All of a sudden I felt like a deer in the headlights. I knew I should run, but I was frozen in place.

He waited, but after a minute of me saying nothing, he said, "Your mom still won't let you talk?"

I said another real intelligent, "Uh . . ." because Casey doesn't know anything about my living illegally with my grandmother or any of that, and I didn't know how to explain that I *wanted* to give him my phone number, but that doing so made me traceable, not just to him but potentially to someone very dangerous.

He let out a dejected sigh. "So you call me then, okay?"

All of a sudden I'd had enough. Enough lying to him, deceiving him, enough just *avoiding* him. Here I was, stinky, burnt, flaky, and matted, and he *still* wanted my phone number.

What kind of amazing guy was this?

So I pulled him farther away from the others and said, "Can you promise me—and I mean really *promise* me—that my phone number will never wind up in Heather's possession?"

"Heather? *That's* what you're worried about? I thought your mom—"

"Don't ask questions, okay? It's complicated and . . . and let's just say that if Heather gets my number, it's going to be a very bad scene."

"Because you're going to make her eat dirt again?"

I laughed, then said, "No, because she'd track me down and ruin everything."

His eyebrows went up a little. "She *has* tried to follow you home, you know."

"I know."

"And she's tried to squeeze information out of me, too."

"Exactly! Which is why I've never told you anything that she *could* squeeze you for."

He shook his head. "All this time I thought it was your mom."

"Forget my mom, okay? Focus on this: you've got to keep my number away from your sister, okay?"

"No problem." He was looking right in my eyes. And somehow he'd picked up my other hand, so he was holding on to *both* of them. "So?" he asked, and his eyes were kinda twinkling. And then he started leaning forward.

Closer.

And closer!

At first I didn't understand, but then my heart panicked and my brain screamed, Your lips are a disaster! Run!

"Nine-two-two-eight-eight-four-seven!" I blurted, then broke away.

He grinned. "Nine-two-two-eight-eight-four-seven, got it."

"And it's top secret! Not even Cricket has it . . . !"

"Got it," he said again.

So we tore down camp and cleaned everything up, which took *hours*. And then, while Quinn and Janey drove our packs down to Robin's van, the rest of us hiked out. Downhill without a pack was a breeze! I couldn't believe how fast we got to the parking turnout.

After we'd crammed everything inside the van, Quinn and Janey drove back up the mountain, and we drove down. We were packed in *tight*, too. All of us except Billy, who got to ride shotgun. "He stinks too bad to ride back here!" Bella said. "Keep him away!"

"It's snake sweat!" Billy said back, blowing a whiff-of-jiff from under his arm. "I could sell this as an aphrodisiac!"

"Oh, right!" we all moaned.

So the ride home was cramped but fun, and since Cricket's house was the first stop, I got off there with the excuse that I had to return stuff and, you know, *get* stuff.

Through the van window, Casey gave me the I'll-call-you sign and smiled.

I smiled back and blushed pretty good, too. And after Robin drove off, I went into Cricket's house, but there was really only one thing I wanted to get.

My high-tops.

I put them on and I'll tell you what—my feet have never been so happy.

Then I asked, "Can we unpack tomorrow? I just want to go home and take a shower."

Cricket laughed. "I'm all for that!"

So I headed home, and when I slipped inside the apartment, Grams jumped up from the couch and said, "You're home a day early!"

At first she looked happy, but it didn't take long for her face to fall and the questions to start: "Look how filthy you are! And sunburned! Didn't you bring any sunblock? Where are your things? Oh, look at your poor lips!" And then finally, "What *happened* to you?"

I gave her a cracked-lip smile. "I'm fine, Grams. But I'm real glad to be home." I looked around the tiny apartment. I'd never really appreciated how clean and tidy and bug-free it was. And the couch looked so, *so* comfy. I sometimes grumble about how living at Grams' is like camping out because I sleep on the couch and live out of her bottom dresser drawer, but looking around the apartment, I realized that I hadn't been camping out—I'd been living in luxury.

"But what happened?" she was asking. "And where are all your things?"

"I have to go over to Cricket's tomorrow to sort through stuff and clean up. We were just too beat to do it tonight." Then I smiled and said, "But I've got lots to tell you!"

I was making a beeline for the couch, but she intercepted me and steered me toward the bathroom. "I'd love to hear, but first you're going to take a shower! A long, *hot* shower. And while you're doing that, I'll fix us some dinner."

So I took the longest shower ever. I soaked the athletic tape off my feet, which was slow-going and painful, I washed my hair four times, and then I just sat on the floor, letting the water rain on me. It felt so good.

By the time I was squeaky clean and dressed, Grams had dinner ready. "Trout?" I said, when I sat down at the table.

She flipped open her napkin. "I kept thinking about you being out in the forest. So today when I was at the grocery store and saw trout, I got the urge to have some." She gave me a little smile. "I was picturing you and your friends maybe having a trout supper, too."

I'd already started eating, so I said through a mouthful, "To catch a trout, you'd need a *river*. . . ." Then I launched into how the Phony Forest was dry and dusty and creeping with bloodsucking bugs, poisonous plants, and trees with sudden death disease. And *then* I rattled on about the Lookout, Gabby and Bella fighting, Gabby taking off into the canyon on her own, hearing gunshots, and my killer blisters.

Now, the more I talked, the slower Grams ate. But when I got to the part about bumping into Casey and Billy, she stopped chewing altogether.

I guess it's kinda hard to eat with your jaw dangling.

"You ran into Casey . . . *Acosta*?"

I nodded. "And Billy Pratt."

And even though she was trying to trust me, I could see little thoughts of doubt dancing around the edges of her eyes. So I pointed my fork at her and said, "Would I be telling you about this if I'd planned it?"

She shook her head. "No. No, of course not."

"So?"

She started eating again. "So go on."

So I went on, but I decided to skip over the part about getting stuck in the woods overnight. I compressed everything that happened into one day, because sleeping in the same tent as the guy who everyone tries to make into your boyfriend is not something you want to have to explain to your grandmother.

Or anybody else, for that matter.

Besides, Grams was way more interested in how we'd rescued Marvin, and *especially* how I'd met Grayson Mann, than she was in the details of time.

"You actually shook his hand?" she gasped.

I grinned at her. "I'd let you touch me, but his celebrity cooties have been washed down the drain."

So avoiding the whole boys-and-girls-in-the-same-small-tent subject was actually easy with her. I'm just glad she wasn't with me the next day when I was taking a short-cut through the mall on my way over to Cricket's house.

It turned out to be a very *dangerous* shortcut.

"Hey, loser!" a familiar voice called as I passed by the food court.

I just kept walking.

"Hey, *loser*," I heard again, and this time the voice was right behind me.

Now, it's not that I like to acknowledge that name, but experience has taught me that facing someone who doesn't mind stabbing you in the back is definitely the superior choice when defending yourself.

So I turned around.

Sure enough, it was the Gossip Grenade herself.

The one and only Heather Acosta.

I gave her a prim little smile, and in an English accent I said, "Such a *pity*. We were hoping you'd come back civilized, dear. Did being so near the royals have no effect whatsoever?"

"You shut up and listen to me," she seethed. "When my dad finds out that you and my brother slept together—"

I laughed, but it was like trying to breathe when you've been slugged in the stomach. And it was almost impossible to keep the whole sophisticated-English-accent thing going with my brain gasping for air, trying to figure out how she'd heard this *already,* but I did my best. I shook my head and whispered, "High-class ladies do not let their minds race so freely to the gutter."

She shoved me and sneered. "High class? What would you know about that, huh?"

I brushed off the spot where she'd shoved me and gave her another prim smile. "Apparently more than you." Then I walked away.

"In your dreams!" she shouted after me. "And when my dad finds out that you slept with my brother—"

The whole food court seemed to fall quiet.

The whole *mall* seemed to fall quiet.

I held my head high and kept walking, but inside, I about *died*. Heather wouldn't stop after dropping this one bomb in the mall. She'd drop them all over town! By tomorrow there'd be fallout everywhere!

She was going to annihilate me.

EIGHTEEN

When I got to Cricket's house, she whisked the door open and said, "Good news! Marvin's going to be all right!"

It *was* good news, but at the moment I was having trouble caring. I had bigger problems to deal with than a blasted bird. *I'd* been blasted by a bird of a different kind. The sharp-beaked, razor-taloned predatory kind.

That Heather Acosta is one mean chick.

I walked past Cricket and said, "I ran into Heather in the mall. She's announcing to the world that Casey and I slept together."

"What?"

"You heard me."

"Casey wouldn't have told her that. . . ."

"If he did, that's it—I'm done talking to him forever."
I marched into the kitchen. "Can I use your phone?"

"Sure. But . . . you're going to *call* him?"

I punched in his number, leaned against the wall, and waited.

One ring.

Two rings.

Four rings.

"Hello?" The voice was mumbly. Sleepy.

Well, I was gonna wake him up quick!

"It's Sammy. Did you tell Heather about the camping trip? Because she just announced to the whole mall that we slept together."

There was a moment of silence and then a mumbly, "Casey . . . ! For you . . . !"

My eyes got huge and I almost slammed down the phone.

"What's wrong?" Cricket whispered.

"That was his *dad* . . . !"

"I thought his dad was gone!"

"So did I . . . !"

Casey was on the phone now. "Sammy?"

For the second time in half an hour, I wanted to curl up and die. And the really stupid thing is, I'd done something like this once before when I'd called his house. I'd gone on and on confessing something at lightning speed . . . to his *dad*.

"Sammy, are you there?"

"Did you tell Heather about the camping trip?" I choked out.

"Haven't seen her. She's at my mom's. Why?"

"She knows we slept in the same tent and she's making it sound really . . . bad."

"How the . . ." There was a moment of silence and then, "I'm calling Billy. I'll get back to you."

He was about to hang up, but I wedged in, "I'm at Cricket's. Call me here," and gave him the number.

"Wow," Cricket gasped after I'd hung up. "How embarrassing."

I slid down the wall and held my head. "I can't believe this. I just can't believe it."

"Hey, what's up?"

I looked up and saw Gary. Porcupine hair matted on one side. Acne in full bloom everywhere. My head drooped back into my hands. I was *not* in the mood to talk to Butterfly Boy.

He, apparently, *was* in the mood to talk to us. "Man! I still can't believe you guys rescued a condor." He pulled the milk jug out of the fridge and poured himself a monster glass. "No one can believe it. People are all in awe."

My head clicked up a few notches. "People? What people?"

He stuffed half a Twinkie in his mouth and drowned it in milk. "People I chat with."

"On the computer?" I asked, and yeah, I was starting to get worried.

"What else," Cricket muttered, but she was grinning at him. Like they'd had some sort of brother-sister breakthrough while I'd been gone.

"How much does he know?" I asked Cricket.

She shrugged. "I told him the whole story."

"*Everything*? And he's posted it on the *Internet*?"

"It's not like we did anything wrong. . . ."

"Yeah," Gary said, milky Twinkie oozing between his teeth as he grinned. "It's not like you did anything wrong. . . ."

"*I* know that, *you* know that, but—"

"Don't freak. I'll show you the thread if you want." He shrugged. "It's an awesome story. I'd be proud if I were you." Then he turned to Cricket and said, "*Mom* would be real proud."

Tears sprang into Cricket's eyes, but before she could say anything, the phone rang. She snatched it off the wall, listened, then handed it to me and gave her Twinkie-toothed brother an enormous hug.

"Billy told Danny," came Casey's voice. "So I called Danny and found out Heather called him last night."

I groaned. On top of everything else, I knew that when Marissa found out that Heather was ringing Danny's bell, she was going to be crushed. She has a thing for Danny, and worm that he is, he makes like he's got a thing for her, too.

Casey must have picked up the vibe, because he said, "Don't be too hard on him—he wasn't trying to sabotage anyone. He thought the story was a riot, because, you know, Billy told it. And don't worry—I'll take care of Heather and her twisted interpretation."

Casey's voice had been getting quieter and quieter, and it sounded like he was moving into a different room so he wouldn't be overheard. "I'll tell you what, though— my dad's roasting me pretty good. Especially after the way I had to fast-talk him into letting me and Billy go solo."

"I'm so sorry," I said, but then added, "At least you'll get to explain it to him before Heather does."

"True," he said, and then, as if my life hadn't spun out of control enough for one day, he drops his voice even far-ther and says, "Guess who my dad ran into at that audition in L.A."

So I say, "Who?" but it's a real disinterested *Who*

because I'm still stewing about Heather and, really, I'm not into movie stars so I'm not going to know what celebrity he's talking about anyway.

But then, on the wings of a whisper, he drops the bomb. "Your mom."

Bubble brain engulfs me.

"Sammy? Did you hear me?"

I couldn't move, I couldn't breathe, I couldn't *think*.

So I did the only thing I *could* do—spaz out.

"I've gotta go!" I choked out, and hung up. Then I slid down the wall and just held my head. And it did flash through my mind that Casey was bound to get fed up with all my weirdy-o-syncrasies and drop me, but how was I supposed to act *normal* when my mother makes it so hard? I mean, living illegally with Grams is one thing. It's stressful, but I don't want to go live with my mother in Hollywood. My friends are here, my *life* is here. And even if Santa Martina is a freak-fest of a town, it's *my* town. I know my way around. I know which cops to avoid and which shortcuts actually work.

And who'd want to live in Hollywood? Talk about a *real* freak-fest! The whole town's a walking, talking, living, *breathing* Barbie-and-Ken convention.

What could be scarier than that?

But the *point* is, even though it's not the best situation, living with Grams is manageable. Grams keeps the secret. I keep the secret. . . . We're good at it. So if my mother would just quit interfering, I'd only have the little stresses in life to deal with. Little stresses like how to ditch someone who's trying to find out where I live. Or how to get in and out of the apartment without being seen. Or how to avoid being blackmailed by a neighbor with supersonic hearing.

Little stresses like that.

But my mother *has* been interfering, and when she does, it causes me *huge* stress. She just doesn't seem to think things through. Like at my birthday brunch when she met Casey's dad for the first time and *flirted* with him. That right there was enough to make me want to crawl under a rock, but she was so thrilled that he recognized her from TV that if I hadn't jumped in and said, "Nah— that's not her, she just *looks* like her," she would have told him the truth.

See? What was she thinking? If she and I live in Santa Martina like everyone is supposed to believe, how can she be a soap star in Hollywood?

And now Casey's dad went to L.A. for an audition and he *saw* her? Where? Was it *at* the audition? Was the audition for a part on her soap? What man in his right mind would want to be on a *soap*?

Then again, what man in his right mind would marry Candi Acosta? I've had a few run-ins with her, and let me tell you, that woman is even more psycho than their daughter.

Of course, he *did* divorce her. . . .

So maybe he and my mom just bumped into each other on the street? Or at a restaurant?

But what did she say to him? Since I wasn't there to jump in and remind her that telling my vindictive, gossipy, bloodsucking archenemy's father anything that might kick the feet out from under the lie we'd been living for *years* was not a good idea, she might have blown everything!

I didn't know what to do. I didn't know what to say. I didn't know how to act. Which is why I'd spazzed out on the phone and was now just sitting on Cricket's kitchen floor, holding my head, trying not to explode.

"Are you all right?" Cricket whispered, putting a hand on my shoulder. "What happened?"

I shook my head. "I'm just stressed out."

"Because of Heather?"

I nodded. It was a lie, but then, it wasn't really. These days, all roads seem to lead back to Heather.

Gary pounded the rest of his milk, put the glass in the sink, and left without a word. And who could blame him? The drama of it all was just so . . . teen chick. I hate feeling that way. I hate acting that way. Why does everything get so intense and emotional and out of control? Why can't it just be . . . calm?

"What happened?" Cricket asked again. "You look wiped out."

I took a deep breath. "*Billy* happened. Billy told Danny. Danny told Heather."

She let out a soft whistle. "That was quick."

Then from down the hall Gary shouts, "Hey, Cricket! A contact of mine in India wants to know if you guys are eligible for marriage!"

"Shut *up*."

"I'm serious! Come here!"

Cricket looks at me like, What do you think? And since anything's better than sitting there stressing about the impending doom that is my life, I get up and head for the dungeon.

Sure enough, there's a posting from some guy named Pryze that says, *These wilderness women are eligible for marriage, yes? I have mansion in India. Will pay transport.*

Cricket grunted and said, "Will pay transport? What are we, cows?"

I snickered. "Some guy named *Pryze*—like he's a real *prize*? What a joker."

Gary turned to face me. "Oh, he's for real. He's on here all the time."

"But how do you know he's not really a guy named Harry from Santa Martina? He could be living on Broadway at, say, the Heavenly Hotel."

Gary turned back to the monitor. "You get to know these guys after a while. Pryze is for real. And he's loaded. He bought a marsh fritillary from a guy in Wales for almost six thousand pounds—which is like ten thousand dollars!"

"What's a marsh fritillary?" I asked.

Cricket rolled her eyes. "A butterfly. What else?"

"For ten *thousand* dollars? What is it, luminescent? *Gold?*"

"Actually, it's very ordinary-looking," Gary said. "A lot like the common monarch butterfly. But the population of the marsh fritillary fluctuates madly, and right now it's real low." His shoulder twitched in a halfhearted shrug. "Bad investment, if you ask me, but he paid it, and he'll pay a lot more than that for a four-eyed viperwing." He eyed his sister. "Which is why I'm investing my time in this, okay?" He scrolled through the last few postings in the chat room, then grinned at Cricket. "Hey, too bad it's not the old days when the men bargained off the women. I could probably get big bucks for you, you wilderness woman!"

Cricket snorted. "Thanks a lot. And it was the other way around, wasn't it? It was the girl *and* a dowry." She turned to me. "Right?"

But I was thinking about the marsh fritillary and the four-eyed viperwing . . . rare flying creatures that a guy in India was willing to pay small fortunes for.

"Gary? Can you do a search for *condor* and *will pay*?"

Cricket said, "Huh?" but Gary's fingers rattled like a hail shower across the keyboard. "Forty-five thousand hits," he said. "What are you looking for?"

"I'm looking for a reason someone would go out and bait a condor. I mean, if someone's willing to pay ten *thousand* dollars for a little butterfly, there's got to be someone out there willing to pay a *million* for a condor."

"But it's illegal to own a condor!" Cricket said. "You'd get thrown in jail." She shook her head and muttered, "What Grayson Mann said about those developers makes a lot more sense."

"I'd agree with you, only what we saw in the woods does not mesh with that theory. Plus, it seemed really *small*-time."

She shrugged. "Maybe they hired a small-time guy."

"Like a condor hit man?" I asked.

She laughed. "I don't know! What do I know?" She shrugged. "Could be, right?"

I couldn't help laughing, too. "I guess so. But remember what Gary said about the dodo?"

Gary nodded. "A dodo would be worth a bundle."

"So let's say the condor is like the present-day dodo—"

"But it's not!" Cricket cried. "The condor is not extinct; it's coming *back*."

I eyed her. "Well, if you believe the developer angle, then it makes sense that they're out to kill them all."

Gary was back, rattling his fingers across the keyboard. "Man. That is one chilling thought."

Cricket gasped. "All the condors on earth are either in a cage or wearing a transmitter. They could slip them poison in the zoos! They could track down every one in the wild!" She started for the door. "I've got to call Quinn!"

I grabbed her by the arm. "Do *not* call Quinn."

"Why not?"

I decided to go for a half-truth. "Because he's good friends with the professor, and there's something about that guy that I don't trust."

She quit pulling for the door and looked down. "I don't like him, either. And I have no idea why Quinn does."

"But the good news is, I really don't think someone's out to kill all the condors on earth or even in the area. I think maybe someone like this Pryze guy wants one for their collection."

Gary had been checking sites and different combinations of words for the search engine. "There are cleaning companies and golf products and construction equipment and medical companies using the Condor label . . . and there *are* lots of sites about the condor recovery." He scrolled up to the top of the page. "Locally, the most relevant ones seem to be the Vista Ridge Lookout site and the KSMY site." His fingers flew across the keys. "Here's the Vista Ridge site."

Cricket shook her head. "That's mostly just an educational site."

"Click there," I said, leaning over Gary's shoulder and pointing to a *contacts* link.

A window opened that showed a picture of the Lookout. It had a letter that started *Dear Friends of the Condor* and went on to ask people to donate time, equipment, and especially money.

One of the links in the sidebar next to the letter was *Condor Information Contacts.* So I pointed to it and said, "How about here?"

A page opened with pictures of six people—one from the Audubon Society, one from the Ornithology Club, the Webmaster-slash-intern, and then pictures of three people I knew: Quinn, Pointy Nose Prag, and Robin.

"Robin's on the site?" I asked. I skimmed the description, which cited all the work she and her Scouts had done repairing and maintaining the Lookout.

"She deserves to be," Cricket said. "She works up there every chance she gets."

I thought about this a minute. "Does she always take Bella with her?"

"I think sometimes Bella stays at Gabby's."

Gary was getting impatient. "Want to go somewhere else?"

I said, "Hang on," and read the descriptions for Quinn

and the professor. Quinn was a zone biologist for the Forest Service, condor archive manager for the Natural History Museum, and dedicated to "the reconstruction and maintenance of the Vista Ridge Lookout, the ecosystem, and the condor."

Not much new there.

The professor's section listed all his degrees and awards and then tried to make him sound like a nice guy by adding "this celebrated raptorphile has played a pivotal role in the success of the Lookout project by bringing volunteer interns under his wing. A fan of the backwoods, he often roosts in the wild near his feathered friends."

Not much there, either.

Then something about the whole page hit me. "There are e-mail links for all of these people."

"Yeah," Gary said. "So?"

"So if somebody was interested in contacting any of them or if they wanted to set up a meeting with any of them, it'd be easy."

Cricket's eyebrows went up. "You can't really think one of *them* might be behind this."

"All I'm saying is that if someone wanted to contact somebody about condors in this area, these would be the people to e-mail."

"Seen enough?" Gary asked, and before I could answer, he'd clicked over to the KSMY site. "Hey, there's a video stream of the condor story. You want to see?"

"Yes!" I leaned over his shoulder again and watched Grayson Mann come to life. There was the whole pre-story about condors, footage of Quinn and the professor at the Lookout, footage from a helicopter of the canyon where we'd hiked, the bellybutton caves, and then more of Grayson yakking away in front of the Lookout at sunset, trying to look like a rugged mountain man in hiking boots, a long-sleeved Pendleton, and a bandanna scarf. His hair, though, was anything but rugged, and the closing part of the last segment was so Vegas. ". . . So don't let the sun set on this magnificent creature. Anyone interested in volunteering at the Lookout or contributing to the Condor Recovery Fund can simply go to our Web site at KSMY dot-com and click on *Condor Story*. This is Grayson Mann reporting live from Vista Ridge Lookout."

I guess it was more the delivery than the actual words—the deep, rich voice, the stressed syllables, the e-nun-ci-*a*-tion . . . but he's always like that. Even when he's asking you to help save an endangered species, what he's really saying is, Am I wonderful or what?

Anyway, when the video stream was done, Gary found the *Condor Story* link and clicked on it, and it took us right to the Vista Ridge Lookout home page.

"Hmm," I said. "So anyone who saw the story on the news is directed to the Lookout site and would contact Quinn, Prag, or Robin."

Cricket scowled. "I don't like this line of reasoning. I think we should give it a rest, unpack, and take Robin's stuff back to her."

I shrugged. "Sure."

But Gary kept typing. "I'm gonna ask my butterfly contacts if they know any bird collectors." Then he muttered, "Or maybe I can find a black market thread."

I turned around. "A black market thread?"

He snorted. "Not that half the Internet isn't really just a black market anyway, but—"

"Wait a minute," I said, going back to the computer desk. "Can you look up something else for me?"

"Sure!" He gave me a smile, and it struck me as more kidlike than teen. Like he was genuinely happy.

"Can you look up horse rentals in the area? Like what's the nearest one to Chumash Caves. Is there a way you can find that out?"

Before I knew it, Gary had a short list, complete with phone numbers and addresses, and a map to go with it. "This would be the obvious choice," he said, pointing to the location of a place called Trail Riders. "It's the closest, plus most of these others look like they rent stable space or are part of a country club."

"Awesome. Can you print that out?" I asked.

Again, that smile. "You bet!"

When I had the hard copy, I told Gary, "Thanks!" and headed for the kitchen phone.

Now I just had to figure out who I was going to pretend to be.

NINETEEN

I sat down at the Kuos' kitchen table with a pad of paper and a pencil. "What are you doing?" Cricket asked as I scribbled down notes.

"Shhh," I said. "Thinking."

I have to hand it to her—she was quiet. And when I was as ready as I was ever going to be, I took a deep breath and held it for a minute, trying to relax.

It didn't help a bit.

No, the only way I was going to be able to get my heart beating normally again was to just pick up the phone and do it.

So I punched in the number, and when someone on the other end answered, "Trail Riders," I tried to sound full of confidence as I said, "Yes. My name is Ulma Willis and I'm a marshal for the United States Department of Fish and Wildlife. With whom am I speaking?"

"Uh . . . Thomas Becker, ma'am."

"And you work there in the capacity of . . . ?"

"I'm the owner, ma'am. You sound like there's a problem."

I kept my voice low and professional-sounding. "There

is, Mr. Becker. From witnesses we have interviewed, it appears you rented a horse to a condor poacher."

"I . . . I don't know anything about that, ma'am."

"Hmm. Well, the rental date would have been last Wednesday or Thursday. It was a chestnut mare, probably returned on Friday, quite late in the day."

"Oh! I know who you're talkin' about! He took out Cherry Blossom on Thursday."

My pounding heart doubled in speed. The pencil was shaking in my hand. "Who, Mr. Becker?"

"He was a foreigner, ma'am."

"Oh?"

"Well, I assumed he was a foreigner. He didn't seem to speak English."

"So what did he look like? Height, weight, distinguishing features . . ."

"Uh . . . not real big. Just average-sized. No moles or scars or nothin'. Clean shaven. If I remember right, he was wearin' jeans and a brown T-shirt, sunglasses, and a cowboy hat."

"What about identification, Mr. Becker? Surely you don't rent your horses without identification."

"He didn't seem to understand about the ID, ma'am."

"How convenient," I snorted. "So you want me to believe that you rented one of your horses to a man who didn't speak to you and didn't have ID."

Silence.

"Mr. Becker. The perpetrator is a condor poacher. I think the courts could find you at least tangentially culpable for what's happened if you can't come up with a more credible accounting than this."

There was a second of silence and then he blurted, "I let him have the horse because he left me a thousand-dollar cash deposit."

"Ah," I said. Like, Oh, boy—you're in trouble. "You didn't find that unusual?"

"He was a foreigner, ma'am! I thought it must just be the way things were done in his country."

I harrumphed, just like an adult. "Really, Mr. Becker." Then I said, "Surely there's a form you have your customers fill out?"

"Yes, ma'am."

"Well?"

Gary had come into the kitchen and was sitting next to Cricket, listening to every word. And when he heard me ask about the form, he grabbed a pencil and scribbled a phone number and *Have him fax it* on my pad of paper.

I nodded at him and smiled, while Mr. Horsey Becker rustled through some papers, then said, "I have it right here!"

"I need you to fax that to me right away."

"Yes, ma'am."

So I gave him the number, then said, "Did you happen to notice what this man was driving?"

"No, ma'am. I'm sorry. He had a small daypack with him; that was it."

"When did he return the horse?"

"That's the other thing, ma'am. The horse returned itself."

"How's that?"

"She just wandered in on her own. We found her waiting at the barn on Friday night."

"So your foreigner didn't pick up his one-thousand-dollar deposit?"

"No, ma'am," he mumbled.

"I see. And you're afraid I'll require you to turn it over to the Department?" Before he could answer, I said, "We don't want to deprive you of your windfall, Mr. Becker. Perhaps if you just faxed us that paper and were willing to answer further questions . . ."

"I'll fax it right away! And call me anytime."

"Very good."

When I got off the phone, Cricket and Gary just *stared* at me. Then Gary said, "Tangentially culpable? How'd you come up with that?"

I shrugged. "Just heard it somewhere." My face felt flushed, and my heart was still beating fast. I laughed, "What a trip," then told them everything I'd learned.

When I was done, Cricket jumped up and said, "We need to tell Quinn!"

I grabbed her by the arm and yanked her back into her seat. "Quit running to Quinn, okay?"

"Yeah," Gary said. "I'm with Sammy." He eyed his sister. "I can't stand that dude—thinks he's so smooth."

"He does not! He's—"

I put my hands up. "Forget Quinn. We need to *think*."

Cricket seemed to relax a little, so I went on. "Whoever the horse rider is probably parked off the road somewhere so that no one would be able to describe his vehicle, then loaded and unloaded from there. And there must be big money involved in this because you don't abandon a one-thousand-dollar cash deposit unless you're making a lot more, right?"

They both nodded, and Cricket said, "Which supports the developer theory, Sammy."

"True. But it also supports the theory that someone could get a lot of money for a condor."

Gary stood up. "I'll check the fax. Maybe that'll tell us something."

Less than a minute later he was back with a paper in his hand. Cricket and I swooped in to see, and there in big, bold letters was a name we both recognized.

"Vargus Mayfield!" Cricket gasped.

"But why would he fill in his real name? He could've put Joe Smith."

Cricket nodded. "You're right." Then she added, "Or Dennis Prag."

I laughed. "Right."

"Do you think all this other information is bogus?" Gary asked. "Like this address and phone number?"

I looked at the paper, then dialed Information.

Now while I'm asking for the phone number and address for Vargus Mayfield, the doorbell rings, and when I get off the phone and turn around, there's Casey, standing in Cricket's kitchen.

"Hey," he says with a grin. "I tried calling, but the phone's been busy."

Gary snickers, but in an amused way. "She's been

burning up the line. This girl and a phone are a dangerous combination."

"Don't I know," Casey says with a laugh.

I blush and try not to fall back into freak-out mode while Cricket says, "Casey, meet my brother, Gary. Gary, this is Casey—one of the guys who helped us bring Marvin home."

They shake hands and do all that hey-dude-what's-up stuff while Cricket asks me, "What did you find out?"

"Someone did their homework," I tell her. "The information's right."

"So if it's not Vargus, it's got to be someone who knows him."

I nod. "Looks like."

She hesitates. "Are you *sure* it's not Vargus?"

I think about it a minute, then nod. "Unless he's dumber than we think he is."

She smirks. "That would be tough."

Casey pulls up a chair across the table from me and says, "So catch me up—what's going on?"

Cricket jumps in with, "Well, the *good* news is that Marvin is doing much better. They did surgery on him and took out all the snake shot—"

"*Snake* shot?" I ask. "What's *that*?"

"It's used for shooting snakes," Cricket says. Then she adds, "Robin told me that the pellets are smaller than birdshot and that hunters will sometimes keep a handgun loaded with snake shot because snakes are easy to miss with regular bullets."

"So you'd carry both?" I ask. "Like a rifle with bullets *and* a pistol loaded with snake shot?"

She shrugs. "Or maybe it was two different people." Then, like it's no big deal that her little throwaway comment might chuck any half-baked theory of mine right out the window, she goes on, saying, "But anyway, they got all the shot out and repaired the damage, and Robin says he's doing great." Her face clouds over a little. "But even after he's better, they won't release him until they find a mentor bird for him to live with."

"Is that like a foster parent?" Casey asks.

Cricket says, "Yes. Exactly."

I'm still stuck on the gun thing, though, so I ask, "When you shoot off snake shot, does it make a big noise?"

Cricket shrugs, but Gary says, "It's not loud like a rifle. It's more a big pop."

"So you wouldn't hear it up the canyon?"

He shakes his head. "No way."

Everyone's quiet a second, then Casey asks, "So where are we on Marvin's mom? Is it possible she's still alive?"

So we bring him up to speed on the information we've dug up, and when we're all done talking, he says, "Look. If some guy just wanted the condor dead, he'd kill it and leave it. Or bury it, so no one would know what happened to it. But if he wanted it for a trophy, he'd have to preserve it."

Cricket nods. "Like they do with the animals at the Natural History Museum."

"That's called taxidermy," Gary says.

I sit back a little. "That Janey girl works there, right?"

Cricket nods again.

"And it said on the Web site that *Quinn* was their archive manager or something, right?"

"It's not a paying job," Cricket says. "Mostly he set up the condor display."

"But wait—if someone wanted a *stuffed* condor, they could just break in and steal it, right? They wouldn't have to go through all the trouble of going out in the woods and shooting one."

Cricket shakes her head. "That would not be easy, Sammy. That would actually be really hard."

Then Casey adds, "And they might not know there was one at the museum."

"Okay. So if someone didn't know, they'd need to go to a taxidermy . . . ologist? Or could you do that yourself?"

Gary laughs. "It's a taxidermist, and there's no way you could do it yourself. It takes a lot of experience to make it look right."

Cricket lets out a puffy-cheeked breath. "Why are we even going down this road?" She looks at me. "I know you're good at figuring stuff out, but this all seems so far-fetched. The developer theory makes a lot more sense to me."

I eye her. "I'd agree with you, but who at Luxton Enterprises knows Vargus Mayfield?"

She stares at me a second, then holds the sides of her head like she's trying to keep it from exploding. "This is so confusing!"

I chuckle and say, "Exactly, but I think that's because

we don't have enough information. Maybe it would help to find out about taxidermists. Like, who around here does that? I've never seen a taxidermy shop, have you?"

Casey looks through the phone book but finally says, "There's nothing listed."

So Gary tells him, "Look up the Natural History Museum," then he hands me the phone. "They would know."

So Casey tells me the number, I dial, and a lady answers, "Natural History Museum, Janey speaking."

All of a sudden my heart is hammering in my chest. But I take a deep breath and try to disguise my voice by keeping it low and calm. "Yes, I'm wondering who you use as a taxidermist. They do such an amazing job. . . ."

"That's a man named Lester Blunt. He's located in Santa Martina."

"Could I get his number? And his address?"

"Hang on, I've got it right here."

A minute later I'm off the phone with the digits on one Lester Blunt, taxidermist. "He's across town on Blosser Road."

"What are you going to say to *him*?" Cricket asks, and her voice is kinda breathy. Like she can't believe I'm abusing her phone line this way.

"Actually, I don't think this is something we should do over the phone." I look around at the others. "Anyone up for a little snoop around?"

Gary breaks into a smile. "I'm game."

Cricket looks worried. "What if he comes at us with big needles full of formaldehyde? What if he—"

I laugh. "It can't be any more dangerous than hiking through a forest with ticks and scorpions and rattlesnakes and killer trees. It's just one guy." I give her a wicked grin. "With big needles. And formaldehyde. And rusty saws. And a foaming mouth. And—"

"Stop!" Cricket squeals.

Casey smirks as he scoots back from the table. "No wonder my sister doesn't stand a chance around you."

And with that we're all off to the taxidermist.

TWENTY

Gary's truck took a few tries to fire up, and when it did, it made a tough rumbling sound that was *loud*.

"Sorry!" he said over his shoulder to Casey and me. "Exhaust manifold leak. They want three hundred and fifty bucks to fix it!"

Casey and I were crammed in the small back compartment, sitting in little fold-down jump seats that faced each other. It felt like we were on some sort of military mission as we thundered down the road.

After a minute, Casey leaned forward to talk to me, and I did the same so I could hear him over the racket.

"I've been trying to figure out why you hung up on me."

I'd kinda shoved that little incident out of my mind, but now there I was, trapped in the back of a bomber on wheels having to face him. Face *it*.

I looked away and mumbled, "Sorry."

"But there's got to be a *reason* you freaked out. I don't get what the big deal is."

I pulled a face. "Can we just forget about it?"

He leaned a little closer. "It's like you and this condor thing—I just want to figure it out."

My eyes got wide as it hit me that this was Cosmic Payback Phase Two.

Why was this happening?

How many phases were there going to be?

Was being around me really this much torture?

Casey laughed. "Why are you looking at me like that?"

I shook my head a little. "It's like everything I do to other people is coming back around to me!"

He laughed again. "That's called karma."

"I must have terrible karma!"

"No, you don't. I think you're just paranoid about something you don't need to be paranoid about."

"Like . . . ?"

His mouth scrunched to one side, then the other. His eyebrow went up, then down, and finally he said, "Like the fact that the phone number I have for you is not the same as the phone number my dad has for your mom."

"He has her *phone* number?"

Casey nodded. "And even if it's her cell, it's a different area code."

I slumped back against the hard plastic of my little jump seat. "What an airhead she is! What a complete moron!"

"But what's the big deal? So you live with . . . your dad? Your grandparents? Your aunt? So what? Why all the secrecy?"

I closed my eyes, took a deep breath, and for the first time since I moved into the Senior Highrise, I wondered exactly why I *was* so uptight about it. Why wasn't I just, you know, *casually* secretive? Why was I always on high alert? Why didn't I just tell people I lived with Grams? I didn't have to say *where*, just that I lived with her. It's not like it's a *crime* to live with your grandmother. Who cares?

Maybe it's because when this all started, I was in elementary school and Grams was super-worried that I would spill the beans to someone who shouldn't know. But now I was going into the eighth grade—I wasn't a little kid anymore! Even if I got busted, I could just leave the apartment. I was old enough to live with Holly or Marissa or even Hudson for a while. Grams *probably* wouldn't be evicted. Everything would be fine!

All of a sudden I felt suffocated by the huge tangled web of lies. I wanted to bust out. To break free. To tell Casey everything!

So I leaned forward, looked him right in the eye, and said, "I live with my grandmother in that seniors building on Broadway. Kids are not supposed to even be *in* the building, let alone live there. And since the apartments are government-subsidized for low-income seniors and there's a waiting list to get in, my grams will get evicted if people find out. And since she can't exactly afford to live anywhere else, it's a big deal that I don't blow it. I use the fire escape to sneak in and out of the apartment without being seen. I sleep on the couch, and everything I own fits in my grams' bottom dresser drawer. It's not easy, but my grandmother is great and my mom's a ditz, so I'd rather live this way than move to Hollywood." I took a deep breath and said, "There. Now you know."

He let out a low, kind of airy whistle. "Now *that* makes total sense."

"And besides you, only Marissa, Dot, and Holly know."

"I promise—I swear—I won't tell a soul."

I nodded. "Thanks." Then I added, "Your dad's the one I'm worried about."

"I'll make sure it's cool." Then he asked, "So where's your dad in all this?"

I rolled my eyes. "Who knows? For some reason my mom is embarrassed by him. I don't even know who he is."

His eyebrows went up. "She won't tell you?"

I shook my head. "And believe me, I've asked."

He frowned. "I wouldn't put up with that."

"I know. And I am planning to figure it out. Eventually. Right now I'm just taking things one little crisis at a time."

We just sat there for a minute, surrounded by the thunder of Gary's truck. Then Casey leaned forward again and said, "Don't stress. Your secret's safe with me."

I nodded, and deep down inside I believed that it was.

The address on Blosser Road turned out to be an old clapboard house set back about fifty feet from the street. A short, dilapidated picket fence marked off the property from farm fields on the right and a big electrical supply stockyard on the left. It was like the house had been uprooted from a West Side neighborhood and wedged there as a buffer between industry and agriculture.

Gary pulled into the dirt driveway and cut the motor. And for a minute we all sort of looked at the house, wondering what it was *doing* there. Then we piled out and stood around wondering what *we* were doing there.

"So?" Gary asked me. "What's the plan?"

I shrugged and started for the front door. "See what we see?"

"But . . . are we looking for a condor?" Cricket asked. "Are we splitting into teams? Do we have some sort of escape strategy?"

I grinned. "Sorry, troops. We're just wingin' it."

We went up the creaky steps, rang the bell, and then knocked, but no one answered.

I checked inside the little flip-up mailbox that was mounted near the front door.

Empty.

The curtains were open, so we shielded the light from our eyes and looked inside. There was one overstuffed chair in front of a television and one chair by a table in the kitchen, but the whole rest of the house was taken up by workbenches that were loaded with junk. Newspapers, cardboard boxes, big spools of string, scissors and hammers and knives, metal tubs in a bunch of different sizes, cans of turpentine, jugs of rubbing alcohol and ammonia . . .

There were also hooks and bars with deflated animal heads hanging upside down from the ceiling. A deer. A lynx. A coyote. A ram. The eyes were missing in all of them. They were like the creepiest Halloween masks ever.

"May I help you?"

We all jumped about ten feet in the air, then turned and saw a man with slicked-back hair. He was wearing a dirty white apron and had his left hand inside a mallard duck. It looked like he was ready to put on a puppet show, but the duck's head was all dangly, and it didn't have eyes.

The man himself was pretty normal-looking, except for *his* eyes. One went to the left, one went to the right. It seemed like he was looking behind the house and out to the street at the same time. He cleared his throat. "I *said,* may I help you?"

Cricket, Casey, and Gary all turned to me.

"Uh, yeah. Hi. Are you Lester Blunt?"

"That I am."

"The Natural History Museum told us—"

"Oh, you're here to pick up the bird?" We all sorta looked at each other and nodded, which I guess was good enough for him. He beat his dead ducky puppet with his free hand, sending up a dusty white cloud. "Well, come on back."

We followed him around to the back of the house. "So I guess you've been doing this a long time, huh?" I asked, catching up to him.

He looked at me.

I think.

"My whole life," he said. "Passed down from my dad. And his dad before him." He beat the duck some more, making a white dust cloud around his hand. "Takes years to master the art, which is why I'm the only taximan left in the area. Could take shortcuts, but I believe in a quality job. I don't even buy them prefab bodies. I can always spot a prefab body. They're unnatural lookin'. I make mine from scratch."

"Prefab bodies? What happens to their real bodies?"

"We don't embalm them, if that's what you thought. We just save the skins, then build a body to stretch them over."

"Really? I didn't know that. . . ."

"Mm-hmm."

"So there's no bones or eyeballs or guts?"

He laughed. "Nah. Just skins."

"And feathers?"

"Oh, yeah. Nothing fake about the feathers."

We were at the back steps now. There was a giant freezer purring away off to the side. It had a heavy chain padlocked around it.

"So, uh, what happens to the bodies?"

"Well, for the trophy heads, the hunters usually keep the meat." He opened the back screen door. "For the rest?" He grinned. "It's one of the perks of the job."

"So that duck you've got there . . . ?"

He shrugged. "If it's good meat, why waste it?"

We followed him inside, zigzagging through small rooms with decaying cardboard boxes and dusty animal heads everywhere. It smelled like mothballs and ammonia and turpentine and . . . dust. I looked around for oversized black feathers but didn't see a thing.

"What's the biggest bird you've ever done?" I asked, trying to keep the conversation going.

"Oh, that con—" He stopped, then peered at me with his right eye before turning it on Gary. "You're not the one that called about doing a condor, are you? Because if you are, I told you—you have to have legal papers. I don't do black market."

"Someone called about doing a condor?" I asked. This was not good. "When?"

"Yesterday." His eye focused back on me. "So it wasn't you people?"

"No!" Gary said. "We're just here to, uh, to deliver that bird to the museum."

He gave a little snort and shook his head. "Of course. I'm sorry." Then he muttered to himself, "You're losing touch, Lester. What would kids want with a condor?"

He put down the duck puppet and handed Gary a tiny sandpiper that was mounted on a driftwood base. "Here she is. Beaut, isn't she?"

Gary turned it from side to side, showing it to the rest of us.

"It looks so real," Cricket said.

"Thanks, miss."

Now, for a guy who skinned and stuffed animals, who lived in a no-man's-land between farm fields and spools of electrical wire and had eyes that shot off like billiard balls on a split, I thought Lester Blunt was pretty nice. Pretty *normal.*

But the minute we're piled back into Gary's truck, Cricket turns to face me from the front seat and says, "*That's* why you would wear sunglasses and a cowboy hat!"

I look at her. "Huh?"

"To cover those eyes!" She shivers. "Ooooh. He is so freaky!"

"He seemed pretty normal to me. . . ."

They all three turn to stare at me. *"Normal?"*

I shrug. "Well, you know—in a freaky sort of taxidermy way . . ."

They all snigger and then Casey says, "I think a condor could fit in that freezer, easy."

"And did you see how it was locked?" Cricket whispers. "It's chained up like a vault!"

I shake my head. "But somebody *did* call about a condor yesterday. He wouldn't admit that if he actually had one."

Gary says, "Maybe he was just trying to throw us off?" He fires up the truck and grinds it into reverse. "So where to?" He eyes the sandpiper and says, "I take it I'm on the hook to deliver that wannabe condor to the museum?"

I pull a face. "Do you mind?"

"No problem," he says, backing into the street. And the funny thing is, from the grin on his face I can tell that he's having fun.

More fun than he's had in a long, long time.

TWENTY-ONE

The Natural History Museum charges five bucks for parking, if you can believe that. And they charge seven more to get inside. And I don't care how much they try to describe it as something interesting—a "still-life zoo," "nature's landscape," a "tour of habitats"—the fact is, it's still seven bucks to see a bunch of stuffed dead stuff.

Anyway, all of us voted to walk instead of pay for parking, so we circled around the block.

No parking.

We went a street farther out, keeping our eyes peeled for a place to pull in.

No parking.

So I asked, "Did you guys *want* to go inside? Because I can just run the bird in myself."

Gary looked at me in the rearview mirror. "Aren't we still snooping around?"

I laughed. "Yeah. But I don't really know what we're expecting to find."

"Well, I want to go," he said.

I looked out the window again. "Okay, then we've got to find parking."

All of a sudden Cricket cries, "Look!" but it's not a

parking place that she's pointing to. It's a woman with amazingly long honey blond hair, pulling a blue and orange mountain bike out of the back of a steel blue SUV.

It's Janey, all right, and as we get closer, we watch her shut the back and push her mountain bike up alongside the driver's door. Then, just as we're passing by, she leans in the SUV's open window and plants a kiss on the cheek of some guy wearing a ball cap.

Cricket gasps. "Did she just *kiss* that guy?"

I nod. "It sure looked like it."

"Go around the block!" Cricket tells her brother. "We've got to find out who that is!"

"Why?" Gary asks.

"Janey's two-timing Quinn!"

"Who cares?"

"I do! He will! Go around the block, Gary!"

Gary's still not keen on the idea, but he do-si-dos through traffic and around the block anyway. Trouble is, we hit all red lights and everyone seems to be moving so *slow* that by the time we get back to where the SUV was, it's long gone.

The parking place, though, is still available. So Gary dives in and we all get out to deliver the itty-bitty mounted bird together.

Now, it takes us a little while to get over to the museum. And then, as we're finally shuffling up the entrance steps, the front door comes whooshing open and Janey comes blasting out. And before the door's had a chance to finish closing, *whoosh,* it flies open again, and this time *Quinn* comes running out. "Janey! Janey, wait!" he shouts, but he's too late. Faster than you can say, I'm outta here, Janey is on her bike and *gone.*

Quinn throws his hands in the air and curses, then turns to us and says, "She dumped me! *She* dumped *me.*"

"She was two-timing you," Cricket blurts, like it's the hottest gossip she's ever heard.

"What?" he asks, and suddenly his dark eyes look cold. Dangerous.

Cricket takes a step back. "We . . . we saw her get her bike out of the back of someone's car." She points. "About four blocks that way. Then she went up and kissed the driver." She hesitates and glances around at us. "At least we think it was a kiss."

He just stands there a minute, then starts back up the museum steps muttering, "Girls and their mind games! Why chase a guy if you're just going to dump him?"

Cricket follows him up the steps. "Are you going to tell her you know she was two-timing you when you see her?"

He looks at her like she's crazy. "Why would I see her?"

"Well, she works here. . . ."

"Not anymore. She quit!" He gives her an exasperated look. "Now can I please have some space?"

So Cricket backs off, but I intercept him at the door and push the sandpiper on him. "We're delivering this for Lester Blunt."

He looks at me, then the bird, then me again. "For whom?"

I watch him very carefully. "Lester Blunt."

His forehead's a mess of wrinkles, and they all seem to be shoving in different directions. "Who?"

"You know, the taxidermist in Santa Martina."

His face smoothes a little. "Oh, right." But then his eyebrows scrunch together as he asks, "Dennis asked you to do this? I thought you two hated each other."

"Uh . . . we haven't talked to him." Then I try to sound all nonchalant as I ask, "Is he the one who picks up and drops off projects?"

"Usually."

"But . . . he doesn't work for the museum, does he?"

Quinn pulls the door open and says, "Look, if you don't mind, I *really* need some space," then disappears inside with the bird.

As we start down the steps, Cricket sighs, "Poor guy. He's really hurting."

Gary snorts. "At least he knows why he got dumped." He eyes his sister. "You delivered that news so tactfully—very impressive."

Casey and I kind of grin at each other, and when Cricket realizes her brother is being sarcastic, she blushes and says, "I guess I really didn't like her."

"I guess not!" we all say.

On the way back to the Kuos' we stopped and got dollar burgers because we were all starving, and after that we were wiped-out tired. And since Casey had to get going and Cricket said, "Can we unpack tomorrow?" I just hiked home.

I like walking. Well, not when I have big balloon blisters or if it's icy-windy or pouring down rain, but other than that, I really like walking. My friends all listen to music when they're walking or cruising along on their skateboards or bikes, but I like to listen to the rhythm of moving. It kind of lulls my mind into a place where I can sort things out. Where I can *think*.

And since my feet were feeling a whole lot better, I really *wanted* to walk. There had been so many new people and new places and changes in the last few days that I hadn't really had the chance to get *used* to them. The walk home gave me time to turn all the new bits and pieces and *people* over in my mind. It was kinda like reviewing for a spelling test—it didn't teach me anything *new*, it just got me more comfortable with what was there.

But still. Like a list of spelling words, I couldn't seem to string the bits and pieces and people together in a way that made sense. I was missing verbs. Or maybe my list was *all* verbs. Whatever. The *point* is, I may not have had any revelations, but by the time I got home, I felt better. At least I'd reviewed. At least I wouldn't bomb the test.

Not that there *was* a test, but you know what I'm saying.

Then I walked through the door and discovered that I'd bombed a completely different kind of test.

The trust test.

Grams glared at me from the kitchen, where she was talking on the phone, and I heard her say, "She's home now. . . . No, I'll tell her. . . . No, Lana, I'll do it. Goodbye."

She hung up, and I could tell that whatever she and my mother had been discussing was something that I was going to hate.

221

My knees went wobbly, so I sat down at the kitchen table. "What's wrong?"

She crossed her arms, and I could see her counting to ten.

"Grams? What's wrong?"

Then, in measured, angry words, she said, "You're moving to Hollywood."

I'd been kind of expecting this since my mother had landed the role of an aristocratic amnesiac on *The Lords of Willow Heights*, but I hadn't expected it in this *way*. And I'd expected that instead of agreeing with her, Grams would tell my mom that me moving to Hollywood was a bad idea. She'd tell her that we were getting along fine, that I had good friends and was making decent grades at school. Why mess up all of that and move me to a place I would hate?

I *would* hate it, too. I mean, come on. The only thing worse than going to school with Heather Acosta would be going to school with Barbie and Ken.

But here Grams was, telling me that I was moving. Not discussing, *telling*. And she was angry. Not at my mother, at *me*.

And then it hit me—Casey's dad had told my mom about the overnighter in the tent. And because my mother had then broadsided Grams with this little tidbit of scandal, I was now plastered with poop.

Normally I would have started ranting about how unfair it was that she was telling me I had to move and how she and my mom were, once again, jumping to conclusions. But for some reason I felt more calm than panicked. This really was an overblown misunderstanding.

I had not done anything wrong.

Well, except for that little bit about not telling the whole truth, but I pushed that whisper of doubt out of my mind, looked Grams in the eye, and said, "No, I'm not."

I said it calmly. Certainly. Like there was just no disputing this fact.

She, on the other hand, screamed, "Yes, you are! This is not open to discussion!"

Boy, was she flustered. She didn't know what to do with herself—she was twitching at the face and moving all around this one little area in the kitchen without actually *going* anywhere. Which, for some funny reason, made me feel even calmer.

"No, I'm not."

Grams twitched and sputtered some more, then did something I'd never seen her do before—she threw herself in a chair, buried her head in her arms on the table, and started bawling.

I rushed over. "Grams, it's all right. Everything is going to be—"

Her head snapped up. "I will not go through this again! I will not!"

Right away I knew what she was talking about. And even though I'd never actually thought about what it must have been like for *her* when my mom broke it to her that she was expecting *me,* in a little flash of understanding, I got it.

"Grams. Grams, calm down. You're not going to have to go through that again. I promise." I gave a little laugh. "Grams, I'm thirteen years old!"

Her cheeks were glistening with tears. "But kids grow up so fast these days! I've read statistics and I know that—"

"Grams! Grams, get a grip! I've never even kissed a boy!"

She took off her glasses and wiped away the tears. "But Lana told me—"

"What does she know? Stuff she's heard thirdhand from people who weren't even there!" I held both her hands and said, "I didn't tell you because I *didn't* want you to worry. It was an emergency, okay? There were five of us—three girls and two boys—in one tent. Did you want us to shiver out in the cold all night? Get attacked by coyotes or snakes or centipedes?"

She looked horrified. *"Centipedes?"*

"Or ticks or scorpions?"

She shook her head, her eyes wide.

"Well, neither did we."

"There were *scorpions* out there?"

I snickered. "Oh, yeah."

She looked at me a minute. Just looked. Like she wasn't really sure it was me or not. Finally she said, "You're growing up so fast, Samantha." Her chin quivered. "Can't you stop? Can't you just stay my precocious little granddaughter forever?"

I laughed and sat back in my chair. "No, but I could

stay *here* forever. Or at least a lot longer." I leaned toward her again. "I don't want to go to Hollywood, Grams. I like living with you."

She nodded, then held my cheeks and said, "Thank you."

After she let go, I said, "The person you've really got to be worried about is your daughter."

"Lana? Why?"

"She doesn't *think*, Grams. She gave Warren Acosta her phone number, and obviously he's using it!"

"*That's* how she found out about your camping trip?"

"Bingo."

Grams' jaw dropped. "She told me she'd heard a rumor!"

I snorted. "Way off in Hollywood? *Right.*"

Her eyes got wider and wider as she put the pieces together. "Is she *dating* him?"

"I have no idea."

"But if she winds up marrying Warren Acosta, Heather would become your stepsister!" She stood up. "Oh, this can't be! This cannot happen!" She headed for the phone. "I've got to put a stop to this. I've got to put a stop to this right now!"

I chased after her, grabbed the phone away, and hung it back up. "You can't, Grams. The more you try, the more she'll go after him."

"But why him? Why him of all people?"

"Because she's Lady Lana, Grams."

I said it like it was the reason and the whole reason, but in my gut I had the awful feeling that it might be something even harder to control than my mother.

Something a person really can't change, no matter what they do.

Fate.

TWENTY-TWO

I woke up in the morning with an itch on my arm. A maddening incessant itch on my arm. The more I scratched it, the worse it seemed to get, and when I finally looked at my arm, there was a rash that went from the outside of my elbow clear down to my wrist. "What in the world . . . ?"

Then it hit me.

"Poison oak?" I said, sitting up. "Is this poison oak?"

Grams was making herself a cup of tea in the kitchen. "Let's see." She came into the living room and inspected my bumpy red arm from a safe distance. "Is that the only place you've got it?"

Suddenly my other arm was itching, too. I tried not to scratch, but I just couldn't help it. And sure enough, there were little bumps springing up all over it.

Grams checked my back and my chest, felt my forehead, and said, "I would say yes. That's poison oak."

"How do I make it stop itching?" I asked, and I sounded kinda panicky 'cause it seemed to be getting worse by the minute.

"I don't think we have any calamine lotion." She headed off to the bathroom. "But let me check."

I told myself, "Don't scratch. Don't scratch. Don't

scratch," which worked for all of thirty seconds before I broke down and ripped my fingernails across one arm, then the other.

"You'll spread it that way," Grams said as she returned empty-handed.

"It spreads?"

She nodded. "Watch out for the pus. I've heard that's how it spreads."

"It puses?"

She gave her couch a worried look. "We should probably wash your bedding."

"This itch is driving me crazy!" I wailed.

"Well, the pharmacy's not open this early, and we don't seem to have any anti-itch salves at all. Try icing it."

So I got an ice cube and rubbed it all up and down my arms. It did help some, but not enough for me to think about anything but the itch.

"Your friend Cricket probably has some calamine lotion."

I looked at the wall clock.

7:08 in the morning.

She'd forgive me.

I dialed the number, and the phone got answered on the first ring. "Hello?"

"Uh . . . Gary?" I asked.

"Sammy?" he asked back, then made a sleepy chuckle. "Of course it's you. Who else uses the phone as a weapon?"

I cringed. "Sorry to be calling so early, but do you guys have any calamine lotion?"

"You got poison oak?"

"Yeah, and it's killin' me!"

He chuckled again. "I'm sure we do. Come on over."

I'd barely hung up when the phone rang. And normally I don't answer the phone, because what would I be doing there at seven in the morning answering the phone like I *lived* there? Only I figured it had to be Gary hitting *69 to tell me, Oops, don't bother, we're all out. So I didn't wait for Grams to answer the phone. I just snatched it up and said, "You're out?"

There was a moment of silence and then, "Sammy?"

I lowered my voice. "Casey?"

"Sorry. You're awake, right?"

"Yeah."

"My dad says your mom's making you move to Hollywood. . . . Is that true?"

"Uh . . . it *was*, but now it's not."

"It's not?" He let out a breath, then whispered, "Man, I hate it when parents jerk your chain. I got like zero sleep last night."

My heart did a ridiculous little *aww*. He'd lost sleep over me moving?

I glanced behind me at Grams, which I shouldn't have because it totally gave away that I was having a private conversation. "I'm on my way to the Kuos'," I whispered into the phone. "You want to meet me there?"

"Sure."

So I got off the phone and headed for the bathroom to get dressed, only Grams' voice intercepted me. "Who was that?"

I could have lied and said Cricket, but instead I told the truth. "Casey."

Her eyebrows went up, but they didn't fly up like they would have a year ago.

Or even a day ago.

She blew on her tea and said, "Does he know our situation? Or just our phone number."

I snorted and said, "Our situation. And you can thank Lady Lana for that." Which *was* true. Yeah, I'd given him our phone number, but I'd told him about "our situation" because of my mother.

"Hmm," she said, which was very un-Grams-like. Normally she's a flustery bundle of nerves about "our situation." She blew on her tea again, then said, "That Lady Lana is in some really hot water."

I sputtered, "What?" because Grams is always harping on me to not call her Lady Lana. She thinks it's disrespectful and sarcastic, which, of course, it is. That's the whole point.

Anyway, I got dressed and headed for the Kuos'. And believe me, I didn't walk. I broke a land speed record riding my skateboard.

"Hey," Cricket said, letting me in, and when I showed her my arms, she nodded and said, "Ooooh. That's bad."

"You didn't get it?"

"Not yet."

I followed her down to the bathroom. "Well, where'd I go that you didn't?"

She pulled a small pink bottle of calamine lotion out of a cupboard over the toilet. "Lots of places."

"Nuh-uh! All I did was follow you!"

"Oh, really? How about that campground where you found the boar? That place was covered with poison oak."

I smeared the lotion all over one arm, then the other. It was kinda chalky, but the coolness felt great.

"Better?" she asked.

I nodded, then said, "Bearable is more like it."

She closed the cupboard. "Yeah, time's really the only cure. Today and tomorrow and the next day will be bad; after that it starts to go away. Takes about a week." She smiled and headed up the hallway. "You hungry?"

"Actually, yes!"

"Cereal? Bacon and eggs? Pancakes?"

Out of Gary's dungeon came, "Pancakes!"

She leaned into his room. "You cooking or on KP?"

"I burn stuff; you know that. I'll clean up."

"Deal."

Mr. Kuo was in the kitchen, having a cup of coffee and a muffin as he skimmed the paper and watched the morning news. He said a quick hello to us, then checked his watch and said, "Have fun today, girls," and took off.

So I called Grams and told her I wouldn't be back anytime soon, then got busy helping Cricket whip up pancake batter, grill bacon, and juice oranges. And things were really starting to sizzle when the doorbell rang.

"Oh!" I said, hoping Cricket wouldn't be mad. "It's a really long story, but I told Casey to meet me here."

"Cool!" she said, like she really was happy to have people over, even if they invited themselves.

So I answered the door and said, "Hungry?" which, of

course, being a guy, he was. And then Gary came into the kitchen, and said, "Hey, dude, you're back," like *he* was really happy to see Casey, too. And, I don't know—it was just fun to be cooking and juicing and talking and, you know, hanging out.

Now, the whole time we were cooking, the TV was on the same station that Mr. Kuo had been watching. None of us were paying any attention to it—it was just sort of white noise in the background. But when we sat down to eat, I did a double take at the screen and said, "Hey, it's Pretty Vegas!"

Gary and Cricket said, "Huh?" but Casey eyed the TV, then grinned at me. And something about that grin made me feel stupidly happy. I guess most people would call it an inside joke, but to me it felt like more than that. It felt like the beginning of our own language. You know how you have things you say to your best friend and they know exactly what it means, but there's so much history behind it that trying to explain it to anyone else just sounds jumbled and disjuncted and *lame*. Or it's something so embarrassing that you'd never, ever in a million years tell anyone what it means. For example, "loopy noogies." If Marissa and I were having lunch together and I said, "Mmm, loopy noogies," she would spray whatever she was drinking all over the place and not stop laughing for half an hour.

It goes back to fourth grade and the school cafeteria, and that's all I'm gonna say.

The *point* is, Marissa and I have our own language.

Words that mean an *experience* more than they mean what the dictionary says they mean.

I like having that with Marissa. And I guess I'd never really thought about how we have our own language because we've been best friends for so long and have done so many things together. But now all of that flashed through my head, and it made me glad that I'd trudged through the dusty heat of the Phony Forest and survived ticks and scorpions and attacking trees—even if it meant I'd come down with poison oak. Casey and I could say things like "Sleep Zombie" or "Pretty Vegas" or "snake floss," and instant pictures would pop into our heads. Even "cool your heels" had a whole new meaning since our stinky experience with a certain big bird.

And as much as I'd like to forget about it, the word *drool* will live on in code word infamy.

Anyway, that's how the back of my mind was entertaining itself while we were eating breakfast. It wasn't trying to piece together any puzzles. It wasn't thinking about Marvin or his mom. It was perfectly content to be reviewing the strange words of a new language.

And then Cricket said, "Stop that, Sammy."

I blinked at her. "Huh?"

She pointed to my arm, which I didn't even know I'd been scratching. "It just makes it worse."

I stopped, but the itch didn't want me to. "That calamine lotion doesn't last very long."

"Go put some more on," Cricket said. "You know where it is, right?"

So I went down to the bathroom, got the lotion out of the cabinet, and started recoating my arms. The combination of the rash and the chalky lotion looked awful. Like I had some horrible, ghoulish disease. And it crossed my mind to ask Cricket if I could borrow a long-sleeved shirt. But sleeves against a rash like this? It would drive you crazy!

And that's when I stopped smearing lotion and just stood there.

I was like a zombie, standing there frozen, staring at nothing.

My mind, though, was in overdrive, scratching, clawing, *tearing* through the rash of bumps in my mind. The bumps of information that had been under the surface but were now blossoming and itching and demanding to be scratched.

No calamine lotion could soothe this itch.

No shot from the doctor, no ice.

Only one thing was going to make these bumps go away.

Proof.

TWENTY-THREE

Even after I explained my theory, the others were not convinced. "I don't know, Sammy," Cricket said, breaking off a piece of bacon and popping it into her mouth. "It seems pretty far-fetched."

Gary agreed. "Not a real strong connection, if you ask me."

"Yeah, but it might be the tip of the iceberg. The leak in the well. The gopher hole that leads to a maze of tunnels that leads to the truth!"

Casey laughed and the others rolled their eyes, so I said, "Look. I just want to go there and ask a few questions. If it doesn't get us anywhere, it's no big deal."

Gary gave a friendly little snort and said, "I'm on the hook to drive again?"

I shrugged. "I could ride my skateboard. . . . It's not *that* far."

"I rode mine over," Casey said, giving me a smile, and all of a sudden that sounded like such a blast—just me and him riding boards across town.

But Gary stood up and said, "No, I know a hook when I'm on it—let's go."

So we all got into his truck again and got our eardrums

pounded as we cruised through town again. And we'd almost made it to our destination again, only we got stopped.

By a cop.

Gary pulled over, cut the motor, and banged his head against the steering wheel. And when the policeman came up alongside the truck and peeked inside at the four of us, Gary asked, "Was I speeding?" like he really hoped that he was.

"No, son," the cop said. "You're not driving too fast; you're driving too *loud*."

Gary heaved a sigh. "I know. They want three hundred and fifty bucks to fix it."

The cop nodded. "License and registration, please."

So Gary took his driver's license out of his wallet, flipped down the sun visor and removed a square piece of paper, then handed them both to the cop.

Now, I'd never seen this cop before, so I didn't really know how to help, but I wanted to do *something*, since this whole excursion had been my stupid idea. I mean, I've heard that tickets can be really expensive, and from the way Gary was taking deep breaths and looking so worried, I was sure he was having a panic attack about the cost of the ticket on top of having to pay to fix his truck. So I leaned forward between the front seats and said to the cop, "Hey, do you know Gil Borsch? I haven't seen him much since he got promoted to sergeant. How's he doing?"

The cop sort of cocked his head at me, hesitated, then said, "He's fine."

"So . . . what's he up to?"

He eyed me again. "Actually, he's on vacation."

"Oh." I didn't know what to say after that. The guy was so . . . professional. Maybe he was on loan from a real police department, I don't know. I just know he wasn't anything like the cops I usually run into in this town.

Anyway, I don't think it had anything to do with me, but he only gave Gary a "fix-it ticket." He handed it over, saying, "You've got thirty days to take care of this, Mr. Kuo. After that, you will be cited if you're caught driving this around."

"Uh, thank you, sir."

When he was gone, I said, "I'm really sorry, Gary. I should just have taken my skateboard."

"Not your fault," he grumbled.

I knew he meant it, but I still felt bad about it as he drove us the last four blocks. But then my mind started getting occupied with other things.

I'd never been to a television station before, and I guess I was expecting something much more Hollywood than what I saw. The complex was only one story high. It was made of painted cinder blocks and laid out like giant pieces of pie, with wedges of parking between the buildings.

As we went up the driveway and passed by a fleet of white KSMY vehicles near a bunch of huge satellite dishes, Gary called, "Where do you want me to park?" over the roar of his exhaust leak.

"Anywhere," I called back.

So Gary pulled into a space, and just as he cut the motor, Cricket pointed and said, "Look!"

It was a bike, leaning against the building near a side door.

A royal blue bike with orange trim.

"What is *she* doing here?" Cricket gasped.

"Who?" Gary asked.

"Janey!" She turned to him. "The girl from the museum? The one who dumped Quinn!"

"Maybe it's not her bike?" Casey said.

Cricket got out of the truck. "It sure looks like it!"

I caught up to her as she marched toward the bike, my mind scrambling for a reason Janey would be there. "Remember how Robin said that Quinn being late was, you know, out of the ordinary?"

"Huh? No, I don't remember that." She glanced at me. "But it is."

"Quinn was supposed to be at the Lookout when we got there the first day and he wasn't, remember?"

"Right," she said, but it was a real absentminded *right* because we were nearly at the bike.

"And he was supposed to be at the Lookout again the next morning. When Robin and Bella went after Gabby, remember?" All of a sudden Janey being at the TV station made total sense. I pulled Cricket away from the bike and whispered, "*She* was the reason Quinn was late! She was a decoy!"

"A what?"

Only just then the door latch clicks and the door starts to push open. Casey and Gary are coming toward us, so real quick I flag them back, then grab Cricket by the arm and dive for the bushes.

Two seconds later Janey emerges from the building, only she doesn't just hop on her bike and leave. She glances over her shoulder, then stands there talking to someone who's propping open the door from inside. We can't see who it is because the door is blocking our view, but we *can* hear Janey's side of the conversation.

"Look, if he's arriving at three, we should *leave* at three. . . . I know, but I don't want to get there early. . . . Okay. Quarter of. I'll pick up the meat." She reaches back inside like she's giving a quick hug, then swings onto her bike and pedals off.

"Who *is* that she was talking to?" Cricket whispers.

"Her partner in crime," I mutter, easing out from behind the bushes. "Something's going down at three o'clock, and I'm pretty sure it has to do with Marvin's mom!"

Now it's Cricket's turn to grab *me* by the arm. "What? Where do you get *that*?"

"The meat? It's either to feed a condor or it *is* a condor."

Her jaw drops. "Have you totally lost it? They were talking about a date!" She follows me toward Gary and Casey, who are coming out from around the building. "You know, like going over to somebody's house to barbecue? She's picking up the meat—like, the steaks or whatever."

I snicker and shake my head. "Oh, no. That is *not* what that was. That was—" And then I notice a familiar steel blue SUV parked beside a bright yellow sports car. "Look!"

So we all go over to the SUV. And I was planning just to, you know, peek in the windows, but the dark tinting made it almost impossible to see anything in back, and the front seats had nothing on them but the morning paper. No cowboy hat. No sunglasses. No condor feathers . . . just the stupid newspaper.

But then I saw something—a bottle on its side on the shelf under the CD player in the dash. I moved around so I could see it better, and bingo!

Calamine lotion.

"I want to know who this belongs to!" Cricket whispered.

"I know who it belongs to," I told her, still looking inside the driver's window.

"You do? Who?"

"Grayson Mann."

Her eyes popped. And after she sputtered a minute, she said, "You think Janey's two-timing with *him*? Over *Quinn*? He's way older than she is! And he's so . . . so . . ."

"Vegas?" Casey asked.

"Exactly!"

"You want proof?" I asked, because I'd just noticed that proof was wedged under a black rectangular gizmo that was clipped to the turned-down sun visor.

"Yes, I want proof!" Cricket said. "I can't believe you believe that! There's no way!"

So I snaked my hand through the window, which was vented a few inches.

"What are you *doing*?" Cricket asked, and believe me, I'd never seen her eyes so wide.

"Getting you proof."

"What if the car's alarmed?"

"Apparently it's not," Gary said, but he was looking around nervously.

I wound up pulling both the black rectangular box and the registration paper out through the crack in the window. "Ready?" I asked. And I was so confident that I was right that I didn't even bother to look at the registration before handing it over.

Cricket took the paper, but a few seconds later she cried, "Ha! You're *wrong*."

I snatched it back and just blinked at it for a minute, not believing my eyes. "Oswald Griffin? Who's *that*?"

Just then a car drove into the parking lot, so we all ducked out of view and waited for it to go by. And I was so busy not believing how *stupid* I'd been that I didn't make the connection right away, but it did finally hit me. "Cricket . . . didn't Bella say that Janey's last name was Griffin?"

Her eyes got all big again. She snatched the registration back from me, checked it over, and said, "All this time she's been *married*? She was having an affair with *Quinn*? That's why she broke it off like that? Wait until Quinn hears about this!"

The car we'd been hiding from had left the parking lot, so I stood up and said, "Come on."

"Where to?" Cricket asked. She shoved the registration paper back at me. "You need to put this and that garage door opener back!"

I stopped short.

Garage door opener?

I looked at the little black box and its long, flat activation switch, and my mind went giddy. The registration paper showed the address, and I was holding a remote control to the garage door!

"Why the look?" Cricket asked.

I was dying to tell her, but there's no way she'd want to hear what I was thinking, let alone *do* it. It would go against all the Girl Scout laws or credos or whatever they're called. You know—a Girl Scout is considerate and honest and does good deeds. What a Girl Scout most definitely does *not* do is open other people's garage doors with an opener that's been snaked from a locked vehicle.

"So what's the plan?" Casey asked.

"Uh . . . I think it's time to use my favorite weapon," I said. He produced a cell phone from the pocket of his jeans, but I shook my head. "I don't want it to be traceable."

Cricket snorted. "Oh, like that call you made to Trail Riders when you were impersonating a federal agent?"

I blushed. "Sorry about that . . ."

I spotted a pay phone at a gas station across the street, so we went over there, and luckily the phone book in it was actually pretty much intact.

I looked up the number for KSMY and got connected, and when the receptionist answered, I said, "I'd like to speak with Oswald Griffin."

A few seconds later she said, "I'm sorry, but there are no Griffins or Oswalds in my directory."

I thanked her, hung up, and immediately dialed again.

And when she asked how she could help me, I said, "Grayson Mann, please."

While the transfer went through, I tried to stay cool, but man, my heart was bouncing off the walls. And pretty soon my hands were shaking and my forehead was sweating. It got so bad that I was actually about to just bail on the whole call, when over the line came, "Grayson Mann speaking."

It sounded like someone announcing the king.

"I have information about that condor poacher," I whispered.

There was a slight pause, then, "Speak up, please. I can barely hear you. Did you say you have information about the condor poacher?"

"Yes," I hissed. "I can't speak any louder. This is highly confidential, but I think you should know."

"Go on . . ."

"There's a sting operation planned. It's going down in about an hour."

"A *sting* operation?" I could practically see him sitting up straighter. "They know who's got the bird?"

"They're pretty sure, yes."

"Who? Where?"

"All I know is there's a man named Lester—"

"Blunt? The taxidermist?"

I hesitated, then whispered, "Someone's coming! I'll have to call you back," and hung up quick.

When I turned around, Cricket was holding her head like she thought it might explode, and Gary and Casey were both looking at me like they'd just come off some radical roller coaster.

"What are you *doing*?" Cricket gasped. "What's that going to accomplish?"

I held up a finger and said, "Give it a minute," but it didn't even take a whole minute for the pay phone to start ringing. "Star sixty-nine," I said with a grin, then snatched up the phone. "Natural History Museum."

Click.

I hung up again and said, "Okay, guys. Back to the parking lot."

Cricket said, "Natural History Museum? Why the Natural History Museum?" and Gary said, "I feel like I'm trapped in a pong game." But Casey walked beside me and said, "You're flushing him out, aren't you?"

I grinned. "I'm *twinkling* him out." And for the first time in a week I felt like I was back in the saddle. I knew what I was doing, even if I hadn't really had the time to totally line it out for everybody else.

I looked at Cricket as we hurried across the street. "He asked me, 'They know who's got the bird?'"

"So?"

"So how does he know someone's *got* a condor? All he knows is someone *shot* a condor."

"But . . . how do *you* know what he knows? Maybe Quinn's talked to him! Maybe Robin has!"

I gave her a wry smile. "Or Janey?"

Then Gary said, "Are you sure he didn't say, 'Who *shot* the bird?' 'Who shot' and 'who's got' sound a lot alike."

"Yeah," Cricket said. "And how do Janey and Oswald connect with Grayson Mann?"

"You'll see." We were across the street now, and as we moved through the parking lot, I kept a sharp eye on the door that Janey had come through earlier. "Right here's good," I said when we were close enough but not *too* close. Then we all crouched behind a silver minivan.

Less than a minute later the door where we'd seen Janey opened.

A man stepped out.

He didn't look left, he didn't look right.

He just headed straight for Oswald Griffin's SUV.

TWENTY-FOUR

When my mom moved to Hollywood, she became someone I barely recognized. She changed her hair, her
makeup, the kind of clothes she wore, her *birth date.* . . .
But the thing that bugged me the most was that she
changed her name.

She became Dominique Windsor.

I think it was partly the name itself that I hated. It was
so aristocratic, daaaaahling.

And so phony.

We got into a huge fight over it when I was down there
visiting her, and to make a long story short, one of the
things that changed after we made up was her name.

I really, really, *really* wanted her to go back to being
Lana Keyes, and she did.

Which, it turns out, is one of the *stupidest* things I've
ever wished for. I mean, you see *Dominique Windsor* scroll
by on the credits of some television show and there is no
connection to me. You see *Lana Keyes* scroll by and,
bingo, I'm busted.

So I don't know what I was thinking, wanting her to
switch back to her real name. Maybe I thought she'd also
switch back to being a real mom.

That was quite a while ago, and let's just say there's been a lot of water eroding the bridge since then, so I don't know if it's possible to ever go back to the way we were before she left. Especially now that she's flirting around with Warren Acosta.

Anyway, the *point* is, I have experience with stage names. Lots of it. So when Cricket whispered, "Why is Grayson Mann getting in Oswald Griffin's car?" I whispered back, "He *is* Oswald Griffin. Grayson Mann is his stage name."

"But . . . how do you know that?"

"He's getting in Oswald Griffin's car, right?" I shrugged. "And who'd hire a newscaster named *Oswald*?"

The SUV blazed out of the parking lot, so I stood up and said, "Let's go!"

"There's no way we can tail him," Gary said. "My truck's way too loud."

"So true." I looked at the registration paper. "But I'm betting he's headed to three twenty-two South Lucas Drive. Anyone know where that is?"

Gary nodded. "It's actually pretty near our house."

Cricket did not look happy. "But . . . what are we going to do when we get there?"

"Depends," I said.

"On . . . ?"

"On whether he's there or not."

"Look," Gary said as we piled into his truck, "I think you need to explain this from the top."

So I said, "Okay. Remember how we saw that KSMY video of Grayson Mann on your computer and—" But after Gary fired up the motor, it was way too loud to talk. So I shouted, "I'll tell you when we get there!"

We roared across town, and when we found South Lucas Drive, Gary tried to just putt down the street, but that was like trying to get a lion to meow.

"You were right!" Cricket said when she saw the SUV. "He's home."

So we parked half a block away and watched.

"He didn't back up to the garage," I said, not really knowing if that was a good thing or a bad thing.

"You think it's in there?" Casey whispered.

"It being the condor?" Gary asked, then looked over his shoulder at me. "Explain, okay?"

I took a deep breath. "Grayson Mann did those news segments for KSMY about a month ago. He was up in the forest, getting the tour of the Lookout, helicoptering around the canyon, getting the scoop on the 'plight of the condor.' Footage and a contact number are available on the Internet."

"Check," Gary said.

"Less than a *week* ago, some man in a cowboy hat, sunglasses, and a T-shirt went into the canyon, shot a wild boar, and used it as bait to catch a condor."

"You're speculating," Gary said.

"You're right," I said back.

Something about that made him laugh. "Whatever. Just go on."

"Two days after we heard shots in the canyon, Grayson Mann shows up at the Lookout all agitated about having intercepted radio traffic about a shot condor. He wanted the story. Contact him first, remember? Well, I don't think he wanted the story, I think he wanted to *kill* the story—or at least control it. Remember that whole bit about Luxton Enterprises? I think that was him trying to steer everyone in the wrong direction."

"But how do you know this?" Cricket asked.

"Just listen," Gary said. "She's got license to speculate."

Something about that made *me* laugh. "Well, actually, it's more than speculation. He did two things when he was up there that make him suspicious. One, it was about ninety degrees out and he had on a long-sleeved shirt."

"News guys always wear long-sleeved shirts," Cricket said. "He probably came right up from the news station."

"He wasn't wearing a tie, and he left his sleeves down because he had a horrible rash on his arms." I stuck my arms out. "A rash like this."

Casey nodded. "Which he got in the same place you did."

"That is a *real* stretch," Gary said. "Poison oak is everywhere out there!"

"But it means he was out there! Recently! Or *somewhere* with poison oak." Then I added, "And no, I haven't seen the rash, but there's calamine lotion in his SUV. And here's where it really turns from coincidence or speculation to something solid—remember how he went around introducing himself, giving us all business cards?"

Cricket shrugged. "Yeah?"

"So think about who was there."

She started listing, "Us, Billy, Gabby, Bella, Robin, Quinn, and . . ." She gasped. "Janey! He gave one to Janey—he acted like he'd never met her before!"

"Exactly. Janey was his decoy. She's only been in town a little while. And she got a job at the Natural History Museum. Why? So she could move in on Quinn. It was her job to keep Quinn away from Grayson when he broke into the Lookout and when he went down into the canyon."

"But wait a minute," Cricket said. "What about Vargus? How would he know to use Vargus's name on the rental form for the horse? The only people who know Vargus are Quinn and Professor Prag."

"And Robin," I added. But she was right—how did Grayson Mann know about Vargus Mayfield?

"Are you saying *Robin* had something to do with this?"

"Are you saying *Quinn* did?" I shot back.

"Can we get back to motive?" Casey asked. "What's the endgame? What's the reason?"

I shrugged. "Money. I think someone contacted Grayson Mann via the Internet and offered him a huge amount of money for a live condor."

"Live?" Cricket asked, and her voice sounded so hopeful.

I nodded. "If they wanted a dead one, they could have broken into the Natural History Museum—especially since Janey worked there. And with the way condors keep turning up dead, there are probably stuffed condors hanging from a whole bunch of natural history museum ceilings!" I nodded down the street. "I think Marvin's mom is alive, and I think she's in that garage."

What I didn't say was that now that Cricket had

brought up that bit about Vargus, I had my doubts. Maybe Marvin was in Professor Prag's garage.

Or Quinn's.

Or Robin's.

Well, he wouldn't be in *her* garage, but that didn't mean she couldn't be involved. Maybe there was some special breeding program that the government wouldn't fund! Maybe they'd set up some big underground laboratory for condor breeding! Maybe—

Casey's voice shook me from my spiraling thoughts. "What if Grayson Mann doesn't have it anymore? Or what if he's got it stored somewhere else?"

"That would not be good," I said.

Cricket shook her head. "Sammy, I don't like this. I don't like this one bit. I think we should call the police."

"And say what? Santa Martina's celebrity newsman is a condor poacher, and my proof is that he's got a rash on his arm?"

"You could say more than that! Tell them everything you just told us."

I sighed. "You know, if Officer Borsch wasn't on vacation, I would. But first we'd have to get someone to listen and actually take us seriously. Then they'd have to go through a bunch of red tape like getting search warrants and all of that." I held up the garage door opener and grinned. "Why go through that when we've got this?"

Cricket frowned. "Because one's legal and the other's not?"

"We're not going to break and enter, okay? We're just going to, you know, press and peek."

But the more I thought about it, the more I thought, You know what? This guy shoots things—maybe having the cops on board wouldn't be such a bad idea.

So I put my hand out to Casey and said, "Can I borrow your phone?"

"Watch out," he said, handing it over. "She's armed and dangerous!"

So I called the police station and asked for Debra, who's the main receptionist there. She gets that I'm not some stupid pesky kid or a juvenile delinquent, and I figured I'd ask her to maybe recommend someone besides the Borschman that I could talk to about taking over the stakeout.

What I discovered, though, was that Debra wasn't there. "When will she be back?" I asked.

"Next week. She's on vacation."

Her too?

Man.

So I hung up and gave Casey his phone back, telling Cricket, "I struck out. Sorry."

We were all quiet a minute, just staring at the house. But then Cricket gasped real loud, turned clear around to face me, and said, "The transmitter! I've still got the transmitter! The one that was on the crow? It's in my backpack! If we could sneak it onto his car and get a receiver from Quinn, we could follow him anywhere!"

This time *my* jaw dropped. "That is genius!"

She smiled from ear to ear, then scrambled out of the truck. "I'm going to run home. I'll be right back!"

It seemed to take her a long time, but when she finally threw herself back inside Gary's truck, she was beaming. "I made it!" she panted.

I had to laugh. Pressing and peeking gave her the willies, but she was totally for planting condor surveillance equipment on someone's vehicle and following them.

"Check it out!" she said, pulling one thing after another from a small duffle bag. "The transmitter, three kinds of tape, two Velcro straps if you think those'll work better, gloves, binoculars, and . . . calamine lotion!"

"Oh, thank you!" I said, snatching the lotion.

"Gloves?" Gary asked her.

"I was trying to think of everything," she said, then shrugged. "You don't want to leave fingerprints."

I chuckled as I coated my arms with lotion. "The girl's on a mission!"

"That's right!" She caught her breath and said, "The whole run home I was thinking, What are you so worried about? We're not doing anything illegal, and if this guy really shot Marvin . . . if he's got Marvin's mom . . . I want to catch him!" She turned to me and said, "What do you think about calling Quinn? Or Robin?"

I capped the lotion. "We can do that. But I think we ought to first see if we can come up with anything more concrete than a rash."

"Okay!" she said, totally accepting that. "So where do we plant the transmitter?" Her face was all flushed, her eyes shining.

Gary looked back at Casey. "What do you think, bro?"

"I'd go for the undercarriage."

Gary nodded. "I was thinking the same thing." He eyed Casey. "I'll plant, you play sentry?"

"That's cool."

They looked at Cricket and me, and since they obviously had more car experience than we did, we said, "Go for it!"

Gary turned back to Casey. "So what's the signal?"

Casey thought a minute, then barked like a border collie. *"Ar, ar, ar, aroooo."*

Gary grinned. "Let's do it!"

They vanished between the fenders of parked cars. And after not being able to spot them for about a minute, I whispered to Cricket, "Can I see the binoculars?"

"Good idea!" she whispered back, only instead of handing them over, she looked through them herself.

"You should probably slump."

"Right," she said, sliding down low in her seat.

"Anything?"

She shook her head. "I can't believe how hard my heart is pounding. I'm not even out there!"

"Can I see?"

She handed me the binoculars, but I couldn't spot the guys, either, so I passed them back.

And then all of a sudden with my naked eyes I see a bike coming down the street.

It's blue, with little flashes of orange.

"Oh, no!" Cricket gasps.

We hold our breath and perk our ears, but there's no warning bark. No yips. No yaps. No nothing.

So after an endless minute of watching her cruise toward the house, I panic and go, *"Ar-ar-ar-arooo,"* out the window. *"Ar-ar-ar-arooo. Ar-ar-ar-arooo!"*

It was a mistake.

A big, *big* mistake.

TWENTY-FIVE

Apparently I'm not very good at sounding like a border collie. After my second yip-yap-yowl out the window, Janey's focus zeroed in on the truck.

"Duck!" Cricket cried.

"Stash the binoculars!" I hissed, laying low behind the driver's seat.

Click-click-click-click-click, we heard Janey's bike approaching. *Click-click-click-click-click.*

We were acting suspicious and I knew it, but I was afraid to sit up. Afraid she'd recognize me. And what I was really hoping was that she'd just cruise past or stop before she got to the truck. I mean, come on. What kind of person actually *looks* into other people's cars?

But *click . . . click . . . click . . . click . . . click,* the bike came closer and slowed, until finally it stopped.

Cosmic payback, at work once again.

I knew she was there. I knew she could see Cricket hiding on the floor of the front seat. And rather than just get busted without even attempting to wriggle out of it, I said, "It's gotta be under there—are you sure you can't see it?"

Cricket picked up on what I was doing. "Maybe if I had a flashlight . . ."

"How about a match?"

"Are you crazy?" Cricket banged her head getting up.

I sat up, too, and forced a scream when I saw Janey. I held my heart and said, "Oh, wow . . . you startled me!"

"What are you two *doing*?" she said with a smirk. Like she was annoyed, but kinda amused, too.

"Looking for a dog tag," Cricket blurted.

"Yeah," I said, my mind scrambling around for why we would need a dog tag when neither of us had a dog. "We just got it engraved."

"And if we can't find it, it's eight-fifty down the drain," Cricket said. She ducked her head to look under the seat. "It's gotta be here somewhere!"

Janey just watched, kinda leaning on the open window. "But what are you doing *here*? In this truck, which you're obviously not old enough to drive."

"Waiting for her annoying brother to finish returning something to a friend of his," I said, rolling my eyes. "He takes forever to do *anything*." And since I could tell she'd keep right on interrogating *us* if I didn't do something about it, I started interrogating *her*. "Do you live around here?"

"Just out for a ride," she said, slick as snake oil.

Cricket came up from her pretend search and oh-so-innocently asked, "So how's Quinn?"

Janey pulled away from the window and tightened the straps of the backpack she was wearing. "You can have him, honey—he's a narcissistic bore."

Cricket blushed, and I guess that was satisfaction enough for Janey, because she laughed and said, "Good luck finding that tag," and pushed off.

We watched through the back window as she pedaled down to the first intersection and hung a right. "That was close!" Cricket whispered.

"I'll bet she's got condor food in that backpack. It looked pretty heavy."

"It did!"

Just then the doors flew open and Gary and Casey scrambled into the truck. "Where'd she go?" Gary asked.

I pointed behind us. "Around the block."

"Did you get it planted?" Cricket asked.

Gary nodded and Casey said, "Man, I blew it. I did not see her coming. I was watching the house." He looked at me. "Are we busted?"

I shook my head. "I think we talked our way out of it. But the bad thing is, she now knows this truck."

Gary fired it up. "Let's drive it home and come back on foot." He pointed down the street. "We could split up and use that hedge and those bushes. Even that tree would work."

"All of us?" I asked. "Somebody should stay here."

Cricket nodded. "If Janey spots us driving down the road, she'll expect to see Sammy, me, and Gary."

"Which leaves Casey." I looked at him. "You cool with staying?"

"Sure," he said. "You want me to call the house if something goes down?"

"We're not even going inside," Cricket said. "We'll be right back."

So we took off for the Kuos', keeping our eyes open for Janey. "I'm sure she's around here somewhere, waiting for us to leave," I muttered.

Cricket said, "And if she wasn't trying to hide something, why not just go in the house?"

"I don't think she's married to Grayson, Cricket. He's too old. And neither of them wears a ring. I think she's his daughter."

Cricket looked at me, horrified. "What kind of girl would do a scam with her *dad*?"

I grunted. "What kind of dad would use his daughter as *bait*?"

"One thing's for sure," Gary said. "If this is a scam, it's the weirdest one I've ever heard of." He checked the rearview mirror. "Let's also make sure she doesn't follow *us*."

So for the three blocks back to the Kuos' we checked all around for Janey but didn't see any sign of her. And after we'd parked, Cricket grabbed her duffle and said, "Let's go!"

So we hurried back to South Lucas Drive, but when we reached Casey, the SUV was already gone.

"He took off?" I asked.

"Two minutes ago. Janey showed up right after you left. She went in the front door and opened the garage. Pretty Vegas backed the SUV about halfway in, and before I could even get across the street, they were closing up shop."

"So what did you see?" I ask.

"It was all in shadows, and they moved quick." He grimaced. "Sorry." But then he added, "I did memorize the license."

That, at least, was something, even though all of us were feeling pretty deflated.

But then Cricket started jumping up and down. "Wait a minute, wait a minute! If he is the guy, then *he's* got a receiver!"

We all blinked at her.

"And if he's anything like every single camper I know, he unloaded all his camping stuff inside the garage!"

In a flash, I'd dug the garage door opener out of the duffle and had it aimed through a thin spot in the hedge. I pressed the button, and the garage door sprang to life, squeaking up, up, up.

When we were sure the coast was clear, we hurried across the street.

Even with the door wide open, the garage stank. It was worse than musty. It was like uric acid mixed with cooking mustard greens.

In other words, vile.

There was camping gear stacked to one side, including an old canvas tent and a roll-up sleeping bag.

"It was him!" Cricket gasped, scooping up a cowboy hat and sunglasses. She put them back down and cried, "And here's the receiver!"

Then Gary called, "I found the net shooter!" and I pointed to some super-sized clippers and said, "And bolt cutters!"

Cricket stopped cold. "That monster! If he killed Marvin's mom, I'm going to kill him!"

Not exactly model Girl Scout behavior, but who could blame her?

But Casey shook his head and said, "This place smells rank, but I'm not sure it smells like dead bird."

"Where's the smell coming from, anyway?" Gary asked.

There was a trash bin in the corner of the garage, and when I flipped open the lid and caught a whiff, I about hurled. "Holy putrid buzzard poop!"

Casey held his breath and looked inside at the newspapers slimed with poop and scraps of rancid meat. His eyes were stinging, just like mine. "Oh, *man*," he said, closing the lid.

Cricket grabbed her duffle bag from where I'd dropped it. "I am taking back our stuff. This is *our* stuff!" She shoved in the receiver and power pack, the shooting net, and the record log that Gary had also found.

Then she zipped the bag closed and stood up. "We're calling the police!"

Gary scowled at her. "And what are you planning to tell them, little Miss Break and Enter?"

Cricket's eyes got wide as she understood what her brother was saying. "Oh, no! I compromised the evidence, huh? He can say that *we* put all this stuff in here, huh? He can say it's a big conspiracy! He can . . . oh, no! What are we going to *do*?"

"I don't know," Gary said. He peered outside. "But we really need to get *out* of here!"

So we slunk out of the garage with the duffle bag, pressed the remote to get the door rolling down, then hurried up the sidewalk. And when we were safely up the street, I glanced back at the house.

The garage door was down.

It was like we'd never been inside.

I looked at my watch. It was already after one. Maybe there was enough time to get the police involved, but with my history with the SMPD, I didn't want to stand around wasting time trying. And with the Vargus connection, I still wasn't sure who else might be involved or who we could trust.

No, the more I thought about it, the more I saw only one thing to do.

Follow them.

Follow them and rescue that big ol' mama bird ourselves.

TWENTY-SIX

I told Cricket and the others what I thought we should do and ended with, "If that big mama is still alive, we don't have much time!" Then Gary said, "So let's go rescue Big Mama!"

The funny thing about the bird suddenly having a name was that it all became personal. I mean, up to now figuring out what had happened to Marvin's mom had been more a nagging challenge to me than a passion. But now? I was ready to fight! Big Mama needed us!

Cricket didn't need Big Mama to have a name to feel the way I did. She'd had the beating pulse of it all along. But with what she'd seen and found in the garage and now with the idea of a *rescue,* she was pumped, man. Pumped and ready to do battle with one slimy newscaster and his decoy daughter.

So we hurried back to the Kuos', where Cricket flew around the house shoving things inside her duffle bag, getting ready for our rescue mission. *Whoosh-whoosh-whoosh!* she zoomed, going this way and that. At one point she came to a dead stop, looked at us, and said, "Be prepared!" like it was the secret key to the universe, then whooshed off again.

Gary had disappeared when we'd first arrived at the Kuos', and I hadn't given what he was doing any thought because Casey and I had been trying to figure out how to work the receiver. But then from across the house he called, "Hey, rescue squad! Come here!"

We all channeled down the hall and into the dungeon, where we found him scrolling intently through the pictures on a Web site. "Remember how I sent out a query to my butterfly contacts? Well, Pryze sent me this link to a site put up by some guy who calls himself the Birdman. He's got a one-hundred-acre aviary full of rare, exotic birds!" He pointed to bright red text against a deep blue background. "Check this out!"

So we all hung over his shoulders and read:

My aviary is the BIGGEST and BEST in the world. I have over 450 RARE and EXOTIC screamers and ducks! Kingfishers, hornbills, and allies! Eagles, hawks, and vultures! Passerines! Cranes, rails, trumpeters! Examples of a few of my greatest acquisitions include the crested shelduck and the white-winged duck! Marquesan kingfishers! Hawaiian crows! Gouldian finches! Whooping cranes! Ivory-billed woodpeckers! I also have Azores bullfinches, bald eagles, Kruper's nuthatches, orange-fronted parakeets . . . and coming soon! The legendary thunderbird!

"Who is this guy?" I gasped.
Gary shrugged. "The Birdman."
"Is there a picture of him?"

Gary scrolled through the site quickly. There were pictures of birds and the aviary, but not one of a human.

Casey sort of frowned and said, "I'm not a world traveler or anything, but that doesn't look like anyplace around here."

The steep hills in some of the pictures' background were a lush green, and in every image the sky looked misty or cloudy.

"Japan?" Cricket asked. "Fiji? The Bahamas? South America?"

Gary shook his head. "Could be any of those places."

"But it's definitely not around here," I said. "And *if* this is the right guy, the Poacher and the Decoy are probably headed for—"

"The airport!" everyone cried.

"And once Big Mama's gone, she's *gone*. This Birdman guy's got to be traceable, but if he's in a different country, we'll never get her back!"

Gary rattled through a lockdown sequence and cried, "To the Thunder Truck!"

The Thunder Truck? Casey and I sorta eyed each other and laughed, 'cause over the past couple of days Gary seemed to be morphing from computer geek to cartoony action hero.

But Cricket balked. "So when do we call the police? We can't take down the Birdman *and* the Poacher *and* the Decoy!"

I laughed out loud, because I'd never heard anyone sound more like me. It wasn't what she was saying; it was

265

the way she was saying it. "How about we find them first, okay? *Then* we'll call the police."

So we grabbed the duffle bag and the tracking equipment and followed Gary out the door. And since Casey's and my skateboards were right there on the porch, we grabbed those, which made Cricket do a U-turn back into the house and appear a minute later with two pairs of Rollerblades.

I looked at her like, Huh?

"We don't have skateboards," she said, "but we're fast on blades."

Now, I hadn't thought about the fact that Gary's truck was loud and that it might be useful to have a skateboard to get us closer to where we needed to go—wherever that was. It was more like, There's my skateboard, I'll grab it just in case we don't come back.

But now I saw that Cricket was thinking strategy and that there was no way she was gonna get left behind because she was on foot and we were on boards.

So I kinda grinned at her and said, "Be prepared?"

She gave me a great big smile. "Exactly."

Anyway, we threw our wheels in the bed of the truck, and after we were all seated, Cricket rolled down her window and stuck the receiver antenna outside while Gary fired up the truck.

"Casey and I couldn't get a signal," I called up to Cricket. "Maybe we were doing something wrong?"

But Cricket seemed to be having trouble, too. "I hadn't thought about this before, but what if there's too much interference in town? Buildings, plus radio and TV station transmissions?"

Gary frowned. "That would not be good." He cruised down the street a little ways, then asked, "Anything?"

Cricket shook her head.

"So?" Gary asked, looking over his shoulder at me. "To the airport?"

"To the airport," I called back. "And step on it!"

I've never actually been on an airplane, so I didn't know much about airports. I'd heard they had tight security. And elaborate monitoring devices. And FBI agents dressed as everyday travelers. But we're talking Santa Martina here—not LAX or JFK or XYZ or whatever big airport terminal most people fly in and out of. So I wasn't too worried about elaborate monitoring devices, and I really didn't think the FBI would be a problem. I mean, come on. The planes that fly in and out of here are just oversized crop dusters. Oh, they *pretend* to be sleek, sophisticated *aero*planes, but everyone knows—they're crop dusters in disguise.

Anyway, when we got to the airport, we cruised through the parking lots searching for the steel blue SUV. It only took a few minutes to go up and down all the aisles of both parts of the lot.

No SUV.

Cricket still had the receiver pointed out of the window, and finally she said, "Gary, can you just park? Your truck's so loud I can't tell if there's a signal or not!"

So Gary pulled over and cut the motor, and Cricket

played with the receiver, moving the antenna from left to right across the window opening.

No beep.

"What if we've got the wrong airport? What if they went up to Santa Luisa?" She opened the door and jumped out. "If they're meeting the Birdman at three, we'll never catch them!" She turned slowly, holding the antenna straight out in front of her. We could see the air traffic control tower and heard the buzz of a plane as it came in for a landing.

My heart sank as Cricket kept turning. And all I could think was, Why'd we wait so long to get going? Why didn't we just grab the receiver, hop in the truck, and *go*? Why'd we have to be so "prepared"?

But then all of a sudden Cricket stops. She stops, and very slowly she swings back in the opposite direction. She plays with the controls some, then shouts, "I've got a signal! It's faint, but I've got a signal!"

The rest of us scramble out of the truck. "Where? Which direction?"

"That's what's so weird." She points away from the airport. "Over there."

So we all pile back in the truck and follow a narrow road that leads away from the control tower. There are some office buildings on our left, so we can't see the airfield at all anymore, and it really seems like we're getting farther and farther away from where any *plane* might land. Still, Cricket is hanging out the window with the receiver and she calls, "It's getting stronger!"

So we continue along the road until it Ts to the left and the right. Going right looks like it'll take us up to some more office buildings near the highway, and to the left is a huge area that's fenced off by chain link topped with razor wire. Plus there's a security gate about fifty yards down the road.

Gary pulls off into the weeds, cuts the motor, and says, "What have you got?"

Cricket scans the area with the antenna, and we can all hear the beep get louder as she aims it over at the fenced-off area.

"That must be an airfield back there," Casey says. He points toward the rows of arched buildings on the other side of the security gate. "Those are probably private hangars."

I grabbed the duffle bag and fished out the binoculars. Then I leaned forward between Cricket and Gary and focused on the gate. There was a sign wired to the fence that had SECURE AREA and a bunch of penal code information on it, plus a post with a security box mounted on top where you could enter a secret code to open the gate and drive through.

The bad news was, there was no way we could guess our way inside the gate or climb over the razor wire. And the whole area around the gate was exposed—no trash cans or bushes or trees . . . nothing to use as cover.

The *good* news was, I didn't see any guards.

And there *were* some great bushes about twenty yards from the gate.

"Park over there," I told Gary, pointing to a shady area under some eucalyptus trees. "I've got an idea."

Casey smirked. "Uh-oh."

So I explained what I wanted to do, and even though

nobody was wild about the idea, nobody could come up with anything better.

Except maybe Cricket, who wanted to call the police.

"I agree—we should do that! But let's get in position first."

I did still have a problem with the whole Vargus connection, though. I mean, how *had* Vargus's name wound up on the Trail Riders form if someone who knew Vargus wasn't involved? What if Quinn or Professor Prag or Robin was involved? What if they were sacrificing one condor to help many? What if they could get so much money from the sale of *one* bird that they could keep the condor program going for a decade!

Should we just let them do it?

Anyway, we wind up crouched behind the bushes with our skateboards and Rollerblades and the duffle bag, and after Cricket's done complaining about how ridiculous it is to be hiding in the bushes wearing *Rollerblades,* she gets Casey's phone, looks at me, and says, "You want to do it?"

I shake my head. "I'm terrible at explaining stuff like this."

So she punches in 9-1-1, and she's totally amped, because when someone answers, she starts talking a hundred miles an hour. "We need help. There's a guy—Grayson Mann, actually—the KSMY reporter? He's stolen a condor. Out of the woods? And he's getting ready to sell it for big bucks to some guy from out of the country called the Birdman, and—"

She stops talking suddenly, and then her jaw drops. And after a few seconds of silence she looks at the phone, then snaps it shut, and says to us, "She told me she'd have me arrested if I didn't quit fooling around! Can you believe that? She hung up on me!"

I give a little shrug. Like, yeah, I can totally believe that.

She flips open the phone. "Well, I'm going to call Robin!"

But before she can dial, a bunch of things start happening, all at once.

First, a car turns down the road toward the security gate.

Then from the sky above comes the sound of a plane, and when we look up, *all* our jaws drop.

It's no crop duster, that's for sure. It's a sleek black jet—not big, but not small, either. And it's strange enough that it's black, but it's painted like an angry raven . . . feathers on the wings, eyes and a beak around the cockpit. . . . We all know it's just a jet, but something about it is still unnerving.

"The Birdman!" Cricket gasps. "That must be him!"

And we're just absorbing the urgency of what's in the sky above us when that car drives past us toward the gate. The driver is wearing a uniform, and he's talking on a walkie-talkie type of radio. Not one of those little hand jobbies—a big one.

Like the kind Quinn used up at the Lookout.

"*That's* how he knew!" I gasp, but there's no time to explain. The car's already at the security keypad.

The driver's punching in the code.

The gate's swinging open.

It's time to charge!

TWENTY-SEVEN

If the security gate had been right *next* to the bushes, we could've piggybacked in, no problem. But when the car went through, we were twenty yards away, and no matter how quick any of us might have been at sprinting, we could never have reached the gate before it closed.

But we had wheels, and the instant the car moved forward through the gate, we hit the ground rolling.

Casey and I got a good start and pushed as hard as we could, but even so, the gate was swinging closed *fast* and we were not going to make it.

Then Gary zoomed past us on his Rollerblades. He was leaning way over, his arms pumping high. He was *flying*. And when he got to the gate, he zipped through, then strained to keep the gate open long enough for the rest of us to squeeze by.

When we were safely in the shadows of a plane hangar, I panted, "Grayson Mann got Vargus's name from radio transmissions!"

"What radio transmissions?" Cricket panted back.

"Quinn radioed down to the sheriff when the Lookout was broken into, remember? He also radioed for help when he found us with Marvin. Grayson said that's how he knew about Marvin being hurt, remember? Well, that must also be how he got Vargus's name—he's been listening in on radio transmissions!"

"So what are you saying?" Gary asked.

I was still trying to catch my breath. "I'm saying . . . call Robin! Call Quinn! Call whoever you want! I think we're gonna need some backup!"

Casey whipped out his phone again and Cricket got busy with it while I unzipped the duffle bag and handed Casey and Gary stuff out of it—binoculars, a length of rope, the receiver. . . .

"Robin's not home!" Cricket wailed, punching in another number. "I left a message, but what good's that going to do?" She dialed Quinn's number and muttered, "C'mon, c'mon, c'mon . . ."

I felt so stupid. I'd been putting off calling anyone for hours, and now here we were, in a restricted place where condor poachers and men in evil-looking jets were meeting to engage in high-stakes activities that could get us all shot.

Anyway, Cricket leaves a kinda panicky, kinda garbled, really *long* message on Quinn's machine while the guys hurry over to the far end of the hangar with the receiver and the binoculars. And by the time Cricket's hung up, Gary and Casey are waving us over.

"I got a signal," Gary says as he folds up the receiver. "But we don't need this thing anymore. They're over there somewhere, and the jet's on the tarmac."

He steps aside so Cricket and I can look around the corner, and there on the private runway, about five hangars over, is the Raven Jet.

Casey hands me the binoculars. "The door's not open yet, so I don't think we missed anything."

We watch and we watch and we watch, taking turns with the binoculars, but all that happens is a refueling truck goes up to the plane and fills it with gas. It gives us plenty of time to come up with a plan, though, and it gives Cricket time to try calling Quinn and Robin and the police again.

Then Gary points to a vehicle that's driving slowly onto the tarmac. "Is that Mann's SUV?"

Casey focuses the binoculars on it. "Bingo."

"Okay," Gary says. "Time to move." He grabs the rope. "Just like we talked about—Casey and I approach from this end, you guys circle around from behind. We'll wait for Sammy's signal."

I grab the duffle bag and stuff everything else in it. "And if we get caught, our story is your dad's got a plane in one of the hangars and we're playing hide-and-seek."

"Are we sure we want to say hide-and-seek?" Cricket says, her eyes all panicky. "We're too old for hide-and-seek! It sounds so lame!"

I look her in the eye. "Say it like you mean it and people will believe it."

"That's right," Gary says. "If you act like you're doing something wrong, people will know you're up to something."

She nods like she's got it, but her eyes are still panicky, and she literally *gulps* when she swallows.

"We're running out of time," Casey says. "If we're gonna do this, we've gotta *move*."

So off we go—girls along the back of the hangars, guys across the front. And it was actually kinda interesting, 'cause we just rolled past cars and open doorways and *people,* and nobody stopped us. I mean, there we were, carrying a duffle bag that could have been full of *explosives,* and nobody stopped us.

Anyway, down the roadway between the fourth and fifth hangars we spot the Birdman's jet on the tarmac. "Now what?" Cricket whispers, because between us and the runway are a bunch of vehicles and open doors that lead to little offices or rooms or storage places that are built into the plane hangar.

"We act like we belong," I whisper back, but my heart's hammering and my eyes are shifting around like I do *not* belong. It's too late to turn back, though, so I take a deep breath and say, "Let's go."

We roll along, trying to act all casual-like, but that's hard to do when your heart's hammering and your skateboard's making a racket and you're toting along a duffle bag that looks like it could be packed with explosives.

"Smile," I whisper to Cricket as we approach a guy wearing a blue jumpsuit and a trucker hat. "Smile like you're having fun."

"Hey, kids," Mr. Jumpsuit says, putting up a hand like he's a kiddie-school crossing guard. "You here with someone?"

I smile at him. "My dad's over in hangar B-3. He's jawin' with his aviation buddies, and we got bored."

He nods like he knows all about it and backs away. "Once the bug bites ya, there's no help for it." He kinda waves and says, "Hang around here long enough and it'll bite you, too!"

We start rolling away and I call, "See ya later!" kinda loud so that anyone else in the vicinity'll know we're not hiding anything.

"Wow," Cricket whispers as we move along, "you are smooth."

"I am *shaking*," I whisper back.

When we get to the front side of the hangars, Cricket looks to the left and says, "Where are the guys? I hope they didn't get caught!"

Then, like Casey had read her mind, we hear, *"Ar, ar, ar, aroooo."*

"There they are!" Cricket says, pointing toward a truck that's parked about fifty yards to our left.

There's a bright yellow and blue biplane right in front of us, so we duck around it and take cover. And when I look across the runway through the binoculars, what I see looks like something out of a movie. The Raven Jet is in the background; the SUV has parked about two hundred feet from it. For a moment everything's still, and then the jet door opens and a man carrying a briefcase comes down the steps. From his neck to his toes, he's dressed in black. Just like his jet.

"The Birdman!" Cricket whispers.

And then, coming out of the plane a few steps behind him is a *boy*, maybe ten or twelve years old.

"He brought his *son*?" I whisper, not quite believing my eyes.

"What's he *thinking*?" Cricket whispers back.

Then the doors of the SUV open and Grayson and Janey emerge. My heart is ka-blamming around so hard I can barely breathe. "This is it!" I whisper as the four of them meet up halfway between the SUV and the jet.

The Birdman opens the briefcase. Right there in the middle of the runway in broad daylight, he opens the briefcase.

I zero in on it with the binoculars.

It's full of money, all right.

Lots of it.

I stand up, give the guys a wave, and there they go, rolling toward the powwow on the runway.

I dump the binoculars in the duffle bag, grab the bungee cords, and hand Cricket the shooting net. "Let's do it!"

She just stands there, and I can see her knees shaking.

Now, what I really want to do is grab the shooting net and go, but I have zero experience with it. Cricket's the one who knows how to use it. So I tell her, "Think Marvin. Think Marvin and Big Mama and get *mad*. These jerks have no right to steal her! She belongs in the wild with her son!" I lean in a little. "Do you want them to get away with this?"

Cricket takes a deep breath, then her nostrils flare and her face firms up and she says, "No."

I look across the tarmac at Gary and Casey.

They're already halfway there.

And they've been noticed.

I toss down my skateboard and jump on. "Then let's go!"

At first I'm all fired up, but as Cricket and I come in from the opposite direction as Casey and Gary, I start feeling really . . . *weird*. I mean, normally doing stuff like ditching a bad guy or tackling a bad guy or hijacking a bad guy's car helps me get rid of my jitters and *focus*.

But as we're approaching the powwow on the tarmac, I start feeling really *dis*connected. Like I'm floating above my body watching *it* push across the runway on a skateboard.

I feel kinda dizzy.

Kinda weak.

Really *scared*.

And that's when it finally hits me that this whole thing is out of control—I am *way* out of my league.

This is *dangerous*.

Ol' Swoopy Hair is moving toward Casey and Gary, and it's easy to see that he's not planning to pass out business cards. Janey's hanging back with the Birdman, trying to charm him into believing nothing's wrong, reaching for the briefcase as she motions him toward the truck.

And then she sees *us*.

She does a double take, then looks behind her at where Casey and Gary are stretching out a rope as they move toward Grayson.

"Dad!" she shouts, and now the Birdman is looking

both ways, too. And you can tell he's thinking, What's going on here? But we've got an advantage.

We're kids.

I mean, really, how seriously are you supposed to take kids on Rollerblades and skateboards wielding a *rope*?

So the Birdman doesn't race off to his plane and try to zoom his way to freedom. He just kind of stands there whipping his head back and forth while Casey and Gary spread out, stretching the rope tight, aiming it right for Grayson Mann's stomach.

Grayson doesn't know what to do—if he tries to duck, they'll lower the rope. If he tries to jump, they'll raise it. And he probably could have just grabbed the rope and pulled, but instead he runs back toward Janey and the Birdman.

And *that's* when the Birdman finally understands that something is terribly wrong. He looks back and forth a few more times, but then his *son* grabs the briefcase and charges for his jet.

"Wait!" Janey cries, chasing after the boy. And there's no way Grayson Mann is going to let a gazillion bucks fly off into the sunset—he chases after him, too. But the Birdman turns around and blocks them, trying to protect his kid.

"Now, Cricket! Now!" I shout as we move in, and then POP! she sends the capture net flying. It sails through the air like a giant fishnet stocking, quivering and wobbling and finally gulping them up.

"Great shot!" I shout, only the Birdman is on the far end of it and manages to scramble free.

Grayson and Janey, though, stumble and tangle, and then *splat,* they hit the tarmac like a big blob of poacher pudding. And while Casey and Gary chase after the Birdman, Cricket and I pounce on them, pinning them down. But they're punching and flailing and fighting like crazy to get free, and net or not, there's no way we're going to be able to hold them down for long. "Help!" I shout over to the guys because the Birdman's out of reach anyway, bounding up the steps to his getaway jet.

Sirens start up somewhere in the distance. And before either of our netted villains can wrestle free, Casey and Gary glide in and loop the rope around them. I hop off and start to bungee kicking and flailing and *cussing* body parts together through the netting. "How's it feel, *Oswald?*" I call. "You and your decoy daughter are gonna get stuck in a nice little cage where you can spend time wishing for *your* freedom."

"Look!" Casey shouts, because the Raven Jet is already taxiing down the runway.

Then all at once people are coming at us from everywhere. There are real cops and airport cops and men in blue jumpsuits with trucker hats. There are people with sirens and golf carts and megaphones. And then there's Quinn. And Robin. And Bella and Gabby. And everyone's talking at once. Everyone but me. I know it's gonna take forever to sort this mess out, and I don't really care who explains why the town's celebrity newscaster is bungeed to his decoy daughter on the tarmac. What I care about is getting over to the SUV.

So I sneak away and try the handle of the back hatch.
It's unlocked.

I swing it open and find myself face to face with . . . a
big white sheet.

But when I throw back the sheet, there, staring right at
me through the bars of a cage, is one big, hunchy, *ugly*
bird.

"Hey, Big Mama," I say with a grin, but what I'm
thinking is, What an amazingly *beautiful* sight.

TWENTY-EIGHT

It did take a while to sort everything out. Adults can be so . . . I want to say dense, but that's not it. And it's not bubble-brained, either. I mean, it isn't that they can't process what you're telling them because it'll shatter them—it's more like their brains can't process it because of *who's* telling them.

I mean, how can *we* know more than they do?

We can't possibly be right.

Or telling the truth.

We're *"kids."*

But a condor in a cage is pretty powerful proof, and after they finally accepted that we *did* know more, that we *were* right *and* telling the truth, *then* we had to suffer through a whole rash of I-can't-believe-you-*did*-that's.

It was so dangerous!

And lawbreaking!

The utter *gall* of it all!

I wish someone would invent a calamine lotion for adult overreaction.

I'd buy buckets.

Anyway, in the end, the evidence spoke for itself and

the birdnappers became jailbirds. A cop at the showdown told us that poaching an endangered species can get you a sentence greater than armed robbery, and if that's true, I can't say I'm sorry that they'll be facing real time in the big cage.

Quinn wasn't sorry, either. He got to face off with Janey right there on the tarmac, and even though she put on this *huge* act of how she hadn't known what her father was doing and how she really *loved* Quinn and still wanted to *see* him, he's no birdbrain. He laughed in her face and said, "The only place I'll see you is in court."

Later, when we were hanging out by Big Mama, he put his hand on Cricket's shoulder and there were actual tears in his eyes. "How can I ever thank you?" he asked her, then kissed her on the temple.

She blushed deep red and I could tell—that was all the thanks she needed.

Grams, on the other hand, was horrified when she heard what had happened. "Grayson Mann? *The* Grayson Mann? That can't be!"

"His real name's Oswald Griffin, Grams. And I'm sorry to break it to you, but his news days are over."

Turns out I was wrong about that. He's been on the news a *lot*. KSMY's competing station out of Santa Luisa has had a *field* day covering the story. And believe me, they haven't been waiting around for him to fix his hair before shooting him.

Anyway, in the days that followed the showdown on the tarmac, a couple of things happened.

First, I went back to the Kuos' and actually unpacked my very stinky backpack and returned stuff to Robin. I saw Gary a lot while I was at the Kuos', and it made me really happy that he'd gone from being a pimply porcupine holed up in his dungeon to a guy who was in and out all the time, joking with his sister and being . . . I don't know . . . one amped teenager.

He was especially hyper when he found out via his connections on the Internet that the Birdman was *not* the man we'd seen at the airport. "He's not really a Bird*man*," he told us, "he's Bird*boy*. He's a twelve-year-old spoiled-to-death *prince*."

"No!" I said. "Was he that kid we saw at the airport?"

"Must've been—which is why he snagged that briefcase of cash!"

We'd already been told that there was probably nothing that could be done about someone from another country trying to buy a condor—that our national laws didn't cross into foreign territories. So maybe Birdboy won't get nailed, but Quinn vowed to shut him down, and between him and Gary working Internet angles, I have no doubt that'll happen.

We also found out from Quinn that Grayson-slash-Oswald said he didn't want to actually *hurt* Marvin, but he'd had to shoot at him because he'd attacked him and *thrown up* on him while he was trying to secure Big Mama.

"He *barfed* on him?" I asked.

Quinn nodded. "It's a defense mechanism."

No kidding.

But anyway, Grayson was also apparently totally miffed that he'd been busted by kids. "He thought he was so clever," Robin told us, "leaving false clues everywhere. Between Luxton Enterprises, throwing beer cans around inside the Lookout, calling the taxidermist, using Vargus's name on the horse rental form . . . he was sure everyone would be completely bamboozled." She grinned at Cricket and me. "Guess he never met a good Scout."

Uh-oh.

Anyway, while I was at the Kuos' unpacking and stuff, I came across that fax we'd gotten from Trail Riders. And seeing it gave me this little hiccup of an idea, which, the more I thought about, the more I wanted to try and pull off.

So I used my favorite weapon one last time to call Trail Riders.

When I had Thomas Becker on the line, I said, "Yes, Mr. Becker, this is Ulma Willis again. Marshal for the United States Department of Fish and Wildlife?"

"Yes, ma'am. Of course I remember you."

"I'm following up to let you know that the issue with the condor poacher has been resolved and that we were mistaken about Vargus Mayfield. He had nothing to do with it and is no longer under investigation."

"Oh. Well, thank you, ma'am, for that information."

Then I told him, "Have a good day, Mr. Becker," and got off the phone.

After that, Cricket and I went back to Grayson Mann's garage for one final press and peek.

Okay, press and *enter*.

And grab!

But all we grabbed was the cowboy hat and sunglasses. Then we hurried back to the Kuos' and got Gary to drive us over to Vargus Mayfield's.

"Hey, Vargus," I said when he answered the door.

"Huh?" he said back, acting more like a junior high kid than an almost college graduate.

So we told him what we wanted, and at first he didn't really believe it, but since money was involved, we managed to twist his arm and drag him out to Trail Riders.

Now, since it would have been kinda suspicious for all of us to go inside, Cricket and Gary waited in the truck while Vargus and I went inside to run our little scam. Vargus was looking as much like Grayson as he could, wearing the cowboy hat and sunglasses, and me, I looked like regular ol' me in my ball cap and jeans.

"May I help you?" the guy behind the counter asked, and I recognized his voice from the telephone.

"Yes," I answered. "My friend here left a one-thousand-dollar deposit on a horse last week. He's here to pick it up." Mr. Becker was just staring at me, so I kinda dropped my voice and said, "He's a mute, so I have to talk for him."

Thomas Becker experienced bubble brain for all of three seconds. Then his face clouded a little and he said, "You can't be serious."

"Why's that?" I ask.

"Because my horse found her own way home!"

"But she *is* home," I say, sounding calm and *very*

reasonable. "Safe and sound." Then I lean in and say, "It's a very complicated story."

He checks Vargus over and says, "This is not the same fella that rented my horse."

"Sure, it is." Then I add, "I don't blame you for not recognizing him. You probably get hundreds of people in here—especially during summertime."

His brow furrows and his mouth wags back and forth once before he says, "Nope. That's not him."

"You need proof?" I turn to Vargus. "Show the man your driver's license, Vargus."

So Vargus pulls out his wallet and hands over his license, then takes off his hat and shades. And after a minute of ol' Tommy Becker comparing the face in front of him to the one on the license, I say, "I understand there were forms he filled out?"

Tommy looks at me, and I can see his brain sputtering with objections, but before he can actually spit any of them out, I say, "Ulma Willis from the Department of Fish and Wildlife assured us there would be no problem collecting the deposit."

He takes one final stare at me, then, without a word, he hands back the license, goes to his desk, and returns with ten one-hundred-dollar bills.

"Much obliged, sir," I tell him, trying to stay cool and calm as he passes the cash to Vargus. Then I move Vargus to the door like he's dumb *and* blind.

Which, in a lot of ways, he is.

Anyway, when we're outside and in the clear, Vargus shakes the fistful of cash and says, "I can't *believe* this!"

I snatch it from him. "You get a *commission,* remember? Not the whole wad."

So I peel off two of the hundreds, which he seems happy enough with, then I get in the truck and tell Gary, "Let's go!"

After we drop Vargus off, I peel off four more hundreds and hand them to Gary. "It's not a four-eyed viperwing, but it'll fix your exhaust manifold."

He just blinks at me.

So I shake it at him and say, "We couldn't have rescued Big Mama without you."

He takes it from me slowly, the biggest grin growing across his face. "You are something," he says, then drives us home.

So I was real happy about all of that. And the other four hundred dollars Cricket and I delivered to Robin to give to Quinn for the Lookout project.

Seemed like the right thing to do.

And while we were there, *she* delivered some good news to *us.*

"Marvin and Big Mama are getting released to their habitat on Friday—would you like to come?"

"Yes!" we both shouted.

So, of course, when we told Gary and Casey, *they* wanted to go along, too, and then the day it was going to happen, *Marissa* called. So I asked her if she wanted to meet us at Robin's house 'cause there was a whole caravan going up to the Lookout. The birds were being taken up by Professor Prag and some bird experts, Robin was riding with Gabby and Bella in Quinn's truck, *Billy* was squeezing in somewhere. . . . "It'll be a huge party up there!" I told her. "You've got to come!"

"Wait," Marissa said. "Aren't condors, like, big buzzard birds? Aren't they really . . . *ugly?*"

"Yeah," I laughed. "Yeah, they are."

She hesitated, then said, "So let me get this straight—you're going to waste your whole day letting some big ugly buzzards go?"

"Yeah," I laughed again. "Yeah, I am."

"Are you sure you don't want to just come over? I've got a ton of stuff to tell you!"

I was dying to catch up with her, but in the end I said, "I'll call you when I get back, okay? This is something I need to do."

"All right. Whatever. But call me—I'm dying to talk to you!"

So Marissa didn't go, but I'm really glad I did. It *was* a big party. Even the ride up was fun. Gary'd gotten his truck fixed, so we could actually hear each other without shouting. We told our favorite jokes, did the name game—you know, like, "If your last name's Weiser, don't name your kid Bud"—we did that for an *hour.* And then we *sang.* It was so corny, but it was fun. Cricket and Gary know a kazillion songs. Old musicals' songs, campfire songs, Beatles songs . . . I felt like I was at a marathon campfire gathering.

And then *Casey* belts out, "*Wild* Thing . . . do-do-da-do-do . . . You make my heart sing . . . do-do-da-do-do . . . You make eeeeverything . . . groovy!" and gives me this real mischievous grin.

So, okay, I totally blushed. And since I was feeling all

flushed and embarrassed, I countered by making up my own words.

"*Wild* things . . . do-do-da-do-do . . . You bite and you sting . . . do-do-da-do-do . . . You make eeeeeverything . . . *itchy*."

Then Gary picked it up, shouting, "C'mon, c'mon, c'mon, c'mon, *wild* things!"

"Do-do-da-do-do!"

"You bite and you sting!"

"Do-do-da-do-do!"

"You make eeeeeverything . . ."

"Itchy!" we all cried, and then busted up.

So the trip up to the Lookout was a blast, and since everyone's vehicle could make it up the last steep five miles, we didn't even have to hike.

Hooray!

When we got to the Lookout, Gary parked his truck but didn't get out right away. He just sat there, real quiet, staring. And when Cricket reached over and held his arm, I realized he was thinking about more than just this place where he hadn't been in ages.

He was thinking about his mom.

Anyway, when we all got out of the truck and joined the others, we discovered that Billy had performed some miracle transformation on Professor Prag on the way up. Ol' Needle Nose was *laughing*. Then he actually came up to me and apologized and said, "We can't thank you enough for rescuing Big Mama."

Him calling her Big Mama instead of AC-34 totally shocked me, so I said, "You mean *Condorus bigbeakybos?*"

He laughed *real* loud, then shook his head at me and Billy. "Ah, you kids."

When he was gone, I looked at Billy and said, "What did you *do* to him?" But I didn't really need an answer. It's just the magic of Billy Pratt.

Anyway, we all stood around and watched as Quinn, Professor Prag, Robin, and some condor handlers decked out in safety glasses and protective gloves got Marvin and his mom ready out near Echo Rock. It took three people to manage each bird—one at the head, one at the body, and one at the feet.

They shoulda just wrapped 'em in a tent and been done with it, but whatever.

And then, when everyone and everything was finally all ready, they let go of the birds and backed away.

Talk about anticlimactic. Those oversized buzzards just *stood* there.

Quinn finally moved toward them with his arms all spread out, which did make them hop forward a few yards, but then they just stood there some more.

But after another few minutes of this breathtaking excitement, Big Mama must've gotten bored, too, because without any warning, she spread her wings and *whoosh,* she went overboard, down into the canyon.

Then all of a sudden *whoosh,* Marvin was gone, too.

We rushed to the edge to see them in flight.

We looked left. We looked right. We looked into the canyon. Across the canyon.

People shielded their eyes.

Binoculars appeared.

But we saw nothing.

Nothing but one stupid caw-y, oily, flappy crow.

"Where'd they go?" Cricket cried, but they were gone.

Just *gone*.

And we were finally just giving up, when all of a sudden from behind us came the sound of distant thunder.

We spun around and there they were, overhead, gliding toward us, broad and black, their wings out straight and steady.

I gasped.

I literally could not believe my eyes.

I knew they were big, but this big?

Their wings seemed to fill the skies as they glided over us. Then they circled once effortlessly around us, looking at us.

It was almost like they were acknowledging us.

Thanking us.

I turned, following them as they circled above. Then off they went, gliding out over the canyon, as free as the wind that carried them.

All of a sudden I was choked up and tears were streaming down my face. Casey came up from behind and wrapped his arms around me. And as we watched them soar away, he put his chin on my shoulder and whispered, "That was the most awesome thing I have ever seen."

And it was.

I mean, yeah, maybe they don't know the difference between human trash and condor kibble, but whose fault is that?

They're the ones who belong in these canyons.

Soaring on the thermals.

Beating thunder through the skies.

I watched them glide through the air like masters of this harsh and unforgiving world, and I got it.

I finally, *truly* got it.